The Detective Joanna Best Mysteries
Book 4

Vengeance is Fine

Cenarth Fox

The Detective Joanna Best Mysteries
Book 4
Vengeance is Fine

First published in 2018 by Fox Plays
www.foxplays.com
www.cenfoxbooks.com

Cover design by Oliviaprodesign

ISBN 978-0-949175-31-1

Dictionary of Australian slang/language

Some of the Australian words and expressions found in this novel.

AFP - Australian Federal Police
ALP - Australian Labor Party, major political party
barbie - barbeque
Barry Crocker - rhyming slang for shocker, terrible
cactus - dead, useless, broken
CBD - Central Business District, Downtown
Children's - Royal Children's Hospital
cricket - summer game
cut lunch and a compass - a long way away
daks - trousers
doddle - if something's a doddle it's easy, not difficult
free kick - Australian football where umpire awards the ball to a player
G'day - hello, hi
gross - off, unpleasant
jiffy - a moment, short period of time
loo - toilet, lavatory
Mildura - regional city a long way from Melbourne
Mum - Mom
OTT - Over the Top, exaggerated, outlandish
paddock - a horse in the paddock eats well, a human puts on weight
pavement - footpath, sidewalk
pinged - caught
public servant - government officer, civil servant
Puffing Billy - locomotive on tourist railway
Reg Grundy's - rhyming slang for undies, underpants
Senior - short for Senior Constable (or Detective Senior Constable)
slow as a wet weekend - very slow, time drags
SOGGIES - (Special Operations Group), elite armed police officers
tacker - a small child
thunderbox/crapper/dunny - toilet
tickety-boo - fine, good, okay
torch - flashlight
two bob's worth - someone's opinion (two bob was about 20 cents)
wardrobe - closet
yonnie - small stone

For MS and BS

1

HELL HATH NO FURY like a man porned. Darren seethed. He'd picked up a babe, a gorgeous ballerina from a sheltered upbringing, and introduced her to the world of sexting, drugs, and rock 'n roll in the hay. He was all class was Darren and when he offered the new chick to his mate Jordan, Elizabeth soon packed her bags and fled. Darren exploded. "No bitch walks out on me", and when Jordan suggested they post a naked photo online of said bitch entertaining the gents, revenge porn was up and running.

Fortunately Elizabeth's sister's old school chum, Detective Senior Constable Jo Best, offered to help. Jo turned to friend and IT whiz, Michael Chan, who created a web site mocking Darren for his caveman-like treatment of women—hence his fury.

Darren was ridiculed in public—actually the web site was on the Dark Web meaning far fewer people got to see it—but ignorant Darren demanded revenge with his plan to attack anyone who made him look like the shit he was—is.

Not being the brightest bulb on the Christmas tree, Darren took time to solve his problem. He thought Jo Best was Joe Best and whacked an innocent bloke. Finally Darren twigged and now knew his target—the bitch, that female copper, Jo Best.

Darren wanted to kill her but Jordan reckoned bumping off the filth was counter-productive. He actually said "fuckin' stupid". They'd tried to rape her. Scarily she survived, just. So the new plan involved ruining her career by having her thrown off the force and into the slammer.

How? Too easy. The lads had already been inside Jo's apartment and once there had "adjusted" the back door making a subsequent entrance a doddle. All they needed now was the evidence, to wit a corpse. Yep, a dead body.

They would place the stiff inside Jo's flat then call the cops. "Try talking your way out that one, bitch. Now, where can we find a stiff?"

Meet Burke and Hare, a.k.a. Darren and Jordan. Burke and Hare, a couple of wee Scottish layabouts, made a quid from body snatching and murder in Edinburgh in the 1820s. Hospitals paid good money for corpses so doctors could tackle Anatomy 101. Burke and Hare liked the seven quid per cadaver. Darren and Jordan had never heard of the Scottish stiff stealers but became a poor man's version thereof.

'Where'll we get a dead body?' asked Jordan, scared of the idea.

'The morgue,' replied Darren. 'People get taken there if it's a sudden or suspicious death. The quacks check them out in case of fowl play.' Darren thought *fowl* instead of *foul* and Jordan thought a homonym was some sort of gay sex game. Late that night they located the Melbourne Morgue, a part of the Coroner's Court in Southbank.

'Are you sure about this?' Jordan felt sick in his guts.

'Shut up and leave it to me.'

They wandered along the vehicle entrance. 'Let's go,' said Jordan.

A vehicle arrived, one for transporting the deceased. Perfect, just pinch the stiff and off to the copper's boudoir we go.

The vehicle stopped and the driver spoke. 'Can I help you, gents?'

Darren was on form. 'G'day bud. Me mate's Gran has just died and he wants to know if she's been brought here.' Jordan looked bereaved.

'Go back. You need the public entrance on Kavanagh Street.'

Darren continued. 'But if we can't find his Gran in here, where will she be?'

The driver had suspicions. 'If the Coroner doesn't need to hold the body, it'll be released to the appropriate funeral parlour. Good luck.' He drove into the building with what the lads wanted.

'What, now?' asked Jordan.

'A funeral parlour.'

'You're mad.'

Darren strode to his vehicle. Jordan ran after him, protesting. 'This'll never work.' But Darren still seethed. *Nobody mocks me and especially not a fucking woman.* He intended to humiliate that cop and make her suffer.

Darren drove out of town. 'There's a funeral parlour near my joint.'

'Oh great. We steal a dead body. What will the family say when their loved one gets pinched?'

'They can have it back after the cop gets busted.'

Darren drove with Jordan complaining and arguing. Darren ignored him thinking about where he last saw a funeral parlour. His memory was good and they parked in a side street.

'Tell me you're joking,' gasped Jordan.

'Are you in this or not? If you're gutless, you can piss off now.'

Jordan *was* gutless but afraid of his mad mate and couldn't accept being branded a wimp. He followed Darren towards the building.

'What if there's someone in there?'

'There will be you idiot but they're dead.'

Jordan shook his head and followed his "leader". They slipped onto the property. The building was in darkness but with the front well lit. Access to the back of the building required fence scaling.

'Follow me,' said Darren and moved to the front verandah. Darren grabbed a bench and looked to Jordan. He muttered disapproval but helped carry the garden furniture round the back.

Using it, Darren scaled the fence. 'Come on,' he hissed. In the dark back garden of the funeral parlour, they surveyed the scene.

'That's a sensor light,' said Darren pointing. 'Stay here. I'll kill it.'

He crept along the wall, stepped up on a water pipe and reached for the light. Ping. On it came in all its brightness.

'Shit,' whispered Jordan. 'Let's go.'

Darren fiddled and darkness returned. He tried the back door without success. He came to a large glass door also locked.

Jordan joined him. 'What now?'

'The back door's alarmed but not this sliding door.'

'How do you know?'

Darren removed a screwdriver from his belt and gently forced the lock. He'd done this before. 'Let's go,' begged a shaking Jordan.

Snap. The lock broke and Darren gently slid the door. No alarm. Large curtains blocked the way. Darren pushed them and disappeared. Jordan followed into a large dark room.

Darren produced a pencil torch. They struck gold. A coffin rested on a table with others upright against walls.

'Bingo,' said Darren. He moved to the coffin on the table and tried to lift the lid.

'No fucking way,' whispered a terrified Jordan. 'I'm outa here.'

'Undo these screws.' Darren got busy unlocking the lid. 'Come on,' he snarled and Jordan was bullied into helping. The screws came loose. 'Now,' breathed Darren as he lifted the coffin lid.

Both men died. Music began. It wasn't loud or inappropriate but rather lush orchestral strings playing an elegant piece. Then subtle lighting flicked on. The music and lights were on a timer. The thugs could see the room but now *they* could be seen.

'Quick,' whispered Darren. 'Lift it.' Right now Jordan was the most unwilling villain in Melbourne but he knew the sooner he did what he was asked to do, the sooner he could nick off. Jordan struggled. The sight of a stiff was not for him and he lifted with his eyes closed. The lid came off but in stepping to one side to place it on the floor, Jordan stumbled. He dropped the lid which landed on his foot. He hopped in pain, lost his balance and fell knocking an upright coffin which wobbled then fell sideways striking another coffin and thus began a game of funeral-parlour dominoes. The noise was loud and as the cacophony warmed up, an alarm sounded and signalled the stampede.

Sans stiff, both thugs clambered for the exit and attacked the fence. They fell over and ran. Their Burke and Hare score now read Body Snatchers 0, Dead Bodies 2.

Darren drove as quickly and as quietly as he could. The language in the car would have made a bikie blush.

'Take me home,' demanded Jordan. Darren kept driving. 'Darren!'

'We've gotta get a body. This is the way to hurt that bitch.'

'Well why don't we murder somebody and be done with it.'

'Bloody good idea,' he said driving faster.

Jordan despaired. 'I was joking. Let me out of the fucking car!'

'I know the spot,' enthused Darren.

'I'm not killing anyone, not murder.'

'Shut up,' said Darren and sounded frightening even to a thug.

When working in Port Melbourne, Darren saw a junk yard and discovered it was homeless city, a refuge for drunks and druggies.

Darren parked and entered the wasteland with Jordan following—reluctantly. Some residents were drinking, some were smoking what was definitely not tobacco. A couple was copulating and advertising the fact. Darren pulled back some canvas. Rude comments flowed from the resident. It wasn't, "I say, do you mind, old chap?" Darren persisted. Jordan thought he'd be killed. Not everyone with a mental illness sleeps safe in their bed at night.

Darren kept searching then stopped. 'This is it, he's dead.'

'How can you tell?'

'Look at him.'

Jordan did. Here was a man in his forties who looked twice as old. His liver was on life-support with the rest of his body racing to catch up. He stank and a strange sound struggled to escape from his mouth.

'He's still alive,' gasped Jordan.

'That's the death rattle. My grandpa made that noise when he snuffed it. Stick him is this tarp,' said Darren getting busy. Together they wrapped their trophy and took it without paying. If any of the residents saw what happened, they said nothing. Around here, the only commandment was "mind your own fuckin' business".

John Doe was unceremoniously dumped in the back of Darren's 4WD which headed to Detective Joanna Best's apartment.

How many Homicide cops keep a stiff in their bath?

Jo wasn't home being out dining with Homicide colleagues. Only Billy Hughes and Jo remained in the restaurant. The waiters were keen for them to go and hovered without success.

'Has the DI said anything about leaving?' asked Jo.

Billy drained her glass. 'You know Steele. He's Mr Secretive. Just rock up in the morning and it'll be business as usual.'

'And still no breakthrough on the murdered judge?'

'Or that poor woman who drowned in the Yarra. There's plenty of work for you, Missy. Forget the DI, put your head down, and I've had too much to drink.' She reached for her phone.

'I can drive you,' offered the sober Senior.

'No you won't. I've fallen in love with Uber.' She belched.

Jo looked at the hovering waiters and smiled. They smiled back with gratitude and relief. The women went into the street.

'How's that IT friend of yours?' asked Billy. 'Matthew ...'

'Michael.'

'Nothing romantic there?'

'Mind your own business, Sarge, and here's your chariot.'

Jo bundled Billy into a most un-taxi like vehicle and waved her boss away. She yelled. 'Homeski, Joanna, and don't spare the horses.'

At Jo's Homeski, Darren and Jordan carried their trophy around the back of Jo's apartment. They opened the side gate and headed to the ground floor back door. Having "fixed" it on a previous visit, they were soon inside. The deceased person, a former merchant banker, Jeffrey Delaney, had fallen on addictive hard times and refused to help with the heavy lifting.

The hoons got him inside. 'Where do we put him?' asked a heavy breathing Jordan.

'In the bathroom—it's the best place to murder someone.'

Jordan panicked. 'How the fuck do you know that?'

The hoons lumped Jeff to the bathroom where Darren unwrapped the corpse. 'He's still warm. That'll put real pressure on the bitch.'

'That's gross.'

Darren ordered Jordan to gather accoutrements for the laying out ceremony. He didn't say *accoutrements* but, 'Grab her underwear.'

'What?' This was going from disgusting to weird.

'Do it,' snarled Darren and Jordan complied. He returned with some of Jo's smalls. Darren sniffed them. 'Nice. We would have enjoyed the bitch,' he said remembering their attempted rape of the police officer in her bedroom not long ago.

'Come on, let's go,' urged Jordan. Burke was enjoying this but not Hare. No wonder he grassed up his buddy.

Darren placed the tights around the corpse's neck, the bra and panties in their appropriate locations then admired his handiwork.

'Try talking y'self out of this one, bitch,' he said removing his phone. 'We'll call the cops then hang around outside and wait till they rock up.' He punched the digits then spoke in a terrible American accent. It was somewhere between New Joisey and Norlins. 'Police? I wanna report a dead body.' He gave the details then panicked when the operator asked a question. He put his hand over the phone and whispered. 'What's the address?' Jordan looked dumb. 'Go and look,' hissed Darren. 'We're checkin',' he said to the operator in an accent now a cross between LA and Houston.

Darren gave some implausible excuse about breaking in to rob the flat only to discover a dead body in the bathroom. He saw nothing paradoxical in criminals reporting a crime. And no, they wouldn't be giving their names. Jordan returned with the flat and street number which was relayed by Darren. He hung up and celebrated.

'Got the bitch. Right, let's get outside and wait for the cops.'

They looked at the corpse and Darren bent to make a small adjustment to the decorative garments. He froze. Jordan was glad they were in the bathroom because right now he desperately needed the lavatory or, as he would say, the shitter. The lads' change of attitude occurred because the stiff replaced his death rattle with a groan.

Both thugs had a problem with their underwear. Neither spoke. Jeffrey, the merchant banker cum homeless person turned stiff in residence was doing a brilliant impression of someone who was alive.

'He's alive,' gasped Jordan. He spoke much louder and with fear embedded in his language. 'He's fucking alive!'

Even Darren applied to join the *I'm Shitting Myself Club*.

The thugs stared at the corpse which wasn't a corpse. It groaned.

Darren panicked. 'We have to kill him,' he said reaching for the pantyhose around Jeff's neck.

'Are you fucking insane?' screamed Jordan. 'Leave him. Let's go.'

'A drunk won't hurt the bitch. It has to be a stiff.'

Darren grabbed the pantyhose and strangled Jeff who gurgled and groaned. Jordan grabbed Darren and strangled his mate. Mate? Neither strangler was winning and when a police siren was heard, all strangling ceased and poor Jeffrey was let go meaning his head fell back and hit the bowl of the lavatory (he'd also never call it that) meaning his groaning took on a new meaning. Now his sore head added to his multiplicity of woes.

Jordan fled. A furious Darren followed. They flung open the backdoor and died. A uniformed policeman, who was large of body and fierce of mind, was about to bang on the door. His colleague was already rat-tat-tatting out front.

'Good evening, gentlemen,' was all the cop got to say before Burke and Hare charged into him in their bid for freedom. They were out the back gate and into the street with the gendarme, if he had a whistle, blowing his whistle in pursuit. He attracted the attention of his colleague who saw the fleeing footpads and joined the chase.

Benny Hill grabbed his saxophone. Darren ran for his vehicle but Jordan ran for his namesake, near Syria. A cop closed in on each crook. The Chief Commissioner would have been delighted with the fitness level of his officers. They outran the bumbling Burke and Hare, arrested then frogmarched them back to the scene of the crime. Later, Darren and Jordan did time and copped plenty of mocking publicity which was ironical as they did all this because of being mocked.

The police radioed their situation and another two patrol cars arrived with flashing lights. The locals were up for some free entertainment. Inside, Jeffrey was gasping and could have murdered a beer. Just as the party began, who should arrive but the occupier of the flat in question? Jo Best pulled up and stared at the circus.

Welcome back to Homicide, Detective.

2

IF YOU THINK GOING VIRAL on a social media platform is all pervasive, you should check the police gossip grapevine. It smashes everything. When Jo arrived at Homicide the next morning, the whole building knew about the bloke in her bathroom. One story had him as Jo's secret lover, dressed in drag and entertaining her neighbours. Had it been the lead story on TV and retweeted a trillion times, it would not have been as public as cops telling cops.

As Jo walked into Homicide, she remembered her first day in the job only a few months ago. Heaps had happened since she became a detective and here she was starting again—for the third time. She wanted a low-key entrance. Fat chance.

She entered the Incident Room where cheering, whistles and applause with desk-thumping greeted her arrival. Colleagues made her welcome but boy did they stir the pot. Even her former fiercest enemy, Senior Constable Stephen Payne was modestly polite in his ribbing. Everyone made facetious remarks about strange men and her choice of boyfriend. DI Richelieu made serious eye contact. Jo thought he was wearing contact lenses because his blue eyes had turned a more Pacific Ocean hue with a touch of sunshine and white beaches.

'Bienvenue Mademoiselle,' he oozed kissing her hand. *So, not all bad then* thought Jo.

After the razzamatazz settled, Billy Hughes called the troops together. She'd been given the task of co-ordinating the two current homicide investigations—the supermarket worker and the Supreme Court judge—what a duo. No sooner had Billy begun then the boss walked in. DI Steele would often slide in and sit observing not so much the status of the case being discussed but rather the behaviour of his colleagues. *Who is a threat to me?*

9

Today was different. He waited causing Billy to pause. 'Sir?'

He sniffed in an exaggerated way. 'Thank you, Sergeant.' She moved aside. He was up for an announcement. 'I want you to be the first to know I've been appointed to a senior position within the AFP.' He waited for a reaction hoping congratulations would ensue. Silence. Many wanted to react in an honest way but reckoned wild cheering would not go down well.

Richelieu saved the DI from total embarrassment, more as a salute to a fellow senior officer. 'Félicitations, Inspecteur.' Steele continued.

'My position here will be advertised but until the new appointment, DI Richelieu will be Acting Head of Homicide.'

This time the troops found their voice. The French Aussie was slapped on the back, people applauded with all feelings sincere. Steele took it as a slap in the face—which it was. Jo felt a twinge of unease. *Will the repressed sexual tension between me and the DI continue now he's the head honcho?*

Steele announced he would take leave making his Homicide exit immediate and, true to his word, he left. Nobody called him back to thank him or wish him well. Nobody planned a farewell drink. Right now the two happiest people in Homicide were Steele and Best.

He was glad to get away from a job he disliked and she was glad to see the back of the man who hated her, she reckoned, because she got results.

Jo waited for Richelieu to receive the last of his congratulatory comments then approached him with a smile. She held out a hand. He grasped it but she manoeuvred his hand, said, 'Félicitations, Inspecteur,' raised his hand and kissed it, then returned to her chair. Richelieu wasn't sure if that was a "You're even more attractive now" line or a "Dear John" message in vocal form.

Most of the room either didn't notice the Best and Richelieu "incident" or, if they did, regarded it as typical behaviour for anyone dealing with the dapper Francophile. Billy saw it and thought otherwise. *I need to speak to that girl.*

'Well, sir,' said Billy, indicating the new head of Homicide, 'if I may continue.'

'Oui Sergeant ..."

The whole room finished his sentence. '... s'il vous plait.' The laughter was loud and friendly and carried down the corridor to DI Steele's office. He didn't care. He was outa here.

Ken Galbraith worried. His wife had recently been fished out of the Yarra near their home in Warburton, about 50 miles north of Melbourne. Why was he worried? Surely he'd be devastated or distraught even shattered. No, he worried because he couldn't tell the police where he was on the night his wife died. Well he could but he sure as hell didn't want to. That night Ken was playing away.

Bethany Pieterson worried. Her lover's wife had recently been fished out of the Yarra near her home in Warburton and Bethany was the alibi for Karen's hubby. He couldn't have murdered his wife, assuming she was murdered, because he was being intimate with his lover. This made it tough for Bethany. She didn't want to give Ken an alibi because that might mean her husband, Brandon, would discover that Bethany and Ken were an item. Oh dear. What a tangled web and all that jazz.

To make it worse, Bethany's hubby Brandon already knew about his wife playing away but was yet to inform the lovers of that fact.

For the cheating couple, lying seemed the only option. Ken and Bethany were able to discuss their predicament because they taught together at the nearby Yarra Junction High School. They had a regular date when on yard duty.

'What happened?' whispered Bethany.

'No idea,' replied Ken tossing a basketball back to a student.

'What did you tell the police?'

'Nothing, yet. The Homicide cops are coming to see me tomorrow.'

'I think Brandon knows about us.'

Ken tried to hide his astonishment. 'You're kidding.'

'If we lie to the police and he tells them about us, we're in trouble.'

'Why? We didn't kill her.'

'Was she killed or was it an accident?'

The bell sounded and students moved. Ken dropped his banana skin in a bin and they headed inside 'Don't send me any texts. Okay?' Bethany looked sad. 'And we tell the cops we were planning the school camp. We tell them we were together on school business.'

'So what we were doing in your car was school business?'

He gave her a certain look. 'Just do it.'

Jo was delighted to be heading to see the police pathologist but wary that she sat beside the now acting head of Homicide. Richelieu asked Jo to drive. He sounded his usual polite and gentlemanly self but really it gave him the chance to ponder the young detective he wanted to bed. That's bed not wed.

'Mademoiselle, it is magnifique to have you back in 'omicide.'

'Thank you, sir,' she replied keeping her eyes on the road.

'I 'ope you will not allow my recent promotion to interrupt our beautiful friendship.'

What the hell does that mean?

She gave a weak smile and changed the subject. 'I'm not up to speed on either of these murders, sir. Please allow me time to catch up.'

'You can 'ave all the time in the world, ma chére.'

'So, no confessions or persons of interest?'

'Certainly no confessions but there are several persons of interest. One problem, 'owever, is that we are not certain the drowning in Warburton is a murder. This trip may 'elp us reach that conclusion.'

They parked and Jo felt excited as they approached the pathologist, the fiery Dr Gabrielle Strange. She beamed, shrieked and threw wide her arms. They embraced.

'It's the deranged detective. Hello, you gorgeous girl.'

'Good morning, Doctor Strange. Long-time no see.'

'Far too long.' She spoke to Richelieu. 'I order you to give this detective your finest homicides.'

'Naturellement,' smiled Richelieu.

Jo became serious. 'You should be more respectful, madam.' Strange looked strange. 'DI Richelieu is the new head of Homicide.'

'Acting, s'il vous plait,' he said smiling at the pathologist.

'Does this mean the man of steel has upped and flown away?'

'It does,' said Jo, 'to the Feds.'

'Pity the Feds. Now,' she said looking for her notes. 'The woman in the river is a mystery.'

'Mystery, Madame?' asked the DI.

'No DNA, hardly a sign of a struggle and I reckon the coroner could easily record a verdict of death by misadventure.'

The police were thrown. 'Are you trying to put us out of a job, Doctor?' asked Jo.

'I'm told the woman could swim and the river's not exactly full fathom five. Why didn't she walk out? Was she depressed?'

'Are you suggesting suicide, Doctor?' asked Richelieu.

'Not my job, Monsieur l'inspecteur. I assume there were no stones in her pockets?' The police stared. 'Was she going mad like Virginia Woolf?' Silence reigned. 'That poor woman filled her coat pockets with stones and walked into the River Ouse—not found for weeks.'

Richelieu cleared his throat. 'So are you recommending we do not investigate this death, Madame?'

'Not necessarily.' Strange was usually a person of definite opinions but here she hedged her bets. 'But I'm not fence sitting with His Honour.' She produced a file and spoke with an American accent. 'Here come da judge.' She looked at her notes. 'This was no accident.'

'Are you stating the bleeding obvious, Madame?' asked the DI.

'Oui and bizarre doesn't begin to cover it.' Jo was fascinated. Being back in Homicide made her feel alive and the harder or more bizarre the case, the more she liked it. 'He was drugged and there are no defensive marks. He sat there and they drove into him.'

'Please elaborate, Madame, s'il vous plait.'

She smiled. 'All in my report, Monsieur l'inspecteur.'

3

OF COURSE ALL MURDERS should be treated equally. Of course the police should thoroughly investigate every homicide with the same dedication, resources and professionalism. But human nature being it what it is, the murder of a Supreme Court judge, meant the Victoria Police Homicide Squad found itself under abnormal pressure.

Both sides of politics jumped on the law and order bandwagon. The Premier gave the Chief Commissioner a call. He rang the Assistant Commissioner Crime and he contacted Homicide where the current boss was one DI Pierre Richelieu and, talented as he was, the pressure from above and the need for a speedy arrest, tested the handsome investigator. He addressed his fellow detectives.

'Mesdames and Monsieurs, we 'ave pressure from our masters to solve this judicial 'omicide as soon as possible, n'est-ce pas?'

'Are we giving this murder priority, sir?' asked DS Hughes.

'Please Sergeant, I 'ave enough of the leading questions already. We 'ave no confirmation that the drowning in Warburton is in fact an 'omicide and DS Fleming will investigate that case.'

'Sir,' replied Fleming looking displeased.

'You, DS Hughes will take charge of the murder of 'is 'onour. Gather your teams and I require daily reports on the judge's 'omicide because that is what the powers that be 'ave demanded of me. Any questions?' Nobody spoke. 'Begin, s'il vous plaît.'

Jo was hoping Billy Hughes would assign her to the judge's murder so when Justin Fleming approached, she crumbled inside.

'You're with me, Senior.' Jo looked at Hughes who met her eye then looked away. 'It's a trip to the Yarra Valley, so grab y'gumboots.'

Jo drove as Fleming poured over the pathologist's report and notes from local police and detectives who were the first responders.

'I hate these homicides,' he said. 'Did she jump or was she pushed?'

'That's if it *is* a homicide, Sarge. Dr Strange expressed doubts.'

'We'll have small town secrets with nobody talking or, if they do, saying nothing of value.'

'I didn't have you down as Mr Prejudice, Sarge.' She kept her eyes on the road. *Have I ruined a beautiful friendship on our first date?*

He sniffed. 'I've heard about you. Cracked a case or two and put a few noses out of joint. Well remember, Detective, you're only as good as your last gig. Screw up on this and you're back in the pack.'

For a while, they drove in silence. Then she started. 'May I ask why you chose me, Sarge?'

'Ah, your first mistake—making assumptions is mucho dangerous.'

Jo let that sink in. She twigged. 'So you didn't choose me. Sergeant Hughes rejected me.'

'Correct, only I think you'll find the direction came from Poirot flexing his newly-acquired muscle.'

That hurt. *Why would the DI push me out of town when the juiciest murder in ages was there for the taking?*

'I think Monsieur Poirot was Belgian, Sarge. Perhaps the DI's code name should be Maigret.' He looked at her and sniffed. Touché.

Billy Hughes led her two Senior Constables down the drive of the late Ranald Slight's South Yarra property. Baldwin and Payne were keen to impress but wondered why the golden girl had been sent to the sticks.

'Doctor Strange described it as a bizarre murder. What did she mean?' asked Hughes.

'Killed by your own car is not a conventional weapon,' said Baldwin.

'And in your own driveway,' added Payne.

'We're under serious pressure to solve this case quickly and quietly.'

'Quietly, Sarge?' asked Payne.

'There's a long list of VIPs to be interviewed and right now the DI is comparing notes with the AC. We do the nuts and bolts and he does the bowing and scraping.' The two Senior Constables looked at one another. They'd been told. 'So tell me, how did he die and why?'

'It's number 44,' said Fleming, 'there.' Jo pulled up outside a friendly weatherboard with a friendly garden. The police had an appointment with Ken Galbraith, widower and adulterer.

He opened the door and smiled. 'Good morning.' His heart raced.

'Mr Galbraith?' asked Fleming. There were introductions all round and the trio sat in the friendly lounge. There was a lot of friendliness in this part of Warburton.

Fleming offered their condolences and then cut to the chase. Jo liked his style. 'Tell us about your wife, Mr Galbraith.'

Short, thought Jo, *to the point and pressure immediately on the interviewee. No simple answer. Make him talk.*

Galbraith seemed to relax. He was prepared more for the "Did you kill your wife, sir?" type question.

'Well, she was a friendly,' (there's that word again) 'and kind lady. She was a wonderful wife and mother.'

'You have children, sir?'

'A son. He's staying with a mate at the moment. I thought it best to get him away from ... well, from missing his mother.'

'Of course,' said Fleming playing the caring parent role. 'And can we go back to the day your wife died? When did you last see her alive?'

Galbraith's Fit Bit kicked in. 'When I left for work.'

'And what time was that?'

'About 7.'

'7 am.'

'No, 7 pm.'

'In the evening?'

'Yes, I went back to school for a meeting to plan the Year 7 camp.'

'And they reckon teachers have a cushy job.' Fleming added a smile and Galbraith returned a weaker one. Jo noticed the widower's body language. *This man is under pressure and it doesn't look like grief.*

'So after the meeting, Mr Galbraith, when did you get home?'

'About 10 I think. Karen wasn't home. My son, Darren was watching TV.' *Karen and Darren*, thought Jo. 'I asked him where his mother was and he didn't know. 'She went out,' he said. 'Then the police came and told us what happened.'

Fleming had 112 questions. Jo had more. Galbraith knew the pressure was coming and it did.

'So who was at the meeting for the Year 8 school camp?'

Jo liked Fleming's deliberate mistake. *I think it was deliberate.*

Galbraith didn't correct the detective. 'Just me and another teacher, Bethany Pieterson.'

Both the police heard alarm bells. Fleming cut to the chase.

'What do you think happened to your wife, Mr Galbraith?'

He was expecting a grilling about his "meeting" with the lovely Bethany. Jo liked the tactic of switching subjects when least expected. Ken was flustered. 'Ah, she drowned. I thought you knew that.'

They did of course but wanted to know why, and if anyone helped her to die. 'Was your wife under any stress, sir?'

Again Jo liked the short questions. *Make them blunt and put the pressure back on the interviewee.*

'No, I don't think so.'

'You don't know if your wife was unwell?' More pressure.

'No, I do know she wasn't unwell. She would have said.'

'You would have noticed, surely?'

'Yes. Yes, of course.'

'And this other teacher you mentioned ...'

'Bethany Pieterson,' said Jo glancing at her notes.

Fleming appreciated Jo's support. 'Was Ms Pieterson at the meeting until it ended?'

'Yes. In fact I drove her home.'

'And where does she live?'

Oh shit, thought Ken. He gave the detectives his lover's details.

DI Richelieu entered the chambers of the late Ranald Slight. His associate, Ms Freya Dunkeld wore a "Neat as a pin" badge on her cardigan. Her hair in a bun was controlled by Praetorian Guard bobby pins. If Richelieu wanted information, it was at her fingertips.

They sat in the late judge's chambers although not behind his desk. 'Tell me, Mademoiselle, 'ow long 'ave you worked for Judge Slight?' Richelieu was reluctant to refer to the judge as His Honour due to his pronunciation being 'is 'onour.

'Four years, sir.'

Richelieu wasn't sure if that was *for* or *four* years. 'And what can you tell me about 'im?'

Freya had a lump in her throat and moist eyes. 'He was a wonderful man, a brilliant jurist, and kind.' She choked. Richelieu gave her time.

'It is indeed a tragedy that 'is 'onour,' (It just slipped out) 'should die so young. I can assure you, the police will do everything to bring whoever is responsible to justice.' He paused.

She dabbed her eyes. 'Thank you,' escaped as a whisper.

'Did the judge receive threats from people 'e sentenced?'

Her head shook. 'None. Everyone admired him.'

High praise indeed. Was the woman in love with her boss?

'Can you give me a list of the people 'e was close to 'ere in the Court?' She nodded. 'And a list of people 'e was close too outside the Court.' She looked at him. 'S'il vous plait?' She nodded again and thought. *Are all Frenchmen so charming?* He paused. 'Can you think of anything that may be relevant to 'is murder?'

The poor man is dead, she thought. *It is better coming from me.* She related an incident many years ago when the judge, then a humble solicitor, helped a barrister friend avoid jail.

Richelieu smiled. 'Merci, Mademoiselle. And do you know of anyone who may 'ave wished to 'arm the judge?'

That was far more threatening than asking for a list of contacts. She felt the pressure. Richelieu sensed her fear.

'I'm not sure,' she murmured.

'Is that because you don't know or because you're reluctant to say?'

That made things worse. She felt trapped. Richelieu slowed the pace, lowered the pressure and subtly encouraged her to reply.

'I'm not sure I wish to answer that question,' she said.

'Please Mademoiselle, anything you say will be 'eld in the strictest confidence. I give you my word as a police officer and a gentleman.'

She handed him a USB stick. 'These emails may be of interest.' She gave a faint smile, summoned up the courage, and spoke the name of the person she believed had ordered the murder of the judge.

4

BETHANY GOT THE CALL from Ken. 'The cops are coming to you.'

'What will I say?'

'The truth, as we agreed.'

'What, the truth about us?'

'Just that we planned the school camp and I drove you home. That's all I told them. Oh, and that I've no idea what happened to Karen.'

'I'm worried.'

'We had nothing to do with Karen's death.'

'Not Karen, Brandon. I think he knows.'

That stopped Ken. He felt reasonably confident he could handle the cops but Bethany's husband was big and red-headed with a temper to match. Ken reckoned there should be a warning on the frontispiece of the *Handbook for Blokes who Sleep With Married Women*. "Make sure her old man's a wimp".

'They're here,' said Bethany as a car pulled up outside her house.

'Stay calm,' said Ken and hung up. He didn't take his own advice.

Bethany let them in and the interview began.

'Did you know Karen Galbraith, Bethany?' asked Fleming.

She nodded. Her nerves were nervous. 'Yes. But we weren't close.'

'And what were you doing on the night Karen died, from say 7 pm?'

What part of the truth can I mention? Will I destroy my marriage?

'I stayed at school and did some marking and lesson preparation.'

'Wow, I'm impressed with you dedicated teachers.' Fleming smiled. 'And what happened next?' He stopped smiling.

'Ah Mr Galbraith, arrived and we made plans for the Year 7 camp.'

'Until when?' Bethany paused. Uncomfortable didn't even come close. 'I can't be sure of the time.'

'Have a guess. An hour, two?'

'Two,' she said and Jo felt sorry for her. She didn't lie well.

'How did you get home, Bethany?'

'Ken drove me.'

'You don't have a car?'

'My husband had the car at his work, and because Ken drives past my place, he gives me a lift.'

Fleming wanted to ask if that was all he gave her. 'When did you hear about Mrs Galbraith's death?'

'Um, later that night, I'm not sure of the time.'

'And how did you hear the news?'

'Ken sent me a text.'

Fleming let things settle. He was sure, well certain, that Bethany was holding back something but uncertain if that something was pertinent to the drowning. He still wasn't calling it murder.

'How would you describe the Galbraith marriage?'

Warning bells clanged. This was quicksand territory. Bethany knew the wrong answer could trap her and worse. Brandon was good at losing his temper. She flipped. The pressure got to her and she lost it.

'I don't know,' she said, her words partly lost in her cries. The police exchanged glances. Fleming nodded to Jo as in, "You have a go".

She paused allowing the woman to settle. 'We know it's difficult, Bethany. All we want to do is find out how Karen died. If you can help us, we'll be extremely grateful.' Jo paused. 'Would you like a cuppa?'

Bethany recovered and stood. 'I'll make it.' She went to the kitchen.

Fleming spoke softly. 'Good work. Do your female bonding thing.'

Jo wondered if this was a branch of mansplaining and followed Bethany. Fleming took a close look at some family photos. A few minutes later Jo emerged alone.

'We're done, Sarge.' He looked puzzled. 'Now.' She left. He looked towards the kitchen, shrugged and followed Jo.

In the car he muttered. 'I'm starting to feel redundant. Don't tell me she confessed to the murder or told you whodunit?'

'It's as we guessed. She and Ken are lovers and she feels bad. Her boyfriend's wife is dead and her husband knows about the affair.'

'Feeling sorry for people ain't in the Homicide manual, madam.'

'She and Ken were too busy making whoopee to drown poor Karen. If she was murdered, it wasn't by them.'

Fleming grunted. 'I was warned about you when I came back to Homicide.' He didn't know what else to say and Jo said nothing. He changed topics. 'Next stop is Karen's sister.' He spoke to the GPS mimicking an American accent. 'Toin left at the next crossroad.'

Richelieu worried. The AC Crime had decreed. 'This case is important, Pierre. Do not upset, antagonise or in any way intimidate the legal profession. Clear any questionable decisions with me first.'

'Sir,' replied the French Australian.

'If you're thinking of applying for the Homicide job, you'll have Buckley's if you screw up the judge's murder.'

'Sir,' he said again. He wanted to say he disliked his new role and had no intention of applying for same but for now kept schtum. He worried because the murdered judge's associate, Freya Dunkeld, had given Richelieu the name of the person she believed conspired to murder the judge. The name was a senior person in the criminal justice system and one which would certainly need to be passed to the AC, if not higher. Richelieu stood on the CBD pavement and called his boss.

'Crowley.'

'It's DI Richelieu, sir. I need to see you immediately.'

'What's happened? Does this require a face to face meeting?'

'It does.'

'I'm at home. Come down the drive.'

Karen's sister grieved. Denise Wallington was older than her deceased sister, a spinster and a retired children's librarian. She was the first person the police encountered in mourning. The sisters were obviously close and with their parents dead and no other siblings, Denise felt the strain. It was easy for the detectives to be sympathetic.

Jo admired the softer side of Fleming. But she wondered if the sister's grief hid something. Plenty of distraught relatives had later turned out to be the one what done it, guv'nor.

'It's a mystery,' said Denise. 'Everyone loved Karen. I can't think of anyone who would want to hurt let alone murder her.' She slipped back into her sadness.

'Can you think of any reason why she would go out on the night she died?' asked Fleming.

Big sister shook her head. 'And why didn't she tell Darren where she was going? It doesn't make sense. Sometimes the supermarket calls her in if they're short of staff but they didn't.'

Fleming looked at Jo inviting her to ask the difficult questions.

'Denise, was there anything troubling Karen? Did she have money or marriage problems, anything which may have caused her to ...'

Denise came alive. 'Kill herself? No! That is ridiculous.'

Jo paused. 'I'm sorry but we have to ask these tough questions.'

'She told me her husband was having an affair.'

Her husband? Why not use his name?

'When did she tell you this?'

'Her name's Bethany Pieterson and they teach at the same school in Yarra Junction.' Denise felt better. She wanted to say that.

Jo looked at Fleming. He gave a mini nod. "Keep going".

'And you can't think of anyone who might wish to harm Karen?'

That was too hard. If there *was* someone, thinking about it ramped up her distress. Fleming asked a couple more questions but Denise was not for interviewing. The death of her sister hit hard, it punched below the belt. Denise walked them to the door and she addressed Fleming.

'When will they release her body? I want to bury my sister.'

'The Coroner needs to be satisfied Karen didn't meet with foul play. But as soon as the investigation's complete, you'll be told.'

'Where is the Coroner based? Is it near the Supreme Court?'

Fleming explained. Jo thought. *Why mention the Supreme Court?*

They thanked Denise and left, drove into town and bought some lunch. Fleming ate rubbish because his wife wasn't there. Jo ate healthy. They sat by the river and Fleming gave her the third degree.

'Who have we missed, Senior?'

'Darren Galbraith. He may know why his mother left the house.'

'How old is he?'

'Sixteen.'

'If Ken and Bethany give each other an alibi, what's their motive to kill Karen?'

'And was Denise genuinely upset or using her grief to cover her anger towards her sister?'

Fleming choked on his sausage roll. 'What?'

'Just asking. Billy Hughes taught me to disbelieve everything.'

Fleming wiped the sauce from his face and the pastry flakes from his jacket. *Bloody women.*

Richelieu walked down the drive of the AC's expensive abode in Kew. His study was tucked away at the rear overlooking a glorious garden.

'Come in, Pierre. Coffee?'

'Merci, Monsieur.'

The AC passed the cup. It wasn't instant. 'So what's so important a phone call wouldn't do?'

The DI sipped his coffee. The AC sensed the issue was serious. 'I 'ave met the judge's associate, a woman who 'as a 'igh regard for the judge. She is sensible and 'ow you say, down to earth.' Another coffee sip pushed the tension higher. 'She told me the names of people the judge 'ad contact with both in the court and outside.'

'And?'

'These people can be investigated discreetly.'

The AC reckoned Richelieu would not make a good head of Homicide. *These basic matters don't require my attention. A good leader understands that.* But then the AC got the news.

'I asked the young woman if she knew of anyone who may 'ave wished to 'arm the judge?' The AC forgot about his coffee. 'She gave me one name—the Attorney-General.'

'The current Victorian Attorney-General?' Richelieu nodded. 'He murdered Judge Slight?' Richelieu shrugged. The AC stared at his visitor in disbelief. *No wonder Richelieu wanted a face to face.*

'Or conspired to do so,' said the DI. That ramped up the pressure.

'Is this a wild guess, a fantasy from a dedicated employee, what?'

Richelieu opened his brief case and removed a tablet. He opened a file and handed the tablet to his host.

'These are emails the associate says are from the AG.' Crowley read and his mouth opened.

'But there's no ID. How could she know the sender?'

'The judge stated they could only be from one person, someone who knew something about an incident in the life of Ranald Slight.'

'What incident?'

'The judge and the AG fell out as Law students at Melbourne. The associate told me the judge 'elped a friend get out of a crime many years ago and the AG knew about it. Those emails carry specific threats against Slight with the sender clearly trying to intimidate the judge.'

The AC scrolled through the emails. 'These are fantastic, dynamite.'

'If we can discover who sent the emails, sir, we 'ave grounds to interview the AG.'

'Under caution?'

'Under caution,' repeated the DI.

'Jesus, Mary and Joseph,' said the AC blowing air. 'I'll have to take this upstairs.' Richelieu shrugged. 'How did you get these?'

'The associate made copies before Judge Slight deleted them. She 'ad access to 'is papers, emails, letters, the lot. 'e obviously trusted 'er.'

'Can *we* trust her?'

'Oui, I think so.'

'But can you discover who sent the emails?'

'There is an IT expert we 'ave used in the past?'

Crowley remembered his involvement with Jo Best. 'Is that Senior Constable Best's colleague?'

Richelieu was impressed. 'Oui, that is 'im.'

The AC took control. 'Right, we keep this under wraps. If we talk on the phone we refer to "the evidence". Understood?'

'Sir. But I will 'ave to speak to Senior Constable Best if I am to involve 'er computer friend.'

'Okay, but she must tell nobody. I'll contact the Chief Commissioner and you deal with Best. Do nothing till you hear from me. My god, this could bring down the government.' The men walked to Richelieu's car. 'Well done, Pierre. Are you thinking of applying for the Homicide job?'

'Non, Monsieur. I am 'appy to be Napoleon's general but not the Emperor 'imself. Find someone else to take the job, s'il vous plait.'

5

DS FLEMING AND JO tracked down Darren Galbraith, the teenage son of the woman who drowned in the Yarra. His father wanted to attend any interview and so all four met in the park in the main street.

The teen was up for a chat, thinking the whole experience was cool, something to tell his mates. His father didn't share that enthusiasm.

Fleming began. 'On the night your Mum sadly drowned, Darren, where were you?'

'At home.'

'What were you doing?'

'Watching TV in me room.'

'Can you remember the show?'

'It was a movie but I can't remember the name.'

'Was it a thriller, romantic comedy, what?'

'Actually I think it was a zombie film on DVD my mate gave me.'

The cops looked at one another. Forget timelines.

'So you were watching a movie and where was your Mum?'

'In the lounge I think or maybe the kitchen.'

'And what happened?'

'I think she said she was going out for a minute.'

Jo took notes and Fleming asked questions. 'That's what she said? I'm going out for a minute?' Darren nodded. His father seemed relieved. 'Did she get a phone call, a text, did someone come to the front door?'

Darren needed think music. 'I don't think so. No, wait. I think I heard the doorbell.'

'You never told me that,' said his father.

'Please, Mr Galbraith,' interrupted Fleming who switched back to the lad. 'You *think* you heard the doorbell but you're not sure?'

'No, I did hear it. Then me Mum called out.'

'And she said what?'

Darren had to think. The police wanted to know if he'd repeat what he said before. 'Darren, I'm going out for a minute.'

Fleming looked at Ken. 'Any thoughts, Mr Galbraith?'

He shook his head. 'Sorry.'

'The time is super important here, Darren. Can you think what time it was when your Mum left?'

He didn't have a clue. 'Nuh.'

'Was it before your father came home?'

More think music. 'All I can remember is that when me Dad came home, he smelled of perfume.'

Ouch.

The drive back to Melbourne involved discussion about the people they'd interviewed, what they discovered and what needed to be done. Jo was driving when her phone rang, in her bag on the back seat.

'Would you mind, Sarge?'

Fleming fished out her phone and answered it. 'Detective Jo Best's phone, DS Fleming speaking.' The caller was surprised. 'She's driving, sir. I'll put you on speaker.' He whispered. 'It's the DI.'

'Hello sir.'

'Something 'as come up, Mademoiselle and I need to contact your computer friend.'

'Michael Chan?'

'Oui. When you are back in Melbourne, please give me a call.'

'Something important, sir?'

There was a pause. Richelieu remembered the AC's order about confidentiality. 'Not so important it cannot wait. 'ow did your trip to the country go?'

'I'll let DS Fleming tell you, sir.' She looked at her companion.

'Ah, good and bad, sir. Lots of lies and half-truths but the two main questions remain unanswered.'

'Two main questions?'

'Why did the dead woman leave the house and was she murdered, and if so, by whom?'

'That's three questions.'

'Sorry?'

'And the answers?'

'All the same, sir, we don't know. Any luck with the judge?'

'I would not call it luck, Sergeant. Drive carefully. Au revoir.'

The DI ended the call and the detectives looked at one another. Fleming replaced Jo's phone. 'I didn't know the DI did cryptic. So what's with your computer friend?'

Jo spoke with a French accent. 'I 'ave no idea, Monsieur.' Fleming laughed. Jo was thinking. *Why does Pierre want to contact Michael? And why didn't he discuss his interview over the phone?*

It was late Saturday afternoon when Jo made it home. She delayed ringing Richelieu and couldn't be sure why. *Is he using Michael Chan as an excuse to get me alone? Does he think his current promotion makes him even more attractive? What is it with me and the Heads of Homicide? Who can I ask? Billy? No way. The pathetic pathologist? Too risky. Come on, Joanna. Pick up the bloody phone.*

His dulcet tones had a warming effect on certain parts of her body. 'Bonjour, Mademoiselle. What kept you? I was beginning to worry.'

'Sorry sir, minor matter of bare cupboards. How can I help?'

'I 'ave a difficult situation, ma chère. I need a favour from your friend Michael.' Jo was intrigued. 'It is 'ighly confidential and I can only discuss this when gazing into your beautiful eyes.'

Jo had that conflicted emotions moment. *Yes please* and *no thank you* both shouted their POV.

'I see,' was all she could muster.

'Let me take you to dinner and we can make a plan to tackle this case together.'

That was either a bloody good offer or else a bloody good offer. She decided to take the bloody good offer option.

'As always, you sound intriguing, sir.'

'I will call for you in 'alf an 'our. Oui?'

'Oui,' she replied, disconnected the call and made another.

'Michael Chan speaking.'

'Joanna Best speaking.'

He laughed. 'Hello stranger. I thought you must have died.'

'Not this week. How are you, Michael? And Alan?'

'We're both well. Now I could be polite and continue this small talk but something tells me that would be delaying the inevitable. So please, why don't I say "sorry, I'm not available" before you even start.'

'I am insisting you get paid.'

He wasn't expecting that and was hooked. 'Paid for what?'

'I can't say now but I believe it's big.' She was lying because she suspected the DI was spinning a yarn to get her into his bed.

'You can't say? You expect me to participate in another of your hair-brain schemes sight unseen?'

'Exactly, only this time, you'll get folding stuff in your hand.'

He ramped up the sarcasm. 'Where do I sign?'

'I'll call you to arrange a meet.'

'A meet! Have you joined the text-speak revolution?'

She laughed. 'It's lovely to hear you, Michael. I'll be in touch. Bye.'

She smiled. She liked Michael Chan. He smiled. He liked Jo Best.

Richelieu knocked on Jo's door. He was always on time and held out a small but expensive bouquet of flowers. Someone had spent time on this arrangement. He didn't speak but smiled and Jo thought a flash of light may have pinged off his teeth.

'Oh thank you, they're beautiful. Come in, I'll pop them in water.' He still hadn't said a word and the silence unnerved her. 'Lost your tongue—sir?'

He smiled again. 'It is wonderful to 'ave you back in 'omicide.' He took her hand and kissed it.

Come on, what's not to like about this bloke?

He took her to a Turkish restaurant in Sydney Road. It was busy and noisy which is what he wanted. They ordered and he told all.

'Something major 'as 'appened with the case from South Yarra. I 'ave told the AC Crime and 'e 'as given permission for me to tell you.'

This wasn't a romantic meeting—so far—but it sure got Jo's attention. Richelieu explained the emails and their alleged source.

'Wow,' she mouthed.

'So I am 'oping your computer friend can 'elp find the sender. Can you please ask 'im?'

'I can.'

'And will 'e keep the matter a secret?'

'He will.'

Their food arrived. Richelieu asked about Warburton with Jo telling all. Richelieu ate and stopped speaking. Jo sensed his concern.

'Is something troubling you, sir?'

'I 'ave a favour to ask, Joanna, s'il vous plait.' She tensed. 'When we are alone like so, I would like you to call me Pierre—please.'

The word *please* sounded foreign and she smiled. 'Naturellement.'

He smiled and she melted faster than the cheese and avocado on her grilled chicken.

'I wish to tell you I am not a candidate for the 'omicide position.'

'Oh?'

'Being an ambitious leader is not, 'ow you say, my thing. I 'ope there will soon be a permanent new 'ead of 'omicide.'

'Well let's hope you go out with a bang.' She whispered. 'Arresting the state's senior legal officer for conspiracy to murder would place a very large feather in your cap.' Their glasses clinked.

'Merci Mademoiselle, Merci.'

He drove her home. She wanted to invite him in for coffee but didn't trust herself. She couldn't resist expensive chocolates or the lips of the man who took her to dinner.

'I will make a time with Michael and we can pay him a visit.'

'As you wish,' said Richelieu disappointed their evening was about to end. They looked at one another. She held her bag in front of her chest. This ruled out an embrace but not osculation. They both moved and the lip connection lasted a nanosecond short of three seconds.

6

JOHN CLINGTON RAPED WOMEN. Experts declared him a psychopath, extremely dangerous and someone who would continue offending unless caught. The police reckoned that was stating the bleeding obvious and wanted him caught yesterday. They dealt with the aftermath in the person of a traumatised female who would probably suffer from her ordeal until her dying day. In fact it wouldn't surprise to learn she'd have the odd shudder in her grave.

Clington didn't stop at one victim. His sordid lifestyle had no use-by date. He lived for his next thrill. He was yet to murder but that seemed only a matter of time.

The police had Clington as a person of interest with a bullet against his name. Not as in shoot him, although many wanted to do that, no, this was a bullet as in rising up the charts. Clington was destined to become rapist #1.

The detectives were excited when the latest victim identified him from mug shots. Finally they had enough evidence to make an arrest. They planned the raid in minute detail. The man was nabbed and gave up without a struggle. His mother was angry, not shocked, but furious.

'He didn't do it. How dare you arrest my son. This is an outrage.'

The police concentrated on the only rape for which they had a good chance of a conviction. They built a watertight case. Without boasting, they took enormous pride in a job well done until disaster struck.

A woman, Gwenda Balance, came forward to make a statement that John Clington and his mother were in her home the night the alleged rape took place and so therefore Mr Clington could not be guilty.

Detectives interviewed Mrs Balance. She'd known the Clingtons for years. They used to be neighbours. And Mrs Balance was adamant.

Mrs Clington and her boy dined at her home that night. Even Gwenda's son, Eddie, who often rang his Mum, told police he was sure his mother told him the Clingtons were with her that night.

'You don't sound certain, Mr Balance,' said the officer taking his statement.

'I definitely remember Mum talking about the Clingtons.'

'But was she saying they were in the house at that time or were due tomorrow, next week or some other time?'

Eddie shook his head. 'That doesn't ring a bell.'

The detectives from the Sexual Offences Team groaned. This was a major setback. It was a battle lost but hopefully not the war.

And so rapist John Clington was released. The charges were dropped, (some officers preferred pending), the police were ropeable, the victims suicidal, and the criminal was free to rape again.

After the visits to Warburton, South Yarra and the Supreme Court, Homicide officers gathered in the Incident Room. Richelieu was not there. He told two people he wasn't interested in the Homicide vacancy. He told the highest and the lowest—the Assistant Commissioner and Jo Best—but gossip didn't need a leak to thrive.

'I heard the new boss is DI Reynolds.'

'Who's he?'

'Mate of Steele's only worse.'

'Why didn't DI Richelieu apply?'

'Why don't you shut up and get on with your work?' berated Billy Hughes who entered the room. Then Richelieu appeared and everyone went super quiet. 'Bonjour Mesdames et Messieurs.'

Mutterings of 'Morning', 'Good morning' and 'Bonjour' were heard.

'We 'ave a busy day. So, reports, s'il vous plait.'

Fleming and Hughes gave details of their progress in the Warburton and South Yarra murders. What a contrast. There was the death of an unknown woman who may not even have been murdered, followed by the homicide of a prominent judge who suffered a bizarre death. Were the police looking for one or two murderers? Was one of them the highest-ranked legal officer in the state?

After both Detective Sergeants finished and issues were discussed, Richelieu gave new tasks. He behaved like he loved the job and wanted it permanently. But his joy was from his decision to not apply.

Officers broke up and got working. Richelieu approached Jo. 'Time to visit your friend, Detective, s'il vous plaît.'

'Yes sir, he's expecting us any time after 10.'

They left with Hughes taking note. As they passed Reception, Beryl called. 'Oh, Senior Constable Best.' They stopped and Beryl brought forth a beautiful bunch of roses. 'For you, my dear. Just delivered.'

Jo was embarrassed and looked a tad sternly at her boss. He made a face as if to say, "Not me this time".

'Thanks Beryl. Is there a card?' She handed it to Jo. 'Why don't you keep them for your office?' Beryl beamed.

'Beautiful flowers for a beautiful lady,' oozed Richelieu. Beryl beamed again. The Francophile was good with the blarney.

Michael opened his door and met the DI. Michael and Jo kissed in a friendly way which sparked a mini burst of envy within the DI. The trio sat and Jo commenced.

'Before I get DI Richelieu to explain things, Michael, I want you to know this is a professional proposal and if you choose to help, there will be a contract for you as a consultant with appropriate payment.'

'So no life or death car chases and gun fights?'

He and Jo smiled. 'And I should tell you that DI Richelieu is now the head of the Homicide squad.'

'Acting head,' said the DI.

'Congratulations, sir,' said Michael who seemed to have lost some of his hometown humility. 'So what happened to your hero, DI Steele?'

'He's moved to Canberra and the AFP,' replied Jo feeling uncomfortable with her friend's flippant attitude. It continued.

'I bet he hasn't asked you to join him.'

'Thank you, Michael, that's enough.' All were embarrassed.

'I apologise,' said Michael with his half smile. 'How can I help?'

Jo looked at her boss. He began. 'First Monsieur, if you take this task, you will be required to sign a document agreeing to never disclose information you are shown.'

Michael was back to being flippant. 'The Official Secrets' Act, wow.'

'Michael, please,' begged Jo.

Richelieu worried about his colleague's friend. 'Monsieur, we are dealing with 'ighly confidential material which must never become available to outside sources.'

'The media?'

'Oui.' Richelieu paused. 'You agree, Monsieur?'

'Oui,' said Michael without a trace of sarcasm or rudeness.

'We are trying to trace the person or persons who sent a number of emails. We 'ave the emails but they 'ave no sender's name.'

'Is that it? You want to find the source of some emails?' Both detectives worried. 'Look I'm happy to take your money but this is not Alan Turing Enigma machine stuff.' More confusion for the detectives. 'If you type *Trace an email address* into YouTube you'll probably find 20 clips showing you how it's done—and quickly.'

The detectives looked surprised. 'Really?' asked Jo.

'Mind you,' continued Michael, 'all you can find is the IP address of the computer, the country and city where it's located, its geographical co-ordinates, and its ISP but that won't give you the sender. I mean, if you could trace an email to this computer, any one of us could have sent it.' He looked at his visitors. 'That'll be 5 dollars 75 thank you.'

His jesting embarrassed them. If the malicious emails came from a computer in the Attorney-General's office, they could have been sent by anyone from his Chief of Staff to the cleaner.

The solving of the murder of Judge Ranald Slight got even harder.

Richelieu phoned the AC to discuss "the evidence". He told him of the difficulty in pinpointing the actual sender. The AC went quiet. This murder was not so much a hot potato as a ticking time bomb.

'We need the Bomb Disposal Squad for this one, Inspector.'

'Sir?'

'Keep me informed.'

Home alone, Jo pondered the two cases. Interesting homicides are great, not solving them a pain. Her phone rang.

'Hello Mother, how are you?'

'I thought you'd forgotten me.'

'Never. I didn't want to interrupt your exciting love life.'

33

'Don't be cheeky.' Jo's divorced mother, Shirley was tickled pink at having found love late in life. Italian Antonio Carboni fell for Jo's mother and Jo thought Tony was lovely and enjoyed his company.

'And how is Signor Carboni?'

'He's well and excited about our cruise. But I have some sad news.' Jo tensed. 'Marjorie's had a fall. They think she's broken her hip.'

'Oh no.' Jo felt sadness for her mother's godmother, a lovely, kind woman who was an extra grandmother to Jo and her sister Caitlyn.

'Antonio and I went to see her today but she hasn't got anyone else. All her friends are dead or dying.'

'Of course I'll go. Where is she?'

'She's at Box Hill and would love to see you.'

'Mum, I said I'll go. I'll ring you once I've seen her. Bye.'

Pensioner Marjorie was in a public ward and her smile when Jo arrived was worth the trip. The pair embraced and Marjorie's joy overrode her discomfort. One of the old lady's many fine qualities was her ability to listen. She took a genuine interest in the Best girls. With Joanna, she wanted all her news, gossip and plans for the future.

The women in adjoining beds were fascinated with Jo's tales and especially with Shirley's new love life and Jo's French-speaking Inspector. Mouths opened and hearing aids buzzed. The other patients wanted Jo to visit every day.

Not wanting to tire the dear woman, Jo gave Marjorie a loving farewell and promised to return soon. At the entrance to the ward, Jo turned and waved. Marjorie and all three of the other patients returned the wave. One even called, 'Come again, soon.'

The lift opened as Jo walked past. She hopped in, reached the crowded foyer and made her way towards the exit when she saw a familiar face. It belonged to Peg Carr, mother of Dr Jack Carr and grandmother to the gorgeous Grace and Harry. Jo stopped dead because Peg was certainly not smiling. In fact she looked terrible.

7

JO MOVED TO THE GRANDMOTHER. 'Peg? Are you okay?'

Peg struggled to speak. Jo felt sick, afraid to ask another question. Then Peg's husband Hugh arrived with his grandson. Hugh managed a smile of sorts but 6 year old Harry lit up with joy.

'Detective Jo,' he beamed and stood to attention and saluted. This simple act gave a shot of happiness to the three adults.

'Hello, young man.' Jo saluted him. 'It's lovely to see you.'

'Have you come to see Grace?' he asked and Jo looked at his grandparents.

Hugh was able to speak. 'There's been an accident. Grace was in the back of our car and she's been injured.'

Jo's heart got pumping. She didn't want to ask the next question. She stopped as Peg found her voice.

'She's in intensive care. Jack's with her and ...' Peg turned away from her grandson. 'We're trying to distract someone.'

Jo responded. 'How about Harry and I go and find an ice-cream?' The boy's face lit up, as much from the idea of an adventure with his favourite policewoman as the prospect of a chocolate chip delight. His grandparents smiled. Peg hugged Jo and whispered, 'Thank you.'

Jo took Harry's hand. 'Come on, young man.' She looked at the grandparents. 'Back here in say 20 minutes?' They nodded and watched their excited grandson head off with his new friend.

Gwenda Balance was a single mother. Her only son, Edward (Eddie) taught Business Studies in a newly-formed, so-called college in the Melbourne CBD. Eddie was gay but didn't advertise the fact and while his mother knew, she never spoke about it, not even to the boy himself.

Gwenda was unwell and late coming downstairs. When she did, the smell hit her. 'Oh Barnaby,' she exclaimed. 'You're a very naughty boy.'

The dog had failed to exit via the dog door and perform his bowel movements on the back lawn. 'What's the matter with you? You're not a puppy anymore. Why now?'

Gwenda cleaned up, kept reprimanding the poor canine, and then unlocked and opened the back door. She screamed so loud and for so long, Barnaby made a pact with the keeper of the Rainbow Bridge that he would never crap indoors again.

The doggy door was blocked by the body of Gwenda's darling boy. Eddie Balance had been murdered and neatly placed against the back door of the property he one day was due to inherit. Not now he won't.

Jo had a grand old time with Harry Carr. She kept talking about anything other than the accident. But the little boy seemed okay with what happened. He matter-of-factly told his favourite police officer that Pop's car had been in a crash and Grace was hurt. Jo checked her watch and decided it was time to face the music. She failed the *How to Pray* test but kept having hopeful thoughts that young Grace would get through and be okay.

'Now young man, it's time to go back to see Gran and Pop. Okay?'

'And Dad.'

'And Dad, of course.'

He saluted. They set off with Harry bouncing and happy. Jo spotted the Carrs and moved to them. They turned and in doing so revealed their son. Jo's eyes met Jack's and her heart pumped harder. Harry ran to his family with the news about his ice-cream tasting. Hugh and Peg whisked their grandson away leaving the quack and the cop alone with only about 50 strangers for company.

'Hello,' said Jack.

'Jack, I'm so, so sorry. How is Grace?'

'Not good. She's in IC and may be moved to the Children's.'

Jo was lost for words and wanted to cry. 'What can I do?'

He couldn't hold back and tears appeared. Jo hugged him and didn't let go. Mutual back rubbing became popular. The best killer for romance is mortality. Finally they separated. He was embarrassed, unnecessarily so, with his tears. 'How are you,' he asked, 'and why are you here? Are you okay?'

She explained and then they were stuck for words. 'If you want me to take Harry to the movies or wherever, to give you and your folks a break, please, I'd love to do it.'

'So would he,' half-smiled Jack. 'He keeps talking about you, non-stop.' They fell into another snippet of silence. 'He was over the moon when he saw you on TV having found that little girl.' Jo smiled. 'Congratulations by the way. You were brilliant—*are* brilliant.'

Now the atmosphere shifted, not massively but the arrow on the wheel of feelings moved from death and dying towards life and love.

Jo's phone pinged. She checked the text. 'Jack, I'm sorry, I have to get going. Can I call you to check on Grace?'

'Of course, any time.'

She leant in and kissed his cheek, squeezed his arm and walked away. Jack's mother watched from afar.

Several Homicide detectives arrived at the Balance house. Poor Gwenda reclined on a settee having been sedated by her family doctor. Eddie remained on the back verandah, dead as the proverbial. Billy Hughes led the investigation.

'Nasty,' she said. Charlie Baldwin and Jo Best hung back as their sergeant knelt and looked closely at the body.

Three forensics officers arrived and began work. Billy stepped away. 'Start with the neighbours,' she said to her colleagues, 'one each side of the road. I'll take the mother.'

Jo and Baldwin walked to the street. 'Oh no, here's trouble,' said Baldwin as the police pathologist hove into view. Hove was appropriate as Dr Strange had been in the paddock of late.

'We can't go on meeting like this,' she said. 'Have you lot finished already?'

'Just starting,' said Jo.

'We're off to play at being Mormons,' added Baldwin.

The pathologist laughed and left to negotiate right of way with the scientific mob. She usually won. Billy joined her.

'Hello, Doctor.'

'I'm pleased to see you've finally come to your senses.'

Billy didn't understand. Many people didn't understand the non-sequiters from the medical guru. 'Pardon?'

'Senior Constable Best is back where she belongs.'

'Yes, and likely to stay now that DI Steele is off the scene.'

'Hallelujah. Now your corpse. At first glance there's a lot of feeling in this one.'

'Meaning?'

'It appears the poor man's been strangled then sodomized with something inanimate.'

Hughes winced. 'Ouch.'

'Ouch indeed. I'll send you my report.'

'Thank you, Doctor.'

'So who's the new Homicide boss? Is it you?'

'Hardly.'

'I recommend Senior Constable Best.'

'So would I,' said Billy to herself and went to find Mrs Balance.

Back at Homicide, the squad gathered to discuss the latest murder. The board listed three homicides with the current score, Murderers 3, Cops 0.

'Where's the DI?' asked Billy Hughes.

Fleming replied. 'With the AC, and no, I don't have any news. So, what do we know about our latest homicide?'

Baldwin announced details of Edward Balance, his age, job, family and complete lack of any police record. A photo of the poor fellow stared back from the notice board.

'Witnesses? Neighbours?'

Jo reported that the three wise monkeys were alive and well. Nobody saw, heard or said anything of use.

Billy got serious. 'You don't need me to tell you the body count. We've got three unsolved homicides and not one person of interest. Not good, folks. We need a bigger and better effort from everyone.'

'You applying for the top job, Sarge?' asked a cheeky minion.

Some laughed, not so much because the remark was funny, but because everyone was under pressure and the gag became a safety valve releasing steam. Then the laughter stopped instantly when three people walked into the room. Billy retreated.

The AC Crime paused then addressed the group. 'Good afternoon, ladies and gentlemen.' The detectives replied. 'As you know, DI Richelieu has been acting head of the squad. He has advised he does not wish to continue in the role and I am delighted to introduce you to your new commanding officer, DI Eleanor Rose.'

Everyone who wasn't already looking at the elegant woman soon was. She remained rock steady without an eye blink or facial muscle twitch. Her hair, suit and blouse were immaculate. The male detectives checked out her pins while the females her shoes. Lots of ticks all round. She wore a wedding ring.

'Before I hand over to DI Rose, I wish to tell you that the investigation of the murder of Judge Slight has uncovered some serious evidence with possible links to prominent individuals. That evidence, like all evidence, must never be discussed outside this room and never to anyone not directly involved in the case. Is that clear?'

'Sir,' replied the masses.

'I will make it my personal goal to deal with anyone who leaks information.' He paused and looked at the officers before him. His look spoke volumes. He broke into a smile, turned and shook hands with DI Rose then left the room. DI Richelieu moved back amongst the troops leaving DI Rose up front and alone.

Silence dominated. One question hovered. *Who is this woman?*

'Good afternoon.' The troops replied. 'I think it's fair to say there's a certain amount of surprise in this room with me the most surprised.' Jo liked her. 'I used to be a member of this squad. I cut my detective teeth in Homicide joining way back in the mid-nineties when the boss was Detective Chief Inspector John Robertson.' Jo tingled. 'Robbo taught me many things one of which was to keep my mouth shut unless I had something worth saying.' Officers warmed to her. 'So that's my plan. I'll leave the talking to you. However, after consultation with the Assistant Commissioner and DI Richelieu, I'm appointing three OICs, one for each of the murders currently on our plate.' She looked at the board. 'Number 4 hasn't bobbed up since I started speaking has it?' This prompted a sprinkling of laughter. 'So DI Richelieu will run the legal homicide, DS Fleming the woman in the river, and DS Hughes the young man discovered ... when was that?'

'Today, ma'am,' said Payne hoping to impress.

'Forgive me not knowing your names. For me, that's a priority. But now, firm up your teams, methodology, and get cracking. Questions?'

'Pardon ma'am,' said DS Fleming, 'but how should we address you?'

'Politely.' That got another murmur of appreciation. 'Until we're drinking buddies, I'm ma'am as in charm and never ma-am as in jam. Anyone using an American accent can expect regular all-night shifts.' She looked around. 'Right, crack on.'

8

JO WAS BUSTING TO MEET her new boss and to tell Pop about her. And now being teamed with Richelieu, Jo's excitement grew as she moved from the homicide in the sticks to the upmarket death in South Yarra. Richelieu and Jo met to discuss the judge's murder.

'I am a new man, Joanna, an ordinary Inspector again and together we will solve this case, n'est-ce pas?'

'Whatever you say, sir.'

He handed her a list. 'These are people who were close to 'is 'onour. The first name, Simon Beaumont, 'as been underlined.'

Jo looked at the list. Before she could respond, there was a soft knock on the open door and the new boss of Homicide entered. She held out a hand. Jo stood and shook it.

'Senior Constable Joanna Best, ma-am.'

'Not *the* Joanna Best, rescuer of missing children?'

'Ah, yes ma-am ... and granddaughter of the retired DCI Robbo Robertson.'

'Well bugger me,' said Rose. 'Small world. How is the old boy?'

'He's well, ma-am and I'm sure he'll be delighted to know one of his former colleagues has taken his old job.'

Rose turned serious. 'But I understand his wife's not well.'

Jo grimaced. 'No ma-am, she's got dementia and lives in care.'

'I'm sorry. Please remember me to him.'

'I will.'

Rose changed gears. 'Right, I'm not here. Carry on.' She moved to one side and observed.

Richelieu smiled at Jo and like him, she felt uncomfortable with a stranger in their midst. 'I suggest we interview the friend of the judge and then maybe you could return to see your friend and 'ave him search for the computer used for the threatening emails.'

Rose interrupted. 'A brief explanation would help me, Inspector.'

Richelieu handed her the emails and explained the possible connection with the Attorney-General. Rose whistled.

'Not bad for my first day.' She placed the emails on the desk. 'Okay, carry on. I'm off to spy on the others.' She left.

'Ready?' asked the DI. Jo nodded and they set off for leafy Toorak and the residence of barrister Simon Beaumont. He and the dead judge went back a long way. They were at school together and graduated in Law from Melbourne University together. But both men shared a secret. Years ago Simon got greedy and indulged in insider trading. The shit hit the fan and Simon's promising law career looked doomed before it began. Enter the brilliant Ranald Slight who created an economic spreadsheet which cleared the guilty Simon. His gratitude overflowed so when Ranald was brutally murdered, Simon's grief overflowed. Richelieu told Jo the insider trading story.

The detectives buzzed at the front gate of the squillion dollar shack in St George's Road, a posh street in a posh suburb.

'Yes?' asked a female voice.

'Good afternoon,' said a man with a French accent. 'This is the police. We wish to speak with Mr Simon Beaumont, s'il vous plait.'

Mrs Beaumont hesitated. *A Frenchman claiming to be a cop. He's a long way from the Champs Elysees.* 'The police?'

'We understand Mr Beaumont was a friend of the late Judge Slight.'

More hesitation from the woman. 'My husband is not well.'

'We 'ope Monsieur Beaumont can 'elp us find the person who 'as murdered 'is friend.'

Silence. The police waited. Then the front gate swung open.

'I think that's a "yes", sir,' said Jo and they set off on a long journey.

Mrs Beaumont opened the door and the detectives showed their ID. They stepped into the Beaumonts' hall. To Jo it was a ballroom. They were led into the closest sitting-room of which there were several.

'Wait here, please.'

She left and the detectives surveyed the room. It took some time. Neither spoke. Then Simon appeared. What a mess—red eyes, uncombed hair, hunched shoulders and crumpled clothes.

'Can I help?'

The detectives introduced themselves and all sat. Richelieu was about to start but nodded at Jo. She was surprised, excited and began.

'We apologise for the intrusion, sir, but we understand you were close to the late Judge Slight.' Beaumont's head slumped and a hand went to his mouth. Jo paused. 'We would greatly appreciate any assistance you can provide.' Again she paused and Beaumont gave the smallest of nods. 'Can you think of anyone who might have wished to harm your friend?'

Beaumont shook his head. He struggled. 'No-one.' He cleared his throat. 'He was the most kind and caring man.'

The detectives looked at each other. Why then had this kind and caring man been so brutally murdered?

'Did you ever discuss cases with the judge?' Richelieu worried and Jo realised this was either inappropriate or downright rude. How would the barrister, an expert in leading questions, react?

Beaumont showed no reaction. 'Always.'

'And the judge never mentioned any difficult people who came before him or who received a harsh sentence from him?'

More head shaking. 'He was a gentle man and a gentleman. He was fairness personified.' Beaumont paused then broke down and cried in silence. 'And I miss him so much.'

The police looked at one another. Richelieu stood. 'We'll trouble you no more, Monsieur. Thank you for your time. Au revoir.' Richelieu left with Jo in hot pursuit. Mrs Beaumont waited in the ballroom, hall.

'He's taken Ranald's death very badly. They go back a long way.' She walked them to the door. 'He's never told me details but Ranald once saved Simon's bacon and my husband has never forgotten it.'

The detectives thanked the lady of the house and took the long walk back to their car. 'You 'ave an excellent interview technique, Senior Constable. You could even teach me a thing or two.'

Jo wondered if he was sincere or trying his drip-drip method of seduction. Whatever, she felt good.

DI Rose attended briefings on all three murders and later that day, conducted her first full meeting of the Squad. 'I can't remember

Homicide being like this in my day. We've got three cases, no motive, and little evidence or clues.'

'Welcome back, ma-am,' said DS Fleming with tongue in cheek.

'Tell me where I'm wrong. The woman in the river could be a murder, a suicide or an accident. Why would she tell her son she was going out for a minute? I mean if you're only stepping outside the door, why say anything? And he's a teenager so he wouldn't have taken any notice if she'd told him the house was on fire.'

'Got a teenager have we, ma-am?' asked Billy Hughes. No reply.

'Then His Honour is murdered in some brutal and bizarre manner with no DNA, no evidence of a robbery, and nobody can say a bad word about him or his judgements—nobody. The man's a saint and yet he's murdered in what is clearly some sort of revenge killing. Comments?'

'You 'ave summed up the case superbly, Madame,' said Richelieu.

Rose grimaced. 'I should have stayed in Vehicle Crime.' Her throwaway line raised a few eyebrows. 'But it gets worse. This morning, a kind, law-abiding young man is strangled, sodomised and dumped on his mother's verandah, and like the other two homicides, motive is a foreign language. We've got three murders with nothing to link them and next to nothing to even suggest a way to solve them.' She looked at her charges. 'Tell me, please, what have I got wrong?'

'Nothing,' said Fleming.

Silence in the room. Rose cranked up her emotions. 'I'm supposed to inspire you lot, co-ordinate your efforts, help you solve homicides to bring justice to the victim and their family.' She stared at them. 'But right now I feel completely fucking useless.' She looked at Richelieu and spoke delicately. 'Pardon my French, Monsieur.'

That was her best remark all day. It provoked a solid response with laughter and wisecracks.

Thank God, thought Rose. *I was about to resign on my first day.*

Jo went into the corridor and made a call. 'Jack Carr,' said the doctor.

'Hello Jack. It's Jo Best.'

'Hello Jo Best.'

'I'm ringing to see how your beautiful daughter is going.'

She heard him take a breath. 'No change, Jo. I think the term the police use is "serious but stable".'

Jo went to the *Ladies*. 'What are they expecting to happen?'

'With brain injuries, Jo, it's difficult to tell. They don't want to operate until she settles down ... *if* she settles down.'

'Oh God, Jack, I don't know what to say.'

She knew he was crying. 'Losing my wife was horrendous. I don't think I could bear to lose my daughter.'

Jo stood in the *Ladies* her emotions bursting to escape. 'Please tell me if I can do anything, Jack. I mean it. Please, just ask.'

'Thank you. And Harry sends his love. Bye Jo. Bye.'

The call ended with both in tears.

Jo took the emails the judge had received and headed to Michael's converted warehouse in Northcote. She always rang before she dropped in but this time her misery overwhelmed her. All she could think of was little Grace and then her father crying.

Wiping her eyes, Jo rang Michael's doorbell. He took a while to answer. She was about to leave when the door opened. Michael looked strange. His shirt was only partly tucked in, his hair was not its usual slick self and his face seemed flushed. If she didn't know better she would have thought he'd been exercising, fighting or copulating. Michael Chan, the daytime shagger? Surely not?

'Oh, sorry Michael, I didn't call because I'm having a rough day. Can I get you to track the computer which sent these emails? Please?'

He smiled that half smile. 'Sure.' He didn't step back and invite her in. She sensed he didn't want her in. He took the emails. 'No problem. I'll call you tomorrow.'

'Okay. Thanks.' She turned to leave when a female voice was heard.

'Who is it, Mikey?'

Mikey?

Jo thought she knew the voice. Michael thought he was about to be embarrassed. The voice turned into a person and appeared wearing nothing but what Jo could have sworn was one of Michael's shirts. Jo stared at a former colleague, Connie Bryant, the sex-mad senior constable who made a habit of having men for dinner. It was difficult to know who felt what. Jo was surprised, Connie smug and Michael tense.

'Jo Best, fancy seeing you.'

'Hi Connie.' *I can't ask how she's doing because she's obviously doing Michael. No wonder he was a bit strange yesterday when I called in with DI Richelieu.* 'Nice to see you.' *And I've never seen so much of you. Well done, Michael.* 'I'll give you a call, Michael. Bye.'

She climbed into her car and headed for Box Hill. What a day. She met the new head of Homicide who worked with Pop nearly 30 years ago. She heard that little Grace Carr was still close to death. And now she discovered the quiet and gentle Michael Chan was exploring new strategies with the local police force. What a day indeed.

Poor Marjory had broken her hip and going home was a no-no. A nonagenarian, living alone, she would never manage, so a nursing home beckoned. Mind you her hospital stay would take some time.

Jo entered her ward where the other patients each had a visitor or visitors beside their bed. When the other patients spotted Jo, all three had their visitors move giving the patients an uninterrupted view.

Marjory was thrilled to welcome Jo and they chatted with the entire ward busting to hear everything. Jo left when she felt her mother's godmother was tiring. Instead of going home, Jo headed for the ICU and nervously approached the nurses' station.

'Hello,' said a friendly face.

'Hello, I'm Jo Best, a friend of Grace Carr and was wondering how she's going?'

'Are you the policewoman who found the little girl in Castlemaine?'

Jo was surprised. 'Wow, how did you know that?'

'Doctor Carr told everyone about you. Would you like to see Grace?'

'Oh no, I haven't spoken to Doctor Carr and ...'

'He said it was fine. He gave us a list of people who could see Grace and after his family, you're on top. I'll take you in.'

Jo felt pressure and once she entered the room felt depressed. The child looked helpless. She *was* helpless. Wires and tubes were connected to her body. Two nurses worked on different tasks. The beeping and soft whirr of equipment was the only sound.

Can Grace hear those sounds? Can she hear anything?

'Would you like to say something to her?' asked the nurse.

'Can I? Can she hear me?'

'We don't know for sure but it may help.'

Jo moved close to the little girl. 'Hello Grace, it's Jo. Remember the ride we had on Puffing Billy and the strawberries we picked? I do.' Jo felt she was choking. 'We all want you to get well soon, Grace, please. I want to take Rags for a walk and I need you to help me. Okay? I'll see you soon, darling. Bye.'

That was it. Jo's tears took over. She turned to leave and just missed bumping into a machine. She headed for the door and didn't even thank the nurse. She had to get away.

Solving a homicide was something she could do, even, with luck, do well. But helping save a little girl's life was way beyond her pay grade.

9

IT WAS A CHINK OF LIGHT, nothing big or earth-shattering, but a start. Homicide had three murders, well, two and a possible, but with next to nothing in the way of evidence, only one person of interest and no motive, the mood in the squad was bleak before this breakthrough. DS Hughes received a call from a former colleague in SOCIT—the Sexual Offences and Child Abuse Investigation Team.

'G'day Billy, it's Toby Weatherhill.'

'Toby, long time no hear. How are you?'

'Good. Listen, I see you're dealing with a Mr Eddie Balance.'

'The murdered teacher?'

'That's the one.'

'Don't tell me he was a suspect with you guys?'

'Not a suspect.' DS Weatherhill explained how Eddie had supported his mother, Gwenda, in providing a statement which became an alibi for the alleged rapist John Clington. Billy noted the facts, thanked her friend and became moderately excited. She told Charlie Baldwin.

'What's it mean, Sarge?'

'Not sure. If someone knew Eddie gave a suspected rapist an alibi then Eddie got his comeuppance.'

'You mean payback because Eddie was a grass.'

'Possibly.'

Baldwin thought about it. 'So who knew Eddie made his statement?'

'That's your next job, Senior.'

Baldwin grimaced and investigated. He discovered a startling fact and told Billy who told Rose who called a meeting.

DI Rose was excited when offered the position of Homicide boss but with three unsolved and clueless cases, her excitement disappeared. Any news was welcome and when Billy Hughes raised the issue of Eddie Balance and his alibi for the alleged rapist, Rose ran with it.

'We may have a lead,' said the new boss. 'Detective Sergeant.'

Billy told the squad how Eddie had given an arrested rapist an alibi. But it was Baldwin's latest news that got tongues wagging.

'John Clington was released thanks to Eddie and his mother's alibi. We've just heard from SOCIT. Clington has been re-arrested and charged with another rape.'

Rose summed up what everyone was thinking. 'This is gold, people. I'm a friend or relative of an alleged rape victim. The attacker is released thanks to Eddie Balance. Clington is free. How do I feel?'

'Outraged,' said one officer.

'Murderous,' said another.

'Chase this lead. Eddie Balance may have been murdered by someone connected to one of John Clington's victims.'

'But 'ow would anyone know Eddie gave an alibi?' asked Richelieu.

'Corrupt police officer,' said Fleming. That flattened the mood. The thought of a colleague acting illegally turned one's stomach.

'But to confuse matters, ma-am,' added Baldwin, 'Eddie was the support act. His mother gave the alibi for Clington. All Eddie did was back up what his mother said.'

'So why not kill Mum?' asked Hughes. 'Without her statement, Clington would have been charged and this latest rape would never have happened.'

Jo had a thought. 'They killed the son to punish the mother.'

Billy liked it and Rose thought, *that's the sort of logic her grandfather used.*

'Excellent,' said Rose. 'Good work everyone. Look into it, Billy. Contact your mate at SOCIT and see if any of the alleged victims or their families had made threats.'

'Ma-am.'

'Okay, let's keep the good news coming. Anything new on the judge and the woman who drowned?'

Richelieu explained how more searching had failed to find anyone prepared to criticise the dead judge. 'Everyone associated with the dead man reckoned 'is 'onour was Monsieur Fairness and Kindness.'

'What, no known enemies at all?' asked an exasperated Rose.

'There are those emails, ma-am,' added Richelieu.

'Yes, that's ongoing,' said Rose. 'What about the people the judge knew at the Court. Have these been explored?'

'Oui, Madame,' said Richelieu, 'without success.'

'Right, what about the drowned woman? Was she murdered?'

Fleming was blunt. 'Doctor Strange says a definite maybe.'

'Who's he?' asked Rose.

'He's a she ma-am, Doctor Strange is the pathologist.'

'Not Gabrielle Strange of the loud voice and unlimited sarcasm?' That promoted a reaction from the troops. 'My god, she started when I first joined Homicide. What's she got to say?'

'There are faint bruises on both wrists.'

'What, ropes, some sort of tie?'

'She thinks more like hands gripping the victim's wrists and if so, the woman was dragged into the river and held under.'

'By one person?'

'Dr Strange reckons two as the bruising on one hand is more pronounced; one attacker stronger than the other.'

'Why didn't the woman scream?'

'There were tiny amounts of a cotton fibre in her throat which Dr Strange reckons could be material stuffed into the victim's mouth.'

'Well if she was dragged by two people, that suggests a struggle,' said Rose trying to get her team to open up. *Is this job a poisoned chalice?* 'What did Forensics make of the scene where she went in?'

'We don't know where she went in,' added Fleming. 'We know where she was found but the body could have drifted downstream.'

'Did you look?'

Silence. 'They couldn't search until morning, ma-am, and there was heavy overnight rain,' said Fleming.

More frustration from Rose. 'I want another search of the river bank for possible places where she may have gone in. Is there DNA there? And have Forensics consider the material in her throat. Yes?'

'Yes, ma-am,' replied a chastened DS Fleming.

Silence entered the debate. Rose looked at her squad. She was hoping someone had an idea, no matter how weird, anything to help spark some new line of enquiry. 'Well come on, anyone else?'

Jo remembered her first case at Homicide. She made a suggestion and got rubbished. Mind you, it later turned out to be spot on, and despite subsequent success, she still hesitated. Then she let it out.

'Could these three homicides be linked, ma-am?'

That hit the murmur button. Some were ready to scoff. Billy Hughes and the new DI were ready to listen. 'Go on,' said Rose.

'They have a different MO but certain similarities.' To some that seemed ridiculous. Jo explained with the entire squad staring at her. 'You could build an argument to say the three murders are unique. But equally they are the same in that they seemingly have no motive, are professional in execution with no DNA, and they appear unsolvable.'

Jo's last word started a reaction. *Unsolvable* was a dirty word.

Rose ran with Jo's suggestion, a trait she picked up from her former boss, DCI Robertson. 'Okay, let's look at Jo's suggestion. Are these homicides connected? What do they have in common?'

'Innocence,' said Richelieu. Officers looked at him. 'The woman in the river was a saint, the judge 'ad no enemies, and the teacher was a wonderful son and 'ighly respected colleague. They were all perfect. There is no motive, and no reason for any of them to be killed.'

The atmosphere in the Incident Room changed and quickly. Until now, no-one had considered that. Rose sparkled. Jo tingled. Everyone realised something had happened. Did this idea, this theory hold the key to solving the three homicides? If so, what next?

'Brilliant,' said Rose. 'Let's form a fourth team to work on finding a link between the victims. The rest of you, keep this new idea in mind. I'll liaise between all four groups. So, who'll be in this fourth group? Jo, it was your idea, you're one. Who else?' Nobody volunteered. 'Pierre, you're on the same wavelength. Have you two worked together before?' He nodded. 'Successful was it?'

'Oui—I got shot,' said the Gallic charmer and everyone laughed.

Rose continued. 'You and Jo come up with a case as to why the same person killed all three victims. Okay?' Jo and Richelieu nodded.

Jo looked at Richelieu and wondered. *Will my theory be proved right, or will I get lost in the charms of my newly appointed partner?*

10

JO AND RICHELIEU met in Rose's office. She spoke excitedly of Jo's theory, the one suggesting the three murders were linked.

'It's just a bit of thinking outside the box, ma-am,' said Jo.

'Jo, we've got nothing. In our current state, any ideas are welcome. Now you and Pierre have free reign to test your theory.'

She said "your" theory. Is she putting it on me so when it produces nothing, I'll cop the blame?

'Work whatever hours it takes. If you're right, this could be our way to solve all three homicides. Questions?'

The detectives said nothing. Jo thought, *What is he thinking? Is this his dream appointment? Work closely with the woman he fancies? Does the boss know Monsieur Richelieu craves my body?*

The new "team" stood in the corridor. 'How do we tackle this, sir?'

'You are the brains, Mademoiselle. This is your idea.'

He's doing it too—putting it all back on me.

'Thanks for nothing, sir.' He looked miffed. She half apologised. 'How about we both draw up what we think then compare notes.'

'Excellente,' he smiled. 'Are you free this evening?'

Jo had a problem. She was free and could easily agree to a rendezvous. She wanted to. And now that the DI was no longer the acting head of Homicide, any intimate relationship was, well, not so dangerous. Or was it? *I need advice.*

'How about whoever finishes their masterpiece, calls the other?'

He smiled and his whole face lit up. 'Once again, you 'ave the perfect solution. Till tonight.'

They separated and began working on the theory that all three murders were connected in some way. How? Good question.

Heading home, Jo passed Reception and was stopped by Beryl. 'Oh Joanna, more flowers, my dear.'

'*More* flowers?' Jo entered Beryl's office. Jo's last collection of roses decorated the receptionist's desk.

'Came a few minutes ago.' Beryl handed Jo another bouquet, sent anonymously. 'Take them home. They're beautiful.' Jo took the flowers. 'It might not be the same man,' said Beryl with a cheeky grin.

Jo's mind buzzed. *Who sent the flowers? Was it the same person? How is little Grace Carr? Do I fancy DI Richelieu enough to let nature take its course? What is my theory about the three murders being linked? What's for tea?*

At home she opened the card attached to the flowers. Again sent anonymously and again with an obvious expression of love. It read.

To the beautiful detective. That was it.

Jo pottered in the kitchen, ate a salad then tried to write her thesis. Her phone rang. She knew the number but was reluctant to answer.

'Hi Michael, how are you?' *Oops, I'm asking about his love life.*

'I've traced your computer, the one sending threatening emails.'

'Oh great.'

'As I told you, I can only pinpoint co-ordinates and have no idea who sent the emails. It could be the cleaner late at night.'

'Understood. So is it the Russian Mafia as we suspected?'

'Ha, ha. No, the computer resides in a glass monstrosity home to government offices including that of the Attorney-General.'

'Michael, you're a star. I'll make sure you get paid.'

'No thanks, no money required.'

'Michael, you can't work for nothing.'

'Okay, you can take me to dinner.'

Wow, that came as a surprise. 'Okay, sure. When suits you?'

'Any day this millennium. Ciao.' He ended the call.

Jo was stunned. *He wants a date. What's happened to Connie?*

Before she could decipher the messages bouncing around her brain, her phone rang again. Another number she knew by heart.

'Good evening, sir. Please don't tell me you've finished your theory.'

'Bonsoir, Mademoiselle.'

'I haven't started.'

'No, no, this 'as nothing to do with work.' Jo gulped. 'I 'ave 'ad a phone call from my mother who demands I go 'ome for Christmas.'

'To France?'

'Oui, to Paris. Now please do not take this the wrong way, Joanna, but I wish to remind you of my promise to show you the City of Light. If you would enjoy Christmas under the Eiffel Tower, I would be 'appy to escort you. No 'urry but do think about it, s'il vous plait. And now, I will let you get back to your theory. Bonne nuit.'

Bugger me. 'I need a spreadsheet to manage my admirers.' She started to list the murder similarities but kept thinking about dinner dates and outfits for Paris. She made notes for Karen/Ranald/Eddie.

Murder similarities/differences

Fame
unknown victim/well-known victim/unknown victim
Method of killing
drowning/car accident/strangulation
Age of victims
39/49/26
Gender of victims
female/male/male
Marital status
married/single/single
Sexual orientation
heterosexual/unknown/homosexual
Status
middle-class/upper-class/middle-class
Occupation
supermarket worker/supreme court judge/college teacher
Time of death (approx.)
2100/0800/2000
Persons of interest
husband/attorney-general/rape victims
Similarities
few if any known enemies

She looked at her notes. Nothing leapt out except the bit about few enemies. Her bright idea looked dim. She tossed her notes on the sofa and tousled her hair. Her phone rang. Again she knew the number. This time she held back with her heart racing.

'Good evening Doctor Carr.'

'Good evening Detective Best.'

'I hope you have some good news.'

'No change, Jo. She's a fighter, my girl.'

'Is the fact there's no change, good or bad?' Jo cringed not wanting to be insensitive or upset a man who was obviously in pain.

'Hard to say. But look, I wanted to beg a favour if I may.'

'Of course, anything.'

'I was hoping you could take Harry out for a drive, a walk somewhere, anything.'

'Of course, I'd love to.'

'His grandparents and I are a bit down and having someone he likes take him away from miserable people would make a huge difference.'

'Tell me when and I'll be there.'

'That's fantastic. But I know your job gets in the way so why don't you find some time and give me a call and we can go from there?'

'This is too important to put off, Jack. How about Saturday?'

'Are you sure?'

'It's in my diary. Does 10 sound okay?'

'That's perfect. Harry'll be over the moon.'

'I'll see you on Saturday. And give my love to Grace.'

'Thanks Jo. Bye.'

She ended the call and felt drained. Being involved with that family at this time was stressful. *Imagine what it must be like for them.*

Her brain bubbled with questions. She needed a pee. No sooner had she sat on the loo than her phone rang. She called. 'Hang on, I'll be there in a jiffy.' She tried to pee faster. It didn't work. She finished, dressed and headed for the lounge. As she picked up her phone, it stopped. 'Bugger.' She looked at the number. Not shown.

I hate that. Someone knows my number and blocks theirs.

She looked at her notes. They seemed feeble. The murders had nothing in common. *How can I make a case for the one person having murdered all three? Richelieu may have something better. If not, he and DI Rose will think I'm a goose.*

Her phone rang again. No number. She hesitated then answered.

'Hello.'

'Hello, is that Detective Best?'

'Who's speaking?'

'This is Alastair.'

'Alastair?'

'Alastair Dean.'

Who the hell is Alastair Dean? The voice sounds familiar.

'How can I help you, Alastair?'

'I haven't seen you at Forensics for a while and wondered if you were ill.'

Oh, it's Mr Cardigan, Mummy's boy. 'No I'm fine, Alastair. Thank you for asking.'

'I've read about three murders and yet you haven't asked me to examine any evidence.'

'Well they're tricky murders, Alastair. The killers are clever and there's been little to examine.

'I see.'

Jo waited for the scientist with the button-down shirt to say something else. He didn't.

'I'm sure as soon as anything is discovered, you'll be contacted.'

'By you?'

This is creepy. 'I'm only a Senior Constable, Alastair. Decisions are made by Sergeants and Inspectors.'

He changed tack and felt more confident. 'I read about your heroics in finding that little girl. You were absolutely brilliant.'

'Oh, thank you, you're very kind.'

'I told my mother about you.'

Not his mother. Please not his mother.

'That's nice.'

A pause and then he popped the question. 'Did you get the flowers?'

What flowers? Oh those flowers. Okay, that's one mystery solved.

'Yes, yes I did.'

'I sent two lots.'

'They were beautiful.'

'Were? Are they dead already?'

'No they're still beautiful. I have some at work and some at home.'

'Which ones are at work?'

Oh shit. This is getting out of hand.

'Ah, the roses. They're beautiful. And thank you, again.'

'I told Mother about the flowers but only the roses, not the second bunch.'

Don't tell Mother about the second bunch.

'It's nice of you to call, Alastair. And thank you again for the beautiful flowers.' *Surely he'll take the hint. Say goodbye Alastair.*

'Will you have dinner with me?'

Fuck.

'Oh, how kind.'

'I've told Mother I was going to ask you?'

And her mother came too!

'I'm super busy with these three homicides right now, Alastair. And we have a new boss. But once I clear up these cases, I'll get back to you. Is that okay?'

'That's wonderful. I'll wait till I hear from you.'

'Sure.'

'Have you still got my number?'

'I'm sure I do. Yes, I have. I'll call you soon. Bye.'

'Bye,' he echoed her speech pattern.

Jo tossed her phone on the sofa then yelled, 'Ahhhhh!' as her phone pinged. A text arrived. 'No!' She grabbed her phone and saw the text. *I 'ave emailed my document. Sweet dreams. Pierre.*

She screamed again—louder.

11

JO STUDIED RICHELIEU'S THEORY. He covered some of the same ground but added a specific detail. He believed the murders were carried out by a vigilante mob with different killers, each for a separate murder. This would explain the variety of methods of killing. But why vigilantes? According to the former Parisian, they were inspired by religion or politics. Each victim had done something to offend a religious or political group's philosophy. *Fair enough.*

She still reckoned it was the same killer as opposed to Richelieu backing several. Both of them mentioned the fact the victims were nice people. They had no enemies although now that the computer in the government office had been pinpointed, whoever sent the nasty emails was a possible enemy. Someone had it in for the judge. Or did they?

She wrote a summary of her theory, sent it to Richelieu then turned in. She couldn't sleep. Three unsolved murders and three, *count them Mother*, three fellas keen to take her to dinner with one restaurant located in Gay Paree. Sheesh!

Oh and then there's the date with the gorgeous Harry Carr. He's definitely in love with me, and vice versa, but he's more of a giver than a taker. The other three gents all want my body. Sleep, Joanna.

DI Rose was angry. 'Why didn't you tell me immediately?' Jo hadn't seen this side of her new boss before. Meet Ms Impatient.

'It was late when I was told, ma-am. I didn't want to disturb you.'

'Learn one thing, Senior Constable, never fail to inform me of anything relevant to a case, any time, any day. Now tell me again.'

Jo explained how the emails to the dead judge had come from an office occupied by the State Attorney-General. The AC Crime had discussed this issue with Rose when she accepted the job.

'I think we interview the AG as soon as,' said Rose.

Jo didn't know what to say. *Is she asking my opinion?* She was.

'It's a legitimate enquiry, ma-am. Should you ask the AC first?'

'He put me in charge. We'll do it this morning.'

'We, ma-am?'

'What's the matter? Got a prior engagement?'

'No, ma-am. I thought you'd take a more senior officer.'

'If your grandfather knew you were playing the meek and mild card, I think he'd be surprised and disappointed.' *Wow. Where did that come from?* 'Make an appointment with the AG then list issues based on the emails and report back once that's done.'

'Ma-am,' said Jo starting to leave.

'It's a priority, Senior.'

In the corridor Jo bumped into Richelieu. 'ave I missed something?'

'Sir?'

'To discuss our theories on 'ow the murders are connected.'

'The DI called me in to discuss the emails sent from the Attorney General's office. That's all we discussed.'

Richelieu looked crestfallen. 'I will run our ideas by 'er.'

The Attorney-General, Stefan Goulding, was a Labour politician, and a clever lawyer keen to climb the political ladder. His PA listened to Jo.

'The Attorney-General is busy all day.'

'Please tell him it's about the murder of Judge Ranald Slight and communications emanating from the Attorney-General's office.'

Silence at the other end. 'Please hold,' said the PA. Jo flicked through the emails handed over by Judge Slight's associate. The PA returned. 'The Minister can see you at 11 am.'

'Thank you,' said Jo then listed points based on the emails. When finished, she returned to Rose's office where the door was open with DI Richelieu in conversation with his replacement. Jo knocked.

'Come in, Jo. Pierre's been telling me about your theories. What happened with the AG?'

'He's expecting a police delegation at 1100 hours, ma-am.'

'Excellent. And the issues?' Jo handed the document to Rose. 'Well done. We leave at 1030. In the meantime, you two polish your act. When you present to the Squad, I want it watertight.'

She busied herself reading Jo's questions. In the corridor, Richelieu asked the question. 'Would you like to do the presentation, Detective?'

'Mine needs more work and I'm happy for you to do it, sir.'

'But it was your idea, Mademoiselle.'

'All the same, I'd prefer supporting what you say.'

He shrugged. 'You must know that all police officers are not the same. DI Steele was jealous and threatened by officers with ideas. DI Rose is the opposite. She told me she 'as copied the way 'er former DCI encouraged 'is officers—a gentleman with whom you are acquainted.'

A smidgeon of a smile appeared. 'I am.'

The notice board in the Incident Room had not been changed in the last 24 hours. Clues, news and views were not so much thin on the ground as non-existent. Rose entered and called the meeting to order.

'Right I'm off to interview the Attorney-General re threatening emails sent from the AG's office to Judge Slight.'

'That'd make a great headline, ma-am,' said DS Fleming. 'Attorney-general appoints judge then has him bumped off.'

'We'll know more today,' said Rose. 'Now the material found in the drowned woman's throat, any word from Forensics?'

'Not yet, ma-am,' said Charlie Baldwin.

'Do we have a contact, someone we can get to speed things along?'

Jo considered hiding under her seat. *Don't you dare, Charlie.*

Too late as Baldwin began. 'Jo Best is out expert charmer, ma-am. Her smile has a senior scientist dropping everything to finish a job.'

You bastard, Baldwin.

'I assume "dropping everything", is not to be taken literally.' A loud laugh bounced around the room and Jo disguised the grinding of teeth. 'Right, Senior,' added Rose, 'that's another job for you today.'

Jo wanted to scream, protest and plead insanity. After last night's phone conversation with Alastair "Mummy's Boy" Dean, for her to turn up in his laboratory the next day would send all the wrong signals. *He'll think I'm interested. Worse, he'll think I'm keen.*

Rose and Jo entered the reception area of the office of the State Attorney-General and were asked to wait. The interview time came and went. Jo worried because the DI had said nothing about her, Jo's role in the interview.

The politician appeared and introductions followed. 'Please,' he said indicating his office. They sat. 'How can I help?'

Rose was firm but polite. She explained how the late judge had received threatening emails which were sent from a computer in this department. Not a bad opening statement. The AG was shocked.

'Threatening emails? May I see them?'

'I'm sorry, sir, but at this stage they're possible evidence.'

'And you say they came from my office?'

'Our IT expert is able to pinpoint the co-ordinates but we'd need to make an inspection tracking the IP address to locate the computer.'

Goulding looked uncomfortable. 'But finding the computer doesn't necessarily find the person who sent the emails.'

'That's true, sir, but it would give us a list of people who could have sent them and who might have a grudge against Judge Slight.' The AG's mind raced. 'May we examine your department's computers, sir?'

Goulding was a lawyer. He knew about police powers. He wanted as little fuss as possible and most definitely didn't want to blot his copybook, lose his job or, heaven forbid, go to jail.

'I'm sure that can be arranged,' he said failing to smile.

'Can I ask, sir, if you or any of your colleagues knew Judge Slight apart from his legal duties?'

Goulding's heart rate peaked. 'I did. We both went to Melbourne.'

Jo jumped in. 'Do you know a Mr Simon Beaumont, sir?'

Goulding felt he was being ambushed. *Oh shit.*

'Yes, I know Simon. We were all at Melbourne together.'

'And do you know anything of the friendship between the judge and the barrister?'

'I'm not sure I understand or like your question, Detective.'

'Mr Beaumont told us things about the judge and we're looking to corroborate these claims. Any help might help lead us to his killer.'

She's smart, this detective, thought both Rose and Goulding.

'I haven't seen or dealt with Simon for years.'

Rose looked at Jo and got the message, "I'll take over, Senior".

'Do you know anyone in your department, sir, who bore a grudge or had a disagreement with His Honour?'

They know something but what?

Jo watched the man's body language and wished she knew more in this area. The AG leant forward. *What does leaning forward mean?*

'No-one, Inspector.'

'Did you appoint the Judge, sir?'

'I was involved in his appointment but took advice as I always do.'

'Thank you, sir. If we might be permitted to count the computers in your department, we'll leave you in peace.' She paused. 'For now.' Rose stood, Jo stood and the AG felt trapped.

'Certainly,' he said leading the way.

Staff members stopped work when the boss and two unknown females entered their office. Counting commenced and staff wondered what was going on? Exercise over, the police prepared to leave.

'Thank you again, sir,' said Rose extending her hand. 'We'll call to make an appointment for our IT officers.' The police left and the Attorney-General felt ill. His conscience impacted his stomach.

Walking back to their car, Jo was curious. 'Did you really want me to count the computers, ma-am?'

Rose laughed. 'No, it's an old trick your grandfather taught me. Make the suspects think you've done or will do something and watch when the panic sets in.' Jo smiled. *Well done, Pop.*

Rose drove Jo to see Gabrielle Strange. 'I haven't seen the pathologist for 25 years,' said Rose. 'Is she still a loopy genius?'

Jo laughed. 'Good description, ma-am.'

The police entered the antiseptic-smelling premises and interrupted Dr Strange examining a corpse. She downed tools when she saw Jo.

'It's the deranged detective.' Strange wanted to embrace Jo who wasn't keen as the medico's protective clothing had unknown stains. 'I know you,' said the pathologist looking at Rose.

'Hello Doctor. I worked in Homicide back when you started.'

'Don't tell me, don't tell me.' Strange struggled. 'Come on brain cells. Flower.' She snapped her fingers. 'Rose. Detective Senior Constable Something Rose.'

'Well done,' said the smiling DI.

'Be careful, Doctor,' said Jo. 'This is Detective Inspector Rose, the new head of Homicide.'

'Eleanor,' snapped Strange, feeling as proud as punch. Both officers laughed. Rose wanted to crack on.

'I believe you found some material in the throat of the woman who drowned at Warburton.'

Strange searched. 'I did, I did, I did.' She found it. 'Not sure what it is but it's not something you'd ingest by choice.' Jo took the container with the material. 'Hopefully Forensics can identify it.'

'Nothing else, Doctor?' asked Rose. 'We've got three homicides and pretty much zero progress.'

'Sorry. Bits of metal and plastic from the judge's face but I'd say they're from his vehicle. The young man who was strangled had a sex toy up his jacksy but apparently no DNA or prints. Your killers, ladies, are either lucky or professional.'

Rose wanted to leave. 'Nice catching up again, Doctor,' said Rose.

'Likewise,' replied Strange, 'and even better to have the deranged detective back where she belongs.'

Jo winked at Strange and, as the police walked to the car, Jo explained the expressions she and Gabrielle used for each other. En route to Forensics, the now nervous Senior Constable made a request.

'Could I ask a favour, please ma-am?'

'You can ask.'

There's a scientist at Forensics who fancies me and I may have ...'

'Led him on?'

'Yes, I think a court would accept that as a reasonable proposition.'

'So you want me to ward off the amorous boffin?'

Jo squirmed. 'I'd feel safer in a crowd, ma-am.' Rose laughed.

They entered Forensics with Jo dreading having to deal with Alastair in person. It was an anti-climax as the 40 year old who lived with his mother was off sick. The material was handed to another scientist and they left. Jo wished she hadn't told the DI about her private life. *Does she think I'm some kind of femme fatale? Am I?*

'Now please have your IT expert check the AG's computers.'

'Yes, ma-am.'

'Is he reliable, discreet?'

'He is but with such a sensitive operation, would it be better to use some of our own IT people?'

'I want the best person for the job and from reports that's him. Has he signed a confidentially contract?'

'If not I'll see he does.'

'Please do it a.s.a.p. You must know that any unsolved homicide builds pressure but when a Supreme Court judge is the victim, we really cop it. The top brass don't care I'm new. They want results.'

'Yes ma-am.'

'You go with your friend to the AG's office, as a sort of babysitter.'

'Ma-am, Michael told me that finding the guilty computer doesn't tell us who sent the emails.'

'Obviously but one goal of the inspection is to put the wind up the guilty party who in turn may panic.' Jo felt stupid. 'A good detective chases down every lead no matter how small. Many are dead ends but exploring every possibility gives you a chance of finding evidence or obtaining a confession. Even if the lead looks shaky, chase it down.'

Lecture over, Jo remained silent.

She rang Michael and explained the situation. 'You do know I may not be able to pinpoint the guilty computer,' he said.

'The DI thinks the inspection is as important as any discovery.'

'I see. So when is this inspection happening?'

'Would you believe, now?'

'Okay,' he replied.

Typical Michael. Mr Unflappable. 'I'll pick you up in half an hour.'

12

BARRY CHUBB WAS KNOWN AS BARRY GRUB. He was a shock jock, a radio presenter with definite views that stood out like nudists at a funeral. He hated dole recipients, vegans, climate-change believers and women who dared to leave the kitchen. He was single, self-opinionated and selfish. Criticism of his behaviour was met with scorn. Anyone who dared challenge him was hammered by reply broadcast. His employers loved him thanks to the money created from his ratings. Interestingly, there were more people who hated Barry who were rusted on listeners as opposed to people who shared his bigoted views. Some folk listen to be outraged.

Barry's private life was limited. He went to political gatherings of a certain Party, and his passion for tennis saw him attend the Australian Open without fail. His only family was his sister Charlotte, divorced, and her daughter, his niece Pippa.

She was the apple of Uncle Barry's eye. Noel Coward would have advised Pippa to avoid the stage and stick to riding horses. As an equestrian, Pippa missed out on Olympic and Commonwealth Games selection much to Barry's annoyance. He went on a tirade about corrupt Olympic officials and how the selection process of athletes was linked to nepotism and favouritism. Barry was threatened with legal action so went harder in his criticism.

Barry watched Pippa compete, funded her travel and expenses, and desperately wanted his favourite girl to succeed. Imagine then his horror when Barry received a call from his sister.

'Hi Sis, what's news?' Charlotte was hysterical. She blurted out the news. Barry couldn't understand. 'What? Pippa's what?'

Charlotte continued her incomprehensible mutterings with only two words registering in Barry's brain. 'Pippa's dead.'

For once the voice that never stopped did stop. Barry fell silent. The concept was as shocking as it was incredible. Finally he spoke. 'Pippa's dead? What happened?'

Charlotte blurted out the details. 'She fell while riding. A man, found her. She's dead, Barry, my baby's dead.'

'Where are you?'

'At home.'

'I'm on my way.'

Accompanied by Jo Best, Michael Chan checked the computers. The entire Attorney-General's staff knew the story and its leak became a torrent. The media knew but worse, so did the faceless apparatchiks of the ALP. Michael made a detailed examination and found what he was looking for. He wrote his findings and gave the details to Jo.

The next Homicide meeting had something concrete—finally. Rose reported on the material found in the throat of the drowned woman.

'Forensics identified the material as a cotton ball, the sort you can buy anywhere. No DNA but it points to Karen being drowned.'

'With the cotton balls used to silence her en route,' said Fleming.

'And with the marks on her wrists and her mouth stuffed with material, she was dragged into the water and held under. The killers removed most of what was in her mouth but she inadvertently swallowed some of it.'

'Scary way to die,' said Stephen Payne.

'This was no suicide. Karen Galbraith was murdered,' said Rose.

'It may well be a 'omicide,' added Richelieu, 'but of suspects, motive and evidence, 'ave we none, n'est-ce pas?'

Rose didn't like his lack of enthusiasm and changed topics.

'We do have some information from the computer inspection in the Attorney-General's office. Jo.'

'The IT expert, Michael Chan, who some of you will remember from the capture of the Sim bothers and the child kidnap in Castlemaine, examined several computers. The one he reckoned had been used to send emails to Judge Slight's rooms had been doctored. Michael said its hard drive had been replaced possibly to remove its history.'

'Why?' asked Baldwin.

'If the sender had been searching for material about the late judge, and that computer was then used to send threatening emails, whoever used that computer would have questions to answer,' replied Jo.

'Again,' said Richelieu, 'all this is interesting but it does not bring to us the smoking gun, n'est-ce pas?'

Rose again found Richelieu's comments irritating. Playing the devil's advocate was fine but she wanted enthusiasm from her fellow DI.

'Finding the guilty computer is a start,' said Rose. 'Now detectives Richelieu and Best have been working on a theory that all three homicides may be linked. Inspector?'

Richelieu addressed the squad and talked about vigilante killings with a possible political or religious motive. 'Senior Constable Best and I worked independently but we 'ave agreed there are certain linking factors. The victims are law-abiding citizens, there appears to be no motive for the 'omicides, and the victims are linked by not 'aving any enemies.'

Rose invited comments.

'You talk about no enemies but surely the judge had some,' said Baldwin. 'Those emails weren't sent by a friend.'

'True but until we know the sender, we cannot be certain,' replied Richelieu.

Fleming commented. 'Many homicides involve victims who are good people. I don't see any connection other than timing. Had they happened months apart, would we consider a connection?'

'Someone else?' asked Rose. She felt flat. She wanted enthusiasm, support, robust argument. It didn't appear.

Stephen Payne had an idea which in itself was unusual. The fact that his idea sounded credible made it all the more interesting.

'Have we thought about a pattern? Did one homicide have to happen to bring on the second and then the third? If there is a pattern, we could anticipate a fourth.'

This was unexpected and so credible, it silenced the squad.

'So are we looking at a serial killer?' asked Billy Hughes.

'If true, we only need to crack one case,' said Fleming. 'Should we concentrate on the homicide with the best chance of a quick arrest?'

Rose felt better. This is what she wanted—detectives with ideas. Robbo Robertson would encourage his team to think outside the box.

'Anyone else?' asked Rose.

'What are we doing about the emails from the Attorney-General's office?' asked Hughes.

'I'll handle them,' replied Rose, thinking she needed to visit the AC Crime before contemplating an arrest. 'Right, we crack on. We've got three outstanding homicides, and if Senior Constable Payne is right, we crack one, we crack all three.'

But if anyone reckoned Homicide was making progress with even one of their three murders, they would soon drop their collective bundle. As if predicted by Payne, news arrived of an unusual murder, number four, and things got a whole lot worse.

When Alastair Dean heard the love of his life had been in his office, standing beside his desk, he was heartbroken then angry. Mother made him stay home; she had a migraine. *Mother made me miss the wonderful Detective Best arriving to seek my help. No, that was a cover. She came to see me to name the date we would marry. No, that's getting ahead of things, Alastair. She came to set the date on which we would have dinner. Damn you, Mother. Damn you to Hades.* Someone else handled Alastair's forensic task. *Mother, I hate you.*

Many people disbelieved 90% of what Barry Chubb said and queried the remaining 10%. But his latest outburst was outrageous. Barry made a brief investigation of his niece's demise then let rip. He made a claim without evidence. Mind you, he'd been doing that all his life.

Barry tweeted that his darling niece had been murdered. No flowery language, just a simple fact. And being who he was, when Barry Chubb made a claim, the retweets and subsequent media coverage exploded.

A doctor who was called to the scene of the horse-riding accident declared the young woman fell from her horse and suffered a broken neck—a credible diagnosis. The fact the horse was lame only added to the death by accident (misadventure) theory. It had stumbled, thrown Pippa and she was killed.

Homicide had no involvement and worked on their three current homicides. But nobody knew history was about to repeat itself. The unfortunate Pippa was delivered to the pathetic pathologist.

In 1996, when Dr Strange first began performing autopsies, she assisted the then pathologist examining a young man who crashed his motorbike. Police reckoned it was an RTA (Road Traffic Accident), a single person fatality. Ambulance officers and a local doctor agreed and all that remained was to inform the next of kin.

The about-to-retire pathologist, Dr Scales, examined the body and declared death was due to blunt force trauma, to wit the young man's head and a solid eucalyptus tree.

But another medico was present, a young pathologist, one Dr Gabrielle Strange. She claimed the motorcyclist had been murdered. Was she trying to make a name for herself as she began her career? Was she brilliant?

Boy, did her assessment stir the pot? The then head of Homicide, DCI John Robbo Robertson arrived and Dr Strange explained her strange theory. Bottom line was she was right and some clever detective work from the Homicide Squad (including Detective Senior Constable Eleanor Rose) uncovered the truth and arrested and charged two murderers. They got 20 years—each. Was history about to repeat itself?

13

JO SCANNED THE LIST OF MOVIES. She needed something suitable for her date with Harry Carr. She wanted to make this a day to remember. She thought about the zoo, the Melbourne Museum, a train ride at Eltham and even the city skyscraper with the glass floor but a movie and lunch sounded good.

She arrived on time and was greeted by the young man himself. He saluted then gave Jo a hug. Dr Carr stood behind his son, smiling.

'Come in,' he said and Jo was taken in hand by her date. To say he was over the moon would be an understatement.

Jo looked at Jack and mouthed, 'Any news?'

He shook his head. The happiness of the little boy was balanced with the dread of the death-like situation at the nearby hospital. Jack's parents were there and in turn embraced the detective.

'You look smart,' said Peg.

'She always looks smart,' said Hugh.

'Now remember your manners, Harry,' said his father. 'It makes no difference that Detective Jo is a police officer.'

'I promise I'll be good,' he said breaking the adult hearts with his innocence and determination to do the right thing.

Jo set the mood. 'I thought we'd have a talk in the car, young man, and decide all the things we'd like to do. What do you think, Harry?'

'Okay.' Then he remembered. 'Thank you, Detective Jo.'

If it did nothing else, it gave the father and grandparents a reason to smile and relax—anything to lighten the stress and suffering from watching their precious Grace struggling on life support.

After more hugs, Jo and Harry hopped in the car (back seat for the lad), and drove off for their day of fun. Jo plumped for a popular kids' film at a multiplex in South Yarra.

The boy could have been taken to watch paint dry and would have loved it. He was a kid getting up close to his football hero. Just being in Jo's presence was more than enough. Sharing popcorn with his favourite detective was the icing on the cake.

After the film they went for lunch. Jo wasn't sure if popular fast food restaurants were okay for a health-conscious medico's children so went for something a little more upmarket. Harry loved the choices on the menu and took Jo's advice.

There was a noisy children's birthday party being held in the restaurant but Harry didn't notice. He wanted to chat about the movie and school and Little Athletics and about becoming a policeman. Jo didn't raise the topic of his sister but was ready to discuss it if Harry chose to do so. They finished lunch and were at the register when Jo was accosted.

'Hello Auntie Jo,' said one child.

'Hello Auntie Jo,' said another.

Jo was surprised. Her sister's children appeared. Jo liked these kids but didn't get on with her sister and loathed her brother-in-law. Harry was impressed as most kids are with other kids.

'Hello you two. Where did you spring from?'

'We're at our friend's birthday party,' said Millie, pointing.

'You remember Harry from Puffing Billy.' Tim and Harry smiled.

Jo enjoyed a bit of banter, paid the bill and started to leave when big sister appeared. 'Fancy seeing you here,' said Caitlyn. She spoke to her offspring. 'Back you go.' They always did as they were told—now. Jo reckoned as teenagers their rebellion would be worth seeing.

Jo put her arm around her date. 'This is Harry from Puffing Billy.'

Caitlyn looked at the child and fired off a plastic smile, a contender for Insincere Person of the Year Award. 'Hello Harry.' He smiled not understanding the hidden meanings of verbal warfare played by adults. When Caitlyn first met Harry and his sister and father with Jo, big sis assumed Dr Carr was a divorcee having his kids for the weekend. Caitlyn made a sarcastic remark warning her sister to steer clear of the lecherous single dad.

Jo cut her down with a throw-away reply. 'He's a widower and his wife died young from cancer.'

Caitlyn didn't learn from her previous faux pas, turned side on, and spoke softly. 'So now he's got you babysitting. Couldn't you manage both of them?'

Jo remembered her previous retort and went even harder. 'His sister's in Intensive Care fighting for her life.' Jo paused to see the look on her sister's face. 'I'll see ya.' She took Harry's hand and left. The interesting thing about Caitlyn is that she thought her sister was lying.

As Jo and Harry walked back to Jo's car, DI Rose took a phone call. 'Good afternoon Inspector, it's Gabrielle Strange. How would you like another homicide?'

Rose groaned. 'Only if you know whodunit.'

'Tell me, how good is your memory?'

'Not as good as yours, Doctor.'

'Do you remember the murdered motorcyclist in the 1996 RTA?'

'I do, it was one of my first cases.'

'Well I think Barry the Grub is right. His niece *was* murdered.'

That comment needed some explaining but the long and short of it meant the DI's weekend was put on hold. She headed to see the pathologist and wanted one particular officer to accompany her.

Jo checked Harry's seating in the back then prepared to drive. 'I hope you've had a good time, Harry. I know I have.'

'I have too,' he said then added, 'but do I have to go home?'

Jo hit the brakes. *What does he mean?* 'Well I need to take you home after we've had our day of fun, Harry.'

He spoke in a matter of fact way. 'Everyone's sad at my house.'

Jo froze. The boy had said nothing about the horrible situation with his sister and now it all came out. Jo blamed herself for not quietly talking about it before. She thought not mentioning it was the right thing. She was wrong and switched off the engine, undid her seatbelt and turned back to face the child.

'I'm sorry, Harry. I forgot to ask about Grace.'

'Daddy's sad and so is Nan and Pop. I wish Grace could get better.'

'So do I. We all do. We just need to wait a little bit longer.' Jo was struggling. Talking to anyone about a loved one possibly dying was tough. When you're dealing with a child, it's super hard.

'Do you know my Mummy died?'

Jo felt her heart start burning and a lump form in her throat. *Don't cry, woman.* 'Yes, I did, Harry.'

'I cried when she died.' Jo was running out of things to say. 'I think I'll cry when Grace dies.'

'Oh Harry, Grace might get better. We need to hope she does.'

'I asked Daddy because he's a doctor.' Jo stopped breathing. 'He said Grace might stay in the hostipal (his mispronunciation was endearing), for a long time.'

Jo fought hard not to cry. 'Well I wish that Grace gets better soon.'

Harry nodded. 'Me too,' he said. Jo wanted to hop in the back and hold him but knew she would weep and didn't think that would help.

'Let's go home and we can tell your Dad and Nan and Pop about the things we did today.'

'Okay,' he said as if their previous chat didn't happen. Jo buckled up, started the engine and was about to pull out when Harry asked a question. 'Would you like to be my Mummy?'

Jo was lucky not to drive into the car in front of her. *How the hell do I answer that?* Before she could speak, her phone rang. She stopped the car, looked at the number and picked up the phone.

'This is a police call, Harry. Excuse me.' She spoke into the phone. 'Yes ma-am?'

'I need you, Jo. Are you free?'

'I will be soon. What's happened?'

'I'm heading to see Dr Strange who reckons we have another homicide. And it sounds like a case your grandfather once handled. I'd like you to see the body then ask him what he thinks.'

Jo was excited. Tricky, as her emotions were a mess. 'Ma-am I'm driving a young boy home and can't get to you for about an hour.'

'Make it forty minutes.' Click.

The call ended and Jo turned to look at Harry. He was gazing out the window. She headed for the Carr residence. All three adults were waiting. Harry buzzed. He told everyone he'd had the best time ever. There were smiles from Jack and his folks but Jo's smile was forced.

'We're having an early tea. Please stay and join us,' said Jack.

Jo looked as sad as she felt. 'I'd love to but there's been a new homicide and my boss has asked me to attend.'

The adults were disappointed and Harry seriously so.

'Please Detective Jo.'

Jo couldn't speak and thankfully Peg stepped in and saved the day. 'Come on young man, time for a bath and then Pop has a new story to read to you.'

Harry got the message and gave Jo the tightest hug. 'Thank you,' he said his face buried in her body. Then he turned and went inside with his grandparents.

'You're a star,' said Jack.

'We had a great day but he got a little emotional as we drove home.'

'About Grace?' Jo nodded. She was struggling not to cry. 'We all are. Come on, I'll walk you out.'

Jo struggled. 'I didn't know what to say to him. He told me his Mummy had died and he didn't want Grace to die too.'

Neither spoke. The heartbreak was physically painful but when expressed by a small child, the agony bit deep.

He held the door as she put on her seat belt. 'I know you're a busy girl, but any time you feel like dropping in, please do.' She didn't try to speak because she knew she'd cry. She nodded and grimaced. He closed the door and she drove off and only then burst into tears.

Jo arrived and Rose and Strange looked at her red eyes.

'You okay?' asked Rose.

Strange moved to Jo, gripped her shoulders and looked into her eyes. 'Tell me his name and I'll make sure the bastard gets a slap.'

Jo wanted to laugh and cry. 'It *is* a male but he's only six and his eight-year-old sister's on life support.'

Both women shared Jo's pain. 'Go home,' said Rose. 'This can wait.'

Jo wiped her eyes and blew her nose. 'No ma-am. I need to be here to take my mind off the kids. Please.'

The women saw the logic and agreed. Rose explained. 'The victim's a woman who fell from a horse and broke her neck. She's the niece of shock jock Barry Chubb. He's spouting some conspiracy theory that his niece was murdered by one of her rivals for the national equestrian team—a homicide disguised as a riding accident.'

'And in this case,' added Strange, 'for once, the madman is right. I don't know about his conspiracy theory but this woman didn't die falling off a horse. Look here.'

The police stood on one side of the body with Strange on the other. They stood where DCI Robbo Robertson stood when Strange was a spring chicken explaining how another accident was a homicide.

'She has a broken neck which I believe was inflicted after she was killed. The cause of death is suffocation.'

'So she had to get off the horse, surely,' said Rose.

'Or was threatened or pulled off,' added the pathologist. 'She has bruising here on the lips, not I'll bet from Botox, she's bitten her tongue and has bruising inside her mouth.'

'Signs of suffocation?' asked Rose.

'Exactly. And here in her left eye, there are tiny petechial haemorrhages, very rare, but again an indication a person has been suffocated due to being smothered.'

'With what?' asked Rose.

'A pillow, towel, anything.'

'I don't suppose you found any foreign material in her throat?'

'Not the cotton balls from the woman who drowned, sorry, no.'

'But why would she get down from her horse?' queried Jo.

'So you want me to be Monsieur Poirot as well?' Jo half-smiled. 'The killer could have pointed a gun at her, anything.'

'Or worse,' added Rose, 'at her horse. Anyone holding a Stanley knife against the neck of a horse would terrify the rider.'

'Now the horse could be another key,' said Strange. 'I was told the animal was lame.'

'Perfect cover for murder,' said Rose, 'horse stumbles, rider falls.'

'Inspector, I would have that horse examined as soon as. If there's a chance the injury was caused by human intervention then that adds weight to my homicide claim. I'm no farrier but surely jamming something into a hoof would be easy and cause the beast to limp.'

The police looked at Strange. They both knew her wild conspiracies were anything but wild and instead were based on scientific fact.

'Thank you, Doctor and can I ask one enormous favour.'

'More favours?' She pretended the request was a hardship.

'Please do not leak these details. If Barry Chubb discovers his niece *was* murdered, the media will bury us.'

'Mum's the word,' smiled Strange handing Rose her preliminary notes. The officers thanked her and left. Strange called. 'And if I can help with that little girl, you only have to ask.' Jo blew her a kiss.

'My car, Senior,' said Rose and Jo joined her boss. 'According to my abacus we have four unsolved homicides, two of which have the potential to rock the world. If the Attorney-General or Barry Chubb gets wind of what we know, we'll have more leads than a pet shop. I don't mind telling you, Jo, I'm shitting myself in this new job.'

'Why don't you give your old boss a call?'

Rose looked at her. 'Are you serious?'

Jo shrugged. 'I'm a beginner but he once gave me a tip that helped crack a case. What have you got to lose, and you know him already.'

'You're right, thanks.' She paused. 'Would you put in a word?'

Jo took out her phone and hit a number. 'Hi Pop, it's Jo.'

Robbo was tickled pink. They sparred until Jo cut to the chase. 'You told me you remembered our new boss.'

'I do indeed, Elly Rose, one of my old senior constables.'

'I don't think she'd like you calling her old, Pop.' The women exchanged glances. Jo put her hand over her phone and whispered. 'Do you want me to come too?' Rose nodded. 'How about I bring DI Rose out for a chat?' Pop was keen. 'Are you up for a visit in say half an hour?' Rose nodded. Pop agreed. 'We'll see you soon.' She ended the call. 'He's excited.'

'So am I,' grinned Rose. Jo gave her DI Pop's address.

14

ATTORNEY-GENERAL STEFAN GOULDING hated Ranald Slight, the murdered judge. The hatred went back decades to when Slight beat Goulding in a student election. For the aspiring politician, it was a kick in the guts. Fast-forward 25 years and Goulding appointed Slight to the Supreme Court. The enmity continued when His Honour, in private, slammed changes to laws proposed by the AG. So when his Honour was murdered, the AG enjoyed a frisson. *Serves him right.*

But recent events gave Stefan no frisson; instead he panicked. Someone in his office had sent nasty emails to Slight and that brought the police to Stefan's door. *Shit!*

Goulding was ambitious. He fancied becoming Premier but now a giant wrecking ball swung his way. To have cops in his office asking questions was the stuff of nightmares. To have the ALP executive wanting to know what was going on was a political minefield. The murder of Judge Slight meant the likely death of Stefan's career.

It mattered not he had nothing to do with the emails—they came from his office. He was on Death Row and needed facts and luck. That weekend, he summoned his Chief of Staff.

Christian Falange was a natural born public servant. He loved organising things and serving important people. Christian's dream job was working for anyone in power. Riding on powerful coattails was an aphrodisiac. But not now. Now he sensed danger.

'What do you know about cricket, Christian?' This was a rhetorical question as both men knew at school—they both went to Melbourne High— when phys ed was on the timetable, Christian hid.

'You know the answer, Minister.'

'The Chappell brothers were famous Australian cricketers. Two of the three brothers captained their country.' Christian didn't follow. 'As kids the brothers played cricket in the backyard. One game saw a cricket ball smash a window. Their mother told her sons their father would discuss the matter after work. Chappell Senior arrived and made a speech—and this is the bit that applies you, Christian.'

What the hell is he talking about? thought the Chief of Staff.

'You won't get into trouble for breaking the window,' said Dad, 'but you will if you lie.'

Stefan looked at his right hand man. Even for a non-cricketing person, Christian knew exactly what his boss meant.

'I believe in George Washington,' said Christian. Stefan's fury glowed brighter.

'What the fuck are you talking about?' he bellowed. *He* should talk.

'I cannot tell a lie,' replied the public servant. 'Under oath, under the table, Under Milkwood, I am programmed to tell the truth. It's in the DNA of every Chief of Staff.'

'Listen, mate, I am in the shit, big time. You saw the cops, the whole department saw them, and now I'll have to front the executive and explain. If someone hasn't already leaked this ticking time bomb of a tale, they're probably doing so as we speak. The media coverage will be obscene and I'll be seen no more.'

Christian wanted to die. *If he goes, I'll go too.*

The AG's mind was in a panic. 'Who's George Milkwood?'

Christian wasn't crying but his bottom lip trembled. 'It's outrageous Judge Slight said those things about your law reform proposals.'

'He never made a public comment.'

Christian turned feisty. 'Oh please, Stefan. Everyone knows Slight hated your reforms, even the Chief Justice agreed.'

'Slight may have hinted at his displeasure.'

Christian scoffed. 'The man was as subtle as a dentist on drugs.'

Stefan wanted to sack his Chief of Staff but knew it wouldn't kill the scandal. Government ministers had to fly *under* the radar. Thanks to those nasty emails, the AG was giving the Opposition free kicks in front of goal. The world and its mother were gossiping about the AG.

Stefan pondered his position. *Should I jump before I'm pushed?* He teetered on the balcony high above the concrete then froze when his subservient Chief of Staff threw him a lifeline.

'You do know, Minister, Ranald Slight perjured himself by saving his barrister mate, Simon Beaumont, after Simple Simon got sprung with insider trading?'

The AG looked like he'd been shot. 'What?'

'Years ago. I thought you knew.'

Stefan flipped and flapped and screamed. 'Knew what?'

'The highly esteemed barrister was once a crook. He was a director of a tin pot mining company which made a lucky strike.'

'When was this?'

'Before our time, decades ago.'

'What happened?'

'Before the company announced the find, Beaumont bought stock for a song in his father-in-law's name. The share price exploded and barrister Beaumont made a killing.'

The AG was both angry and excited. 'Why wasn't I aware of this?'

'I thought you were. That's why you sent the threatening emails.'

'Me?! What do you mean, *me*? I didn't send them. *You* sent them.'

A silence bomb exploded. The office was littered with quiet. The penny dropped. Both men froze. Each was sure the other was the phantom email sender. Both were wrong.

But if it wasn't them, then who? Stefan twigged. This was the worst possible result. One of his enemies—he could name many within his Party—sent the emails from his department so as to embarrass Stefan. The plot worked. Did it ever? The cops rocked up. Suspicion settled in the AG's office like a fog and that suspicion would see Mr Goulding sent back to some ridiculous portfolio such as Minister for Grande Opera and Horse Racing. The pain on their faces was etched in 3D.

'There is a way out of this,' said the Attorney-General. His sidekick felt sick knowing what was coming. 'I've got an idea.'

Jo arrived at her grandfather's house and waited. Rose arrived and together they stood at his front door. This was a double-barrelled delight for the retired cop. He hugged them both.

'Come in, come in,' he said and they sat and revelled in one another's company. 'Who would've thunk it, hey? My granddaughter's a homicide detective and her boss is my former senior constable.'

Laughter and memories bounced around the room. Finally they got down to the nitty gritty.

'I'd love your advice, sir, on a couple of matters.'

'I've forgotten everything I ever knew, and that wasn't much,' replied the retired detective.

'Don't believe him, ma-am,' said Jo. Robbo was buzzing.

Rose got serious. 'We've got four homicides with none looking easy. When you had multiple cases, did you have a priority list?'

'Is that it?' asked Robbo. 'That's not a problem.'

'Perhaps,' replied Rose, 'but two of the cases are likely to attract massive media coverage and with the world watching, we might struggle to solve what are already difficult cases.'

'Forget fame. Treat high-profile homicides like any other. Don't let the top brass, politicians or the bloody media put you off your stroke. Go by the book.'

That advice alone was worth the trip for Rose. She needed down-to-earth support for what she believed was the right thing. She felt better hearing from someone she trusted and Jo felt better seeing her boss relax. And when Rose told Robbo his granddaughter had a theory about the cases being linked, he became doubly interested.

'Tell me more,' he said.

Jo explained and Robbo considered his verdict.

'Am I on the right track, Pop?'

'Maybe but I'd concentrate on the motive. It's unusual to have a motive-free homicide; four is rare, unheard of. Crack the motive and if they're linked, you'll have a real shot at locating the killer or killers.'

The women liked that answer which sounded great in theory. But they were still short on practical ideas.

After a cuppa and more memories, Rose thanked her former boss and left. Jo washed up and asked about her grandmother. That killed the happy mood. Ida's dementia was here to stay and Robbo's retirement was a drag as every daily visit became a game of charades. Having Jo visit was a highlight for the old man. His daughter and great-grandchildren were infrequent visitors.

'So what do you think of my new boss?'

'I think she's matured. She needed a bit more humanity and from what I saw today, she's picked that up and in spades.'

'Good.'

'Now, what's happening with you? I've heard about your mother's new boyfriend but nothing about yours.'

'Don't *you* start.' They laughed. She wanted to stay longer but left to visit her mother's godmother in hospital and a little girl in an induced coma.

All of Jo's unsolved homicide cases, all her would-be boyfriends counted for nothing when Grace Carr clung to life thanks to medical science. *How can any parent switch off the life-support of their child?*

First visit was to Marjorie who was dozing. *I'll let her rest*, Jo thought and turned to go. The other patients were having none of that.

'Hello love,' said the woman in the closest bed. Then in an even louder voice she said, 'Have you come to visit Marjorie?'

The other two inmates were less subtle. 'Marjorie!' they called. 'You've got a visitor, Marjorie.'

It was pointless Jo asking them to be quiet because Marjorie was soon wide awake and delighted to see her young visitor.

'Hello my dear,' she beamed and Jo sat for the duration.

Visit over, she kissed Marjorie and waved to the entire ward who, thanks to Marjorie, now knew that Jo was a Homicide Detective, single and able to leap tall buildings in a single bound. Several bachelor grandsons were being groomed as a match for Marjorie's mate.

Jo headed for the ICU. She felt her pulse quicken and the knot in her stomach get tighter. She opened the door to Reception and froze. Ten metres away Jack Carr had his back to her and was facing two doctors in white coats—a man and a woman. Jack's head dropped. Both the people in white coats put a hand on Jack to steady him. He would have collapsed had not the others been there. Jo couldn't bear to watch. She turned and fled.

15

IT WAS HELL IN THE Attorney-General's office. Stefan explained his plan to Christian who protested. 'But if I admit to sending the emails, I'll be sacked. I may even be charged and go to prison.'

'You're not listening. You confess to the Party. I tell the executive we planned it together to expose the corrupt judge.'

'We can't prove he was corrupt.'

The AG erupted. 'We don't have to. We spread doubt. We milk the bit where he covered for his barrister mate's insider trading sting.'

Christian couldn't think straight. Having to confess to threatening a judge turned him into a gibbering wreck.

'So if you tell the Party, how will that save me?'

'The Party approved of Slight. If either of us gets whacked, we hint that the press will be delighted to learn why the emails were sent. Slight was corrupt. We wanted him to quit. The Party bigwigs will shit themselves and cover up the whole affair.'

'But the cops will come after me. If I admit to the emails, I'll be their number one murder suspect.'

'You are not listening to me!' roared the AG. 'You only confess to the Party. You say nothing to the cops. And besides, no cop on planet Earth will believe a skinny weakling like you could murder anyone let alone a judge.'

Christian was miffed. *How dare you. And I'm slim, not skinny.*

Sadly that wasn't the end of the plan. 'You're forgetting something,' said Christian, 'the person who sent those emails.'

'I told you it was one of my rivals, someone within the Party.'

'Yes but that person will know my confession is false.'

'And do what? Stand up and call you a liar? It wasn't him, it was me. That won't happen. They did it to ruin me and it's backfired. We've snookered them and if we hold our nerve, this plan is our get-out-of-jail card. Now this is how you'll confess.'

In his palatial apartment, Barry Chubb worked the phones. He was looking for data to promote his conspiracy theory regarding the sudden and tragic death of his beloved niece, Pippa.

Barry's radio show pulled great ratings. With his lead story personal, he needed facts. Barry was not remotely interested in anything which might challenge his claim. He was a black and white opinion giver with no shades of grey. His niece was murdered and he intended to beat that drum until the police danced to his tune.

He wanted details about the sporting officials who selected teams for the equestrian events at the Commonwealth and Olympic Games. Barry "knew" these people favoured family, friends or friends of friends. There was no way on God's Earth, (Barry was big on the Almighty when it suited) his niece could not have been on those teams.

According to Barry, with the next selection announcement due, someone panicked and murdered his brilliant niece to prevent her from winning the recognition she deserved.

He researched other sports. Phar Lap was poisoned by American gangsters and what about that ice skating champion? My God, everyone wants to nobble a champion and Pippa was just that.

Ironically, Barry was correct. All of his loopy conspiracy theories were laughable, and this seemed to fit that description. But for once in his cotton-pickin' on-air nonsensical rantings, Barry was right. His niece *was* murdered. If Dr Gabrielle Strange bothered to listen to Barry, she could have become one of his callers.

"Spot on, Bazz. As sure as I'm Strange, you're right."

He worked on his speech to be delivered live next week.

As he wrote, DI Eleanor Rose sipped a glass of red and studied Dr Strange's notes. *Bloody hell*, she thought. *If that shock jock goes public with his murder theory, it'll look like I'm reacting to an idiot who thinks he can control the police.*

First thing on Monday, Rose reckoned that Jo was still affected by the little girl's suffering.

'Go home, Senior, take a break,' said Rose.

'Thanks but I'm fine, ma-am.'

'Okay but no field work. Spend time seeing if you can expand that theory about the homicides being linked.'

Jo wanted to argue but agreed. 'Okay, ma-am, and thanks.'

Most of her colleagues were out and about. Billy Hughes was running the Eddie Balance homicide, the young man strangled and dumped on his Mum's back verandah. To everyone who knew him, it was a massive shock. It was a motiveless murder. Billy, with Senior Constable Payne at her side, wanted another chat with the mother.

'Remember Stephen, the woman is in mourning and we tread softly. Say nothing other than you don't want a cuppa. Comprende?'

'I'm not sure why I'm here, Sarge.' She stared at him. He nodded.

Gwenda Balance had the shakes. She and the police sat in her sitting-room. She didn't close any doors or offer any refreshment. She was in shock, delayed, ongoing or both. Her beloved son died suddenly and unexpectedly. And when you're the one who finds his corpse, naked from the waist down and with serious injuries to his rectum, that tends to ramp up the appalling pain and shock flooding your body. For Gwenda, tranquilisers were being consumed under medical supervision but at best they only took the edge off her agony.

The detectives didn't fancy their chances of learning anything new let alone substantial. How wrong they were. Gwenda was on fire.

'He was bullied and threatened.'

'Eddie was bullied?' asked Billy in as soft a voice as possible.

'He found out his principal was charging exorbitant fees for Mickey Mouse courses and granting diplomas regardless of what the students did. Some didn't even attend classes.' Billy saw Payne taking notes.

'Eddie told you this?'

'He challenged Mr Souvlakis who told Eddie to mind his own business. Eddie didn't and that's when the threats started. I told him to go to the police.' She broke down. 'Why didn't he go the police? Why?'

Billy let her cry. The woman had obviously been stewing for days about her son's situation. Now she was up for a chat. She wanted the bastard who killed her son to be brought to justice. When the crying stopped, Billy suggested they break for a cup of tea. Gwenda ignored the suggestion.

'And that business with the abuse of his body was a cowardly and cruel attempt to shift the blame onto his ex-boyfriend.'

Billy struggled. *Wow, where did that come from?* 'Who was Eddie's ex-boyfriend?' asked Billy.

Gwenda ignored the question and let fly. 'Everyone knew Eddie was gay. He was proud of who he was. *I* was proud of who he was. But to try and cover the corruption in his college, that bastard had Eddie killed making it look like it was a lover's quarrel.'

Forget Gwenda being tired, *Billy* wanted a break. From a motiveless homicide, she now had a potential fraud, a vindictive fraudster and an angry former lover. Motives and persons of interest sprang out of the woodwork. Where to start?

'I need some details please, Gwenda.' Billy soon had the name and address of Eddie's former boyfriend and the business address of his former employer. She thanked Gwenda, tried to convey some words of comfort, and promised to try and bring justice to her beloved son.

Her suffering seemed overwhelming. Her little dog offered comfort but even he despaired seeing his mistress in such misery.

In the car, the detectives took stock. 'I wasn't expecting that, Sarge,' said Payne. 'From zero suspects and no motive, we've got a choice.'

'Let's have a chat with the ex-boyfriend.'

They headed for one of the now many high-rise apartment blocks in town.

As DS Hughes investigated Eddie Balance, DS Fleming and Charlie Baldwin were in the Yarra Valley for the now confirmed homicide of Karen Galbraith. Their first port of call was the supermarket where she worked. Her former colleagues had given statements and Fleming and Baldwin were to double check them and, if necessary, ask more questions. Nothing new was gleaned until the manager of the night shift turned up. John Grassmere was no oil painting and as he was sleeping rough, looked terrible.

'Bad night, Mr Grassmere?' asked Fleming.

'You could say that.'

'We're going over the statements made about Karen Galbraith.'

'I lied.'

Fleming paused. 'I'm sorry?'

'I lied; on my statement I lied.'

The police stared at him. Had they finally cracked the homicide?

'I told you I was here at work when I wasn't. I pissed off for a bit. I couldn't have seen Karen even if she was here that night.'

'Okay,' said Fleming, 'let's have the truth this time, Mr Grassmere.'

'I've been having an affair with a woman in Millgrove. On the night Karen died, I pissed off for a long meal break. I never told you because I'm married and if I told you I wasn't here, me missus might find out.'

'And?'

'She and the bird in Millgrove have both given me the arse. I look like this 'cos I'm sleepin' in me fuckin' car.'

Fleming kept a straight face. 'Is Warburton the adultery capital of the Yarra Valley?'

Grassmere didn't react. His life at present was down the toilet. 'If the bird in Millgrove doesn't give me an alibi, my phone company will have plenty of history between us.'

'We'll need names and addresses, Mr Grassmere and I warn you, if this latest statement is not the whole truth, you'll be in serious strife.'

'There's something else.' The police stared at him. 'A while back we had a bloke who was sacked for being late, nicking stuff and that. He got the flick and then we had this scare with tampered fruit. Someone put broken glass in watermelons. We got lucky. The first person who bought one was the father of one of our workers. He told us and we removed all the watermelons.'

'Did you find more glass?' asked Fleming.

'Only two had broken glass.'

'Did you call the police?'

Grassmere made a face. 'The boss reckoned we caught all the tampered fruit and we'd get a big hit to business if the story got out.'

'But you know who did it? Was it the guy who got sacked?'

'Karen caught him sneaking around and he threatened her.'

'How?'

'Told her if she told anyone he was here, she'd be sorry.'

'And when was this?'

'The night before the tampered fruit was found.'

'Which was?'

'About a week before she died.'

The detectives looked at one another. From being a motive-free murder, they now had a person of interest, a strong lead and a good chance their homicide could be solved and soon. Karen Galbraith might be about to get some justice.

'So name and address of the sacked worker.'

'Don't know his real name. We called him Alvin.'

'Alvin?'

'Yeah as in *Alvin and the Chipmunks*.' The cops looked puzzled. 'He's got this squeaky kind of voice. The office'll have his details.'

'Does he live in the town?'

'Nah, he's weird, lives off the grid up in the bush, and that's cut lunch and a compass territory. I know he shoots rabbits and you could put a saddle on his dog.'

The detectives wouldn't be interviewing Alvin without backup. The haggard night manager signed a new statement and the cops went to the find Alvin's details. At last they had good news for DI Rose.

16

JO ARRIVED HOME and saw mail in her letterbox. It was an envelope sans stamp but addressed to Mademoiselle Joanna Best. She knew the handwriting and only one person addressed her as Mademoiselle.

She opened the envelope and discovered a brochure headed *Christmas in Paris*. The photos of the famous attractions with night shots showing snow and eerie lights along the Seine were stunning.

She turned it over and saw more highlights for the visitor. There was no note and nothing written on the brochure. Richelieu did things in style. He wasn't pushy. He was smooth, subtle and sensuous. Jo was keen. How keen, she wasn't sure. Her Parisian daydreaming ended when her phone rang.

'Hello ma-am.'

'I wanted you to know how much I enjoyed catching up with the old fella. I'd forgotten how wise and caring he was.'

'Still is.'

'Of course. Listen, I've heard from Billy and Justin and both have struck gold.'

'Ma-am?'

'We have motive and suspects for both the woman in the river and the murdered son. We might have solved two homicides.'

'That's fantastic.'

'What's not fantastic is the shock jock's niece and the judge.'

'But what about Dr Strange's murder theory?'

'That doesn't give us motive or MO.'

'Early days, ma-am.'

'Will you stop interrupting me?' Jo fell silent. 'I'm told Barry Chubb intends to go full volume in the morning pushing the line his niece was murdered. And if that's not enough, the AC has given the green light to have the Attorney General interviewed under caution.'

'Bloody hell.'

'Bloody hell indeed. So I want the entire squad in at 0700 hours. Can do?'

'Yes ma-am.'

'I'll see you then. Oh, and how's that little girl going?' Jo froze. Even if she wanted to speak, she couldn't. Rose understood and spoke softly. 'I'm so sorry.' Another pause. 'Bye.'

Lying in bed, Jo couldn't sleep. She wanted to do something but hated the fact that if she contacted Jack or his parents, she would force them to discuss what must be eating away at their insides.

She wondered why Jack or his parents hadn't contacted her and told her the terrible news. *Maybe I'm not seen as an intimate of the family. But the nurse in ICU told me I was top of the visitor list.*

She got up and made coffee. *This won't help me sleep.* She thought about ringing a nurse she knew. *Could she ring the hospital for me and get some news?*

Her phone pinged and she read the text.

Rags is ready for his walk.

Jo gasped. The text was from Jack Carr. Rags is the loveable dog. *But what does the cryptic text mean? Surely not at a time like this?*

She couldn't wait and hit Jack's number. Her heart doubled as a bass drum.

'Hello Detective Jo,' said the GP. He sounded bright, excited.

'Jack, what's happened?'

'She awake, Jo. My girl is awake.'

Jo lost control as her tear ducts let rip. 'Oh Jack, that's wonderful.'

'She not out of the woods but she's certainly turned the corner. And your little chat came at just the right time.'

Jo was confused. 'I don't understand.'

'The nurses said you told Grace you were going to take Rags for a walk and Grace was coming too. We said all those things to her and she nodded and even gave a tiny smile.'

Jo was so glad she was alone. Her emotions had been under some sort of control until that last comment. Now the dam wall shattered and her flat became the Ruhr Valley with floods of tears. She stood, her head shook, and her legs mimed stamping with her joy unconfined.

'That's wonderful news, Jack. I bet your folks are thrilled.'

'We're all thrilled to bits. Harry cheered.'

Jo lost it again then gradually got some form of control. 'Jack, I came to the hospital today and saw you with two doctors.'

'I didn't see you. You should have come over.'

'I was behind you and you seemed to slump and the doctors caught you and I couldn't bear to see you knowing you'd just been told some terrible news.'

'Not terrible, terrific. They'd told me the latest scans were positive, that she has a chance and that's when I collapsed.'

Jo's period of mourning was over and replaced with relief and joy. Right now she was a mess but it was a nice mess.

'When will Grace be up for visitors?'

'Any time. Give me a call or just drop in.'

'I'll do that but we're a bit stretched at present. We've got the media and politicians front and centre with two homicides. But I'll come and see Grace the first chance I get.'

'Thanks a million, Jo. My kids adore you, my folks think you're the best Best and I know they're right. Get a good night's sleep and look after yourself. Goodnight.'

'Goodnight,' said Jo without much feeling. She was drained. She tossed her phone on the settee, raised her clenched fists above her head and roared. 'Yes!'

The husband stared at the screen. 'Anything?' asked the wife.

'Nothing.'

'He said there'd be something big. What did he mean?'

'That there'd be something big.'

'What do you think he does for a living?'

'I don't know and we don't need to know.'

'I think he must be high up in the world.'

'Possibly.'

'Could he be a cop or work for the cops?'

'Don't think so.'

'Or a judge?'

'Why would a judge order the death of another judge?'

The woman stared at the screen. 'How do you know he's posted something? I thought you said he changes his screen name every time.'

'He does.'

'So?'

'I know his way of speaking. I respond and if I've got it right, he fires off the details.'

In code?'

The man snapped. 'Yes, in code.'

She paused. 'Will we ever get caught?'

'Not if we're careful. The police are looking for multiple killers. And besides, they obviously have no idea about the mixed up formula.'

The man keep staring, scrolling and searching.

'When will we see some change in people's behaviour?'

'No idea. But of that day and hour knoweth no man.'

She paused again. 'Do you think we'll make a difference?'

'All we can do is our job. Now leave me to look for the message.'

She withdrew and waited for the identity of their next victim.

17

DI ROSE CALLED FOR AN EARLY START—0700 hours. Everyone was on time. Was this out of respect for the new boss or because of the massive publicity two of their cases would soon receive? Perhaps both.

'Good morning,' said Rose breezing into the room. The troops replied in kind. They liked her hands-on approach but didn't know she was channelling her former boss, DCI Robbo Robertson.

'There's no news yet on Barry Chubb's broadcast. He usually tweets when he plans to drop a bomb. Word is he's going to publicly demand we investigate the death of his niece as a homicide.'

'So we haven't told him yet?' asked DS Fleming.

'No and we won't. And on top of that media frenzy is the fact that later this morning we're to interview, under caution, the Honourable Stefan Goulding, Attorney-General, regarding threatening emails sent from his office to the late Judge Slight.'

That created a hubbub. Billy Hughes interjected. 'Does Barry know he'll be gazumped by a politician?' That sparked comments.

'No and he won't like it when he discovers we knew about his niece before he did. And the good news keeps coming. We plan arrests for two homicides this morning. DS Fleming and DS Hughes both had productive interviews. Justin, what's happening in Warburton?'

Fleming related the details he and Baldwin gleaned and described the person of interest. 'He's known as Alvin, real name Bradley Michael Ford. The guy has a record for assault, we believe he has an unlicensed firearm and lives in an isolated shack with a dog that eats visitors. The arrest is set for noon and volunteers are welcome.'

That got the troops laughing. Rose was having none of it. 'No volunteers required. This is a job for the SOGGIES. Detectives Fleming and Baldwin will hide in the bushes till it's safe to come out.'

More laughter and Rose was impressive. The contrast between her attitude and the concern she showed for her officers with that of her predecessor, DI Steele, was chalk and cheese. She insisted on safety first by engaging the armed Special Operations Group (SOG) and gave the two Homicide officers the honour of making the arrest.

'Now Billy, what's the state of play with the late Eddie Balance?'

Hughes explained Gwenda's outpourings. 'We tracked down the ex-boyfriend but he was o/s when Mr Balance was murdered. That leaves the shady college principal, Kostos Souvlakis. If he's not involved in the homicide, Fraud wants a word about his dodgy education racket. We're ready to interview him this morning, ma-am.'

'Brilliant. What a difference a day makes.'

The detectives buzzed. Two days ago they had four homicides with basically nothing. Now they had leads aplenty.

'Pardon, Madame,' interrupted Richelieu. 'But what 'ave we to do with 'is 'onour, s'il vous plait?'

'Thank you, Pierre. You and 'is 'onour 'ave not been forgotten.' Others were amused at her mimicking Richelieu. Jo looked at the Francophile to see if he approved. It was hard to tell. 'We have traced the threatening emails sent to the judge to a computer in the office of the Attorney General. You and I, Monsieur, will shortly conduct an interview with the honourable member—under caution.' The hubbub returned. Jo had been replaced. 'Questions?' No reply. 'Right, good luck with your leads and let's make progress.'

Officers departed with Jo on her lonesome. She'd been bumped from Warburton and now the Attorney-General. Rose approached.

'How's that little girl?'

'Good news, ma-am. A long way to go but she's making progress.'

'Brilliant. Now I want you to make a start on Barry Chubb's niece.' Jo felt better. 'Go over the pathologist's notes, study Chubb's tweets and find out all you can about the horse in question. Questions?'

'No ma-am.'

'Call me if you find anything important.'

'Ma-am.' Rose left not noticing Jo's grin.

As the Homicide Squad started its day, the Attorney General and his Chief of Staff did likewise. They were off to the ALP HQ.

'We've got the President and State Secretary,' said Stefan.

'I'm scared,' mumbled Christian.

'Just remember the plan. I'll say the emails were sent by you to embarrass the judge because of his secret and disingenuous opposition to my law reform proposals.'

'Secret and disingenuous?' queried Christian.

Stefan ignored him. 'When they ask the ridiculous questions about the judge's murder, we treat it with the contempt it deserves.'

'That's easy for you to say.'

'When they ask for our resignations, we pull out the big guns.'

'I assume you're using the royal we.'

'Grey tie's good, Christian; sombre subject, sombre attire. Let's go.'

Hughes and Payne found the address of the *Advanced College of Learning*. Billy thought even the name was a crime. Learning what? Advanced in what way? The detectives entered the poky reception area where a young woman sat chewing gum and filing nails.

'Mr Kostos Souvlakis,' said Billy displaying her ID.

'Have you got an appointment?'

'Is he in?'

'You have to make an appointment.' She reached for a diary, 'Hey!' she shouted as Billy and Payne walked around the reception desk and headed down a short corridor. They passed empty classrooms heading for a door marked *Private*. Billy opened it and surprised the occupant.

'What the ...' exclaimed Souvlakis who was on the phone.

The receptionist burst in. 'They pushed past me.'

The officers had ID. 'Police,' said Billy, and Souvlakis hung up.

'Get out,' he snapped at the receptionist who left. Souvlakis produced a fake smile. 'How can I help you, officers?'

'We're investigating the murder of a member of your staff.'

Souvlakis blanched. 'Oh that was terrible, terrible. He was a nice young man and a very good teacher. It's a tragedy.' He indicated the only two chairs in his office. 'Please, take a seat.'

The officers sat and Billy kept firing. 'How would you describe your relationship with Mr Balance?'

'Relationship? It was employer and employee.'

'Did you and Mr Balance get on well together?'

Souvlakis gained a smidgeon of control. 'I have to tell you, I am not happy with your questions, officer.'

'We're not here to make you happy, Mr Souvlakis. We're trying to solve the brutal murder of a man who worked for you.'

Souvlakis dug in. 'I can't help you.'

'Can't or won't?'

'This is not fair. You come into my office and start harassing me when I have done nothing. I want you to go.'

Payne enjoyed these situations. Billy, being a woman, was sometimes regarded as a pushover. Men being interviewed by DS Hughes reckoned they could bluff their way past her. Big mistake.

'You have a choice, Mr Souvlakis. You answer my questions here or I'll arrest you and we can continue the conversation at Homicide.'

'Arrest me?' Souvlakis was genuinely afraid. 'Homicide?'

'What's it to be, sir?'

What a choice. Kostos had a rock to his right and a hard place to his left. He delayed answering. Billy stood with Payne following suit.

'Kostos Souvlakis I'm arresting you on suspicion of the murder of Eddie Balance.'

'No,' wailed the college principal as Payne attached the bracelets. Billy led the two men through Reception. The receptionist's mouth opened. For once she could honestly tell despairing students that the sneaky bastard of a principal was genuinely unavailable.

The SOG officers spent time studying maps and working out a plan to arrest Alvin a.k.a. Bradley Michael Ford. They could only get their vehicle part of the way along the track to Alvin's primitive abode.

There were eight SOG officers and their black outfits looked artistically pleasing in amongst the lush Yarra Valley greenery. Detectives Fleming and Baldwin parked behind the SOG vehicle and began the trek at a safe distance.

Getting too close would set off the Hound of the Barkingvilles so keeping out of sight and upwind was essential. Baldwin drew the short straw meaning Fleming snaffled the only pair of gumboots leaving Charlie, the fashion guru of the Squad, to ruin his fairly new loafers.

SOG Team A approached from the north, Team B from the south. At a distance, the Team A leader, using powerful binoculars, spotted the dog asleep in front of the shack. 'Dog found. No sign of target,' was the message. Then the dog jerked awake as a piece of drugged steak flew through the air and landed near the canine.

The police remained still and silent. The dog stood. It really was a small horse. It investigated then took the bait. Still no sign of Alvin. The beast enjoyed its tasty snack. It's chewing became slower. It took a backward step then another then crumpled.

Team A sent a second message. 'Dog drugged. Still no sign of target.

Team B replied. 'Roger that. Target in sight. Approaching now.'

Officers in the Special Operations Group are highly skilled. They spend ages training for situations dealing with hostages, armed fugitives, terrorists, and more but this project was a first.

Alvin was living off the grid. His mini windmill provided basic lighting. Surrounded by dense bush meant firewood was on tap. His bath time was short and primitive. Shaving and haircuts were homemade and optional. His toilet was sensibly basic. It shifted from time to time. As the second SOG team moved silently through the bush, Alvin was using his thunderbox. Technically speaking it was a hole in the ground, well away from his homestead, with a couple of short saplings placed precariously about a foot above the hole.

Alvin would drop his daks and Reg Grundys, squat to gently place his cheeks on the saplings and then have his brain send a message south that it was time to push. On this sunny afternoon, Alvin was enjoying his al fresco whoopsie time when he got one almighty fright. It scared the shit out him, literally, which was not a problem because of his current sapling-supported position.

As one, four SOG officers, all in black, and with visors down and semi-automatic weapons pointed, sprang from the bush screaming, 'Armed police—stay where you are.' Their screams were not in unison giving a sort of ripple or echo effect.

Alvin froze as the armaments and odds were not in his favour. In fact his only weapon was a copy of the *Upper Yarra Mail*—two week's old—and his alternative to the softest of soft toilet tissue. Online news doesn't offer that benefit.

Following the surge in adrenalin and the emptying of his bowels, Alvin panicked and chose to stand. This was not wise. He managed to rise, then lost his balance and fell backwards. His dunny seat would never win any architectural awards and so heading towards the core of planet Earth, Alvin hit the saplings at speed. They surrendered and alas poor Alvin's buttocks plunged into his well dug hole.

It meant he was shit-sitting in a butt-plugged hole. His arms and legs were free but his arse was anchored to the powder room. The SOG officers moved forward, their lethal weapons aimed at the helpless hermit.

'Hands, let me see your hands,' screamed the SOG leader.

Alvin didn't fancy putting his hands anywhere except as high in the air as he could muster. Team A got the news.

'Target locked down. Repeat, Target locked down.'

It was all too much for the Team B Soggies. They lowered their weapons and laughed. Nothing hysterical at first but it built. Did it ever? They laughed at the victim and at one another as the laughter itself was funny. It drifted towards uncontrollable glee.

Alvin wanted to swear but all he could think to say was *Shit*.

The ALP has been accused of being run by faceless men. In Victoria, the current President and State Secretary both had faces; not particularly attractive one's mind, and they used said dials to show their distaste at the words expressed by the Attorney-General. Christian hadn't looked so miserable since his mother confiscated his X-Box when he failed to eat all his Brussels sprouts.

The President raged. 'You allowed this member of your staff to send abusive emails to a judge of the Supreme Court?' Christian glowered.

'I didn't allow it,' snapped Stefan. 'He did it without my knowledge.'

'Do the police have these emails?' asked the state secretary.

'Why do you think we're here?' fumed Stefan.

The President fumed back. 'Your stupidity will cost us government. A Supreme Court judge is murdered and you've been threatening the dead man. The fucking Liberals will have a field day.' Stefan scoffed. 'Please don't tell me you actually murdered His Worship.'

'It's His Honour,' said Stefan, glad to correct his factional rival.

'The Executive will demand Christian's resignation and you Stefan, will get demoted to something like Drought Relief and Frog Counting.'

'Not necessarily,' replied the Attorney-General.

That comment put a frozen expression on the faceless faces.

'Meaning?' asked the President.

'Let's face facts. If you demote me, you'll give the media another reason to investigate. You'll encourage the cops to snoop further. That'll mean more bad publicity for the Party for longer.'

The President lost it. 'You sent threatening emails to a judge.'

Christian boiled. Stefan kept calm. 'The same judge appointed by this government, who indirectly criticised our proposed law reforms, and who covered up a serious crime as a favour for a friend.' Wow.

The enraged Labor President was punched hard and gasped for air. 'A Supreme Court judge covered up a serious crime for a friend?'

'Insider trading,' said Christian now getting in on the act.

'You have proof?' asked the state secretary.

'No, I made it up,' snorted Stefan. 'Of course we have proof.'

The faceless duo were struck dumb. They knew a smoking gun when they saw one. The Attorney General stared, daring them to act.

'So we're agreed. Christian and I will retain our current positions and plead ignorance to any knowledge of the unfortunate emails should the police ask questions. Comrades?'

The comrades hesitated. They knew the damage the Attorney General could inflict. Demote him and the world will hear the secrets of the dead judge, the one they appointed, and the media coverage of the slain jurist will intensify a thousand times.

Stefan walked from the room with his Chief of Staff scurrying behind, now believing in miracles.

18

ROSE AND RICHELIEU headed to interview the Attorney-General but called on the Assistant Commissioner Crime en route. Crowley was well aware of Barry Chubb and the threatening emails. The two Homicide inspectors sat in his office.

'So where are we with the Attorney-General, Inspector?'

'DI Richelieu and I are about to interview him now, sir.'

'And do what?'

'Ask him who sent the threatening emails to the judge?'

'Too broad,' said the AC. 'Drop the softly-softly routine. Your first question is "Did you send them?" Get stuck in. Don't ever let the status of the suspect cause you to pull your punches.'

'Sir.'

'And ignore the rants from Barry Chubb whatever he claims. What's happening with his niece?'

'We believe she was murdered and hope the world and its mother doesn't get in the way.'

'No thanks to her uncle.' The AC stood. He was big on less chat and more action. 'Good-o. Keep me informed.'

The Inspectors headed for the politician who was expecting them. 'DI Rose,' he beamed with insincerity. She introduced Richelieu. 'Do come in.' His fake bonhomie fairly shone.

Rose fired the opening salvo and Stefan's bonhomie evaporated. 'What do you know about the threatening emails sent to Judge Slight?'

The AG expected an attack. 'Should I have my lawyer present, Inspector?'

'We traced the emails to a computer in your adjoining office, Attorney, and because of your known antipathy towards the deceased judge, we're duty bound to ask if you were involved in any conspiracy?'

Stefan batted away her attack with ease. 'I should reprimand you, Inspector, for your abuse of procedure in not warning me I may be a person of interest in this grievous matter. But I'll let that pass suffice to say that any mention of my name being associated with your investigation will not be treated so lightly.' He smiled and his bonhomie returned. 'Now, how can I help?'

Richelieu joined in. 'Pardon Monsieur but 'ave you 'eard the story about 'ow the late judge once saved the career of 'is friend, the barrister Monsieur Simon Beaumont?'

Oh shit thought the Attorney. *They know about the insider trading.* That elusive bonhomie got elusive again. Stefan lied and showed off.

'Inspecteur de pardon. Je n'ai absolument aucun commentaire.' (Pardon Inspector. I have absolutely no comment.)

Rose was speechless but her colleague nodded. 'Merci Monsieur.'

Rose persisted. 'We would like to speak to the person who uses the computer we discovered in our search.'

'Of course,' replied the AG.

'Did you know that computer had been tampered with, sir?'

It was another bye-bye bonhomie moment. 'I did not, Inspector.'

'And we require a list of staff members who have access to the computers in your outer office.'

'Certainly. Would that include the cleaning staff?'

Smug prick thought Rose. The verbal jousting built in intensity and Stefan felt he was holding his ground until Rose played her trump card. 'Who best knows your staff, sir? Would that be your Chief of Staff, Mr Christian Falange?'

Shit, and in triplicate. Stefan had two strategies in place re Christian. The first was to keep him as far away from the cops as possible. The second was to keep him even further away. If Plans A and B failed, Stefan's instructions to Christian were simple. Admit nothing. You do not know who used the computer to send the emails to the judge. You've never seen the emails. The judge was a fine and noble creature, and you were nowhere near the Texas School Book Depository when JFK was shot.

The two inspectors went in search of Christian with the Attorney-General going in search of anyone's rosary beads.

Having located Christian, Rose and Richelieu interviewed the nervous Chief of Staff. He handed over a list of names all of whom had access to the computer in question and which told the detectives everything and nothing. They returned to Homicide where Jo worked on the horse in the hills homicide.

'What news, Senior?' asked Rose.

Jo explained the facts she'd gleaned. 'I've rung the owner of the property where the horse is stabled.'

'And?'

'I think a visit is required, ma-am.'

'So why are you still here?'

Jo hesitated. 'Right, ma-am.'

Delighted to be back in the saddle, she grabbed her bag and headed for the hills. The animal was stabled on a property in the Dandenong Ranges. Driving out of town, Jo remembered her first homicide. She could even hear the Puffing Billy whistle.

In another part of the hills, Alvin had washed in the presence of the boys in grey (Detectives Fleming and Baldwin) and the boys in black (SOG).

'Who's gunna look after me dog?'

'Who looks after him when you go into Warburton?' asked Fleming.

'He looks after himself.'

'Then put out some food and if you're refused bail, we'll contact the local elephant hunters who can feed him from a distance.'

Alvin was marched back to the vehicles. Baldwin swore because his newish shoes were now only good for gardening. In Melbourne, Alvin was fed and watered then interviewed. He wanted a smoke.

'Tough,' said Fleming who read the suspect his rights. Alvin couldn't be arsed about a solicitor and wanted out. Fleming began.

'Do you know Karen Galbraith?'

Alvin sniffed. 'Might.'

'Listen, Alvin ...'

'Don't call me that,' snapped the suspect.

'Were you sacked from the supermarket in Warburton?'

'You know I was.'

'Were you angry?'

'You know I was. And all I took was stuff they was throwin' out. How is that stealing?'

'Did you go back at night after you were sacked?'

'Yes.'

'Why?'

'Because I wanted some more free food.'

'Is that all you wanted?'

'What do you mean?'

Fleming shook his head. 'Did you speak to anyone the night you came back to steal more food?'

'Might 'ave.'

Who?' Alvin paused. 'Who?' shouted Fleming.

Alvin shouted back. 'Karen Galbraith.'

The two detectives tensed. 'What did you say?'

'I told her to f'get I was ever there.'

'And?'

'And that's it. She ignored me and went back inside.'

'And what did you do?"

'I took some fruit they had in the bin where stuff gets chucked.'

'What fruit?'

'Does it matter?'

'Yes. What fruit did you steal?'

'I took some bananas and three watermelons. So come on. Charge me. What do you get for nickin' watermelons? Ten years?'

'More if you poke glass into it.'

Alvin stared at the police officers. They stared back. 'What?'

'Do you know where Karen Galbraith lives?'

'No idea.'

'How do you think we found you?'

Alvin had to think about that. 'Dunno.'

'Someone gave us your name. Someone told us where you lived. Who was that?'

'How the fuck would I know?'

'Karen Galbraith saw you sneaking around after you were sacked.'

'So?'

'She reported you.'

'So?'

'How did that make you feel?'

Alvin was no Einstein but even he could see where this was headed. 'Well now that I know she grassed me up, I'm pissed. But it's a bit late to give her a slap now 'cos I heard she's cactus.'

Fleming knew he'd lost the battle. He still hoped to win the war.

'This interview is being recorded. Present are Detective Sergeant Deborah Hughes.'

'Senior Constable Stephen Payne.'

'And we're interviewing Mr Kostos Souvlakis with his solicitor ...'

'George Megalos,' said the balding brief.

'Mr Souvlakis,' said Billy, 'we have information you argued with the deceased Edward Balance. What did you argue about?'

Kostos looked at his solicitor who gave a small nod. 'No comment.'

'Was this argument about the alleged fraud Mr Balance claimed to have discovered in your college?'

Kostos didn't need to look at anyone. 'No comment.'

'Is your college being investigated by the Fraud Squad?'

Kostos acted according to his solicitor's instructions. 'No comment.'

'Where were you last Tuesday between 8 pm and 8 am the following morning?'

'No comment.'

Billy lost the formal approach. 'Kostos, I know you're in the shit. You've got a mountain of complaints from angry students, the tabloids are all over you, and Fraud officers are ready to pounce. The last thing you want is a murder charge. Give us an alibi for the night in question and you can be out of here.' She paused. 'All you'll get from a *No comment* is a return to the cells. Come on, talk to me.'

The client's solicitor whispered to Kostos then asked for a break. 'I'd like a word with my client.'

Billy suspended the interview. When they re-commenced, the solicitor read a prepared statement. 'I know nothing about the death of Mr Eddie Balance. On the night he died, I was at home with my wife and children. I would never harm, let alone kill any person.'

The police had plenty of motive but nothing else. Kostos was free to go. Billy blew air and slapped the table. 'The DI ain't gunna like this.'

Using her GPS, Jo found the property near Monbulk. She drove over a cattle grid and along a driveway with tall poplars either side. Obstacles for horse jumping stood in the paddocks. Jo pulled up in the yard and was greeted by a kelpie and a border collie with welcoming smiles.

'Hello,' said Jo patting the tailwaggers. 'Where's your family?'

The canines either didn't know or were told not to speak to cops. Jo climbed the verandah steps and was about to knock on the door when a voice called. 'Can I help you?'

Jo turned. A woman walked towards her. Jo showed her ID.

'Hello, I'm Detective Senior Constable Jo Best. Are you the owner?'

'What kept you?' Jo looked confused. 'We've had private eyes, reporters, camera crews, stickybeaks and busybodies. I was saying to Jacko we've had everyone except the cops.'

'Right,' said Jo feeling flat. 'I'm hoping to talk to someone about the horse that Pippa St Clair was riding the day she died.'

'Killed you mean. Anyways, Jacko's your man. He's in the shed.'

'Thanks,' said Jo and headed to the shed accompanied by two security officers named Buster and Gertie. Buster was the kelpie.

Jacko was weather-beaten with a mane any horse would envy. 'G'day,' he said giving Jo the once over while repairing a saddle. 'Copper, right?'

'Was it my size elevens or the helmet?' asked Jo and Jacko smiled.

'I'll save you asking, girlie. Pippa stabled a couple of her horses here. I got a call from a neighbour who found Pippa. I went and fetched the horse. He was proppy. I checked his feet and there was a stone wedged under the shoe on his front near side. He could have picked it up himself but it didn't look right.'

'I know nothing about horses.'

'There's a saying, "No feet, no horse". Lameness is caused by many things but I always check the feet first. No bruising but tucked inside against the coffin bone was a small stone.' He pointed at Jo. 'Now before you ask, I chucked it. Sorry. But to me, that stone was bloody determined to get where it was or somebody put it there.'

'I bet I'm not the first person you've told about this stone?'

Jacko gave a grimace which tried hard to become a smile. 'Sorry, love. Barry Chubb came in person. He was a mess. Had some private investigator with him and took photos and a movie.'

'Of the horse?'

'Of the horse, me, the stable, everything. Maisie weren't too pleased without her hair being done.'

'Right. So if the horse picked up the stone while riding ...'

'Unlikely.'

'But *if* that happened, would the horse throw the rider?'

'Not that horse and not that rider.'

'What's the alternative?'

'You asking me to do your job?'

Jo smiled. 'I'm asking you to help a dumb detective who doesn't know a horse's arse from its elbow.'

Jacko reckoned this sheila was smart; good-looking too. 'One alternative is that Pippa came off or got off the horse and Sir Galahad was nobbled later.' He looked at Jo. 'But that's purely a guess.'

'Thanks. I'm Jo by the way.' They shook hands.

'Jo By-The-Way? How many hyphens in that?'

Jacko grinned, Jo laughed and he walked her to the car.

'I may need to come back,' said Jo.

'No worries. Dunno if this will help but accident or murder, that radio shock jock took it real bad. Pippa has one shattered uncle.'

Jo drove back to town thinking about that last statement.

19

EARLY NEXT MORNING, Barry Chubb tweeted he would make a statement about his beloved niece. Record numbers of listeners, including many Homicide Squad detectives, tuned in to hear if the man behind the microphone knew anything about his niece's death and more importantly, if he had a heart. He spoke.

Last week I suffered the worst day of life. My darling niece died suddenly doing the thing she loved. She went out riding her favourite horse and never came home. Her horse, Sir Galahad, although injured, remained by her side.

(He paused. It added tension. One was never sure when Barry was acting but this sounded like genuine grief.)

I have investigated Pippa's death and now know for certain she was murdered. I'll repeat that. My niece, Pippa Jane St Clair was murdered by a person or persons unknown and I have now made it my life's goal to see that justice is done.

I say to the Victoria Police, you have a duty to find the evil culprits and to do so without hesitation. Justice delayed is justice denied.

(Another pause. Some Homicide officers wondered why he didn't have solemn music supporting his diatribe.)

I've had a courier deliver a document to the Chief Commissioner, Victoria Police. The document contains details of my darling niece's murder. It explains the motive, persons of interest, and the method of execution used by her callous killer.

I hereby put the police on notice. If we do not hear a response from the state's highest ranking officer in the next 24 hours, explaining what they have done to investigate this crime, I urge you to contact your local member of parliament and demand action be taken. (His voice began to waver.)

If the police refuse to act on my detailed document, I will publish it online and allow my loyal listeners and the rest of the world to see exactly how our so-called guardians of law and order have failed in their duty. I will never ...

(He paused. Listeners could hear a whimpering sound.)

I will never stop until my darling Pippa is given justice and ...

(This time he broke down and couldn't speak. There was that awful sound of dead air until music began.)

Fleming turned off the radio. 'What a moron.' He mimicked the broadcaster. 'I hereby put the police on notice.' He shouted at the radio. 'We already know she was bumped off, you prick.'

Baldwin said what the others were thinking. 'Every nutter will ring Crime Stoppers. This'll be a massive waste of time and resources.' Other officers voiced their opinions. Rose closed the discussion.

'Okay, that's enough. We've made arrests and we need to charge or release. Where are we with the wild man of Borneo?'

Fleming sniffed. 'Nowhere, ma-am.'

'Nowhere?'

'He threatened the victim, nicked produce and behaved like a prat, but we have nothing to charge him with murder.'

Rose felt frustration. 'And Billy, have we got Eddie Balance's killer?'

'Two suspects, ma-am, and both eliminated.'

'Both?' Billy nodded. Rose turned to Jo. 'Senior, what news on Chubb's niece?'

Jo reported on Jacko's pebble-in-the-hoof theory with the pebble lost. 'There are no witnesses and no suspects.'

That wasn't true if Chubb was correct. His list included every equestrian selector and most of the riders on the National team. If Barry posted his document online, the police would be under huge pressure.

That left the judge, and Rose reported on the recent meeting with the Attorney-General. 'He's a clever bastard.'

'He's a politician,' said Fleming.

'He tried to hide his Chief of Staff. If the emails were written by someone in that office, the Chief of Staff is the one most likely to know.'

'The Attorney did not like any mention of barrister Beaumont. Per'aps there is something to discover there,' added Richelieu.

'Perhaps is the key word,' said Rose summing up the mood of the room. 'Four homicides, persons of interest arrested and released, and now bugger all to go on. We are going backwards.'

The mood was flat, ideas were non-existent and the publicity generated by Barrie Chubb was about to build. It was hard enough trying to crack multiple homicides without the media telling the world the cops had nothing. Officers went back to their desks. Pressure continued to build.

Struggling at work, Jo now struggled at home. Her divorced parents didn't speak. Jo's mother, Shirley, called her ex, Malcolm X. He was turning 60. A milestone birthday is a bit like Christmas in that warring family factions have to negotiate terms of engagement at any shared social event. Malcolm would never invite his former wife to his home.

But Malcolm X's grandchildren were Shirley's grandchildren and one of them happened to share a birthday with Grandpa. This was the one occasion when Shirley had to break her vow—never have anything to with that smug bastard again.

'Grandpa's having his birthday on my birthday, Gran,' said granddaughter Millie on the phone to Shirley, 'and I would like you to come, please.' Millie had manners and her father, merchant banker Jeremy, took delight in taunting his hated mother-in-law. He called her Boudicca behind her back.

Jo's phone rang at work. 'Hello Mother. How are you?' Jo wandered into the corridor.

'Terrible. It's that time of the year and I need you to protect me.'

'Why not take Antony? He could protect you and you'd poke a stick in Dad's eye at the same time.'

The idea had crossed Shirley's mind. Here she was, seriously middle-aged and a prime candidate for the First Wives' Club but still able to pull a fella. Antony wasn't on a Zimmer frame, had his own teeth and money, and dressed and behaved as a gentleman.

But Shirley worried something would go wrong. Secretly she feared her new man would find fault with her and do what Malcolm X did and scarper. She dreaded another failed relationship.

'Antony may not be available so I'm relying on you, Joanna. You are my bodyguard for the event and I have no objection to you carrying a firearm. Flash it in front of your father if you wish.'

Jo laughed. 'Stop worrying, Mum. You'll survive. I'll call you.'

'Don't hang up, I haven't finished.' Jo groaned in a loud silent way. 'Would you believe Antony's daughters are putting pressure on their father to make sure I am not a part of his will.'

'What?'

'They think I'm a gold digger out to steal their inheritance.'

Jo stirred. 'And are you?'

Shirley was outraged. 'Of course not. How could you even think such a thing?'

'It's a joke, Mum.' Shirley let off steam. 'So what does Antony say?'

'He's embarrassed and angry.'

'What are his daughters like?'

'I feel sorry for him. How could such a cultured man produce such awful daughters?'

'He might say the same about you and your two.' That knocked Shirley sideways and Jo seized the moment. 'I'll call you before the weekend, Mum. Bye.'

DI Rose faced a quandary. Barry Chubb had publicly challenged the police (and specifically the Homicide Squad) to put up or he would. There was no shut up option. Rose spoke with the AC Crime.

'If I make a public statement, sir,' she said, 'I'm doing his bidding. He says "jump" and I do. If I say nothing, he'll release his document and create even more massive publicity.'

'And possibly impede your investigation.'

'Exactly, sir. I've been in the job five minutes and any advice, preferably an order, would be much appreciated.'

Crowley wasn't impressed. 'You wanted promotion, Inspector. With it comes responsibility. I suggest you have a chat with your squad and make a decision based on their opinions. Good luck.'

The call ended and Rose spoke to herself. 'Thanks for nothing, *sir.*' She entered the Incident Room and called the meeting to order.

'Thank you, I want some advice.'

This was remarkable. It was unheard of for Rose's predecessor, DI Steele, to ever ask colleagues for advice.

'AC Crowley has left the Barry Chubb threat to me. Do I respond to his challenge? I welcome your opinion.'

'Ignore him, ma-am,' said Fleming. Others supported that. 'We can't have Joe Public telling us how to do our job.'

'But if you say nothing,' argued Billy Hughes, 'Chubb will go even harder making our job twice as difficult.'

'He'll post his document online,' added Baldwin.

'Great,' said Rose. 'I'm damned if I do or don't.' The room fell silent. Jo Best had a suggestion.

'How about a statement, ma-am, with no reference to Chubb?'

Rose paused. 'Explain.' The others looked at Jo.

'You could read a statement such as ... "Last week, the Homicide Squad received forensic advice that the death of Ms Pippa St Clair was suspicious. We commenced an investigation on that basis. That investigation continues. A press release will be issued once new information is available. In the meantime we'll continue to investigate that and other possible homicides." Then ma'am, you turn and walk away, ignoring the barrage of questions.'

'Magnifique,' said a certain Inspector.

'I like it,' said Rose. 'I'll do it today.'

Jo continued. 'It takes the wind out of Barry's sails twice. He gets no mention and we announce that we knew about the homicide before he did. We gazump the megaphone.'

Officers laughed and a few applauded. Billy Hughes glowed.

'Thank you, Senior,' said Rose. 'I'll excuse you the midnight shift.'

Nobody spoke. The silence lingered.

'So where to next, ma-am?' asked Fleming.

'If I knew, DS Fleming, I'd tell you. But as my old DCI used to say, "Keep knocking till they bloody well open the door".' Jo glowed. 'I want Forensics to re-examine what we have. Surely there must be some DNA on the judge's car, on Eddie Balance's sex toy or on the horse rider's clothes or the horse's bridle.'

'Only the victims' DNA, ma-am,' said Billy.

'Well the squeaky wheel and all that. Go back to Forensics and apply some pressure.' Jo felt sick. 'Who wants to visit the boffins?'

Officers turned to Jo. She shook her head.

'I've outstayed my welcome, ma-am.'

Rose remembered Jo's secret and felt sorry for her. 'Who will accompany Senior Constable Best?'

It was a smidgeon of mercy. Charlie Baldwin and DI Richelieu both volunteered; Baldwin, because he liked Jo and Richelieu, because he really liked her.

Rose smiled to herself then left calling, 'Sort it out.'

The previous theory about the murders being linked was forgotten. It was back to cracking them one at a time. This meant checking statements, interviews, timelines and reports. The only positive thing was the silence from Barry Chubb. No-one expected that to last.

Richelieu and Baldwin joined Jo. 'Thank you, gentlemen,' she said.

'I bow to seniority,' said Baldwin preparing to back away.

'Non, non,' interrupted Richelieu. 'Mademoiselle Best must choose.'

Bloody hell thought Jo. 'I think we should *all* go.'

'Three of us?' said a surprised Baldwin.

'Oui, all three,' said the Frenchman. 'This will show we're serious.'

'Or desperate,' added Baldwin.

Jo felt good. *Two's company, three's a crowd which might keep me safe from you know who.* They headed off to try and find some forensic answers. One would be fantastic.

Alastair was shocked and delighted. Three detectives entered his laboratory with one of them the girl of his dreams. He stopped working and stood wanting to smile and cry (with happiness and relief) at the same time. His heart pumped faster.

'Hello Alastair,' beamed Jo.

'Detective Best, it's lovely to see you again.'

'You know my colleagues.'

The men acknowledged one another but Alastair had eyes only for the female of the species.

'How can I be of service?' gushed Alastair. It was obvious to everyone that Jo had won a heart and the scientist would do anything for the female Senior Constable. Richelieu felt a sliver of jealousy.

'We have slow progress on our four homicides,' she said.

'Very slow,' added Baldwin.

'Do you have other material for me to examine?' asked Alastair.

'No, but could you re-examine the items from the horse?'

'Ah,' said Alastair, 'you are not the only ones to make that request.' The detectives stared at him. He enjoyed milking the moment.

'Oh?' said Jo.

'A private investigator and two journalists from those current affairs television programmes have been snooping around.'

'I 'ope, Monsieur, you gave them nothing,' said a serious Richelieu.

Alastair looked offended. *How dare you question my loyalty.*

Jo saved the day. 'We know you're a consummate professional, Alastair but yet again we rely on your expertise.' Her eyes dwelt on his. 'Please, if you can help in any way, we'll be extremely grateful.'

Alastair crumbled. 'I'll ring you if I discover anything.'

'Thank you,' beamed Jo and touched his arm. He almost drooled, Baldwin felt nauseous and Richelieu called a halt to proceedings.

'Merci, Monsieur.' He beckoned subtly to his colleagues. Alastair felt annoyed when the males allowed Jo to depart ahead of them denying the scientist the opportunity to wave to his girl.

Driving back to Homicide, the males took it in turn to praise and gently mock their colleague and her puppy love admirer.

Alastair rang Jo that afternoon but had no news. He promised to continue working and hoped to see her back in his lab soon. Jo told Rose the news then returned to work on the Pippa St Clair death.

She rang the horse property and Jacko answered. She asked about horse materials. 'To grab the horse, what would you hold?'

Jacko stated the obvious. 'If someone grabbed the horse to hurt Pippa, wearing gloves would be the way to go.' Jo kicked herself.

20

THAT NIGHT JO'S MIND GOT BUSY. She thought about her relationship with DI Richelieu, her concern about little Grace Carr, her parents and their annual "walking on eggshells" get-together, and the strange behaviour of Michael Chan and Alastair Dean.

But the dominant issue was her theory that the four homicides were linked. She needed advice so made a call.

'I'm Strange,' said the pathetic pathologist.

'This is the deranged detective,' said Jo.

Gabrielle was thrilled to hear from her favourite detective and immediately agreed to Jo's request for a chat.

'And I need someone to help me finish the bottle,' laughed Strange.

Jo worried. The pathologist had been pinged for drink-driving. Jo heard about it and once gave the doctor a lift. *Is she drinking too much?* The answer was *yes* with the problem being that those who knew were few and not brave enough to say, "Physician heal thyself".

In Strange's trendy North Fitzroy home, Jo insisted on coffee. She produced a box of expensive Belgian chocolates which Strange attacked with relish. At least the grog was off the table.

'So what's the burning issue? And don't say men. I got the "Wham Bam" bit right but never the "Thank you Ma'am".'

Jo made a mental note never to ask Dr Strange for boyfriend advice.

'No, it's work. I'd love to know your system of finding the clue or clues that turn a case from an accident to a murder.'

'What system? I haven't got a system.'

'Take the woman on the horse case. First responders, local quack, everyone said accident. Horse goes lame, rider falls, breaks neck, case closed. But not so says Dr Strange.'

'She's brilliant. More coffee?' Jo was topped up.

'Years ago, a motorcyclist crashes in the bush. Ambos, traffic cops and local quack all agree it's an RTA. Speed kills. Then up pops the new and inexperienced Gabrielle Strange and nominates murder.'

'Your grandfather told you this story.'

'What's your system, your trick in cracking cases? If I knew how you do it, maybe I could apply the same method to find killers.'

'You think so?'

Jo considered that. 'It's worth a try.' Another pause. 'Please.'

Gabrielle smiled. 'It's simple as, Missy. I copy the great man.' Jo felt proud. Pop was a star, her hero and it was great to have someone else recognize his talent. 'He had this one saying which always worked for me. "The little things are infinitely the most important".'

Jo thought. *That doesn't sound like Pop.*

'People mock him and pastiche him to death, but his methods have stood the test of time.' Strange saw Jo's confusion. 'Mr Holmes, my dear, the world's greatest detective.'

Oh. No shit, Sherlock.

'He's been in more plays, books and films than any other character.'

'Really.'

'You know there's a UK police software programme called *Home Office Large Major Enquiry System* or HOLMES for short.'

'No, I didn't.'

'Maybe that's your problem, Detective. You should copy the genius of the great man. I still do.'

Jo tried to recover. 'Oh? How?'

'Concentrate on the little things. With that young man on the motorbike, there was a tiny bruise on his arm. That was caused by a syringe when the killers tried to have us believe he was a druggie. Tiny bruise—a little thing.'

'And Pippa St Clair? What tipped you off with her?'

'No impact marks on either hand. If you're falling off a horse, the hands break your fall.' Strange waggled her fingers. 'Not a sausage. Once you've found a little thing, follow that to the big thing.' She paused. 'These choccies are bloody good.'

Jo smiled. She liked the self-deprecating doctor, worried about her drinking and determined to help her. 'Must away, cases to solve.'

'What, no gossip about your love life?'

Jo laughed, pinched another chocolate and hugged her colleague and friend. 'Thanks, Doc, and I'll see you in the soup.'

Driving home to the next suburb took a few minutes. *Concentrate on the little things.* She sat on her settee. With a list of the clues, items and details for each of the four murders, she thought, *little things*.

She concentrated on the latest murder, Pippa St Clair. Nothing leapt out. *What if there are no little things? Worse, what if there are and I can't find them?*

She worked backwards and moved to the brutal slaying of Eddie Balance. *Is there a clue, a little thing in the sexual abuse post mortem? Is that a little thing? Seems pretty major to me.*

On to the judge. *Why was the motor of his Worship's car left running? Why not stab or shoot him and be done with it? Why position him against the garage? And is the suffering of the barrister Beaumont a little thing?*

Finally she came to the first murder, the drowning in the Yarra River at Warburton. Depression crept up behind her ready to pounce. *Bugger all, I've found bugger all.* She studied the notes of the interview with Alvin. Nothing leapt out as being a "little thing". *Did Sherlock Holmes know what he was talking about?*

She slapped her head in frustration and spoke aloud. 'What are you babbling about, Joanna. The man never existed—he's fictional!'

She took a few deep breaths then packed up her notes. The drowning case was on the top of her pile and as she dumped the lot in a cardboard box, her eye caught some underlined words. She stopped and read aloud her own recorded notes.

'The victim's sister asked if the morgue was anywhere near the Supreme Court.' The last two words were underlined.

Jo stared at that sentence. 'Why did she mention the Supreme Court? Think Jo.' She spoke as she wrote possible answers.

'She works at the Supreme Court. She's been on trial there or on jury service. She went to watch a trial or knew someone who was on trial or a witness. Oh no! She knew Judge Slight!' Jo moved into a dead-end alley.

'Well if she worked at the Court, she wouldn't ask where it was. If she'd been on trial, she'd … nah, retired children's librarian an axe murderer? I don't think so. That leaves curious spectator and jury service. She knows that part of town because she went to the Supreme Court for jury service.' She scribbled. 'Find out if Karen's sister served on a jury and, if so, what was the trial and the result?'

It was a little thing. Gabrielle's right. Jo buzzed talking aloud to encourage herself. 'Okay, assume she was on jury service. The result, was acquittal or guilty. Whatever the result, someone didn't like it. The family of the accused reckon their son/daughter/parent was innocent but the jury found otherwise, or the family of the victim reckoned the person charged should have been found guilty but wasn't. Someone wanted revenge. They killed the jury members.'

She threw her pencil on the coffee table and stormed to the kitchen. Her logical investigation brought her to the Texas Chainsaw Massacre. Anger set in.

Her phone pinged as a text arrived from Dr Jack Carr.

Hi Jo. Hope you're well. Great news here. Our darling girl is coming home. We're having a welcome home party on Sunday from 2. If you're free we'd love you to come. P.S. Harry is refusing to attend unless you're there. Jack

Jo smiled. The news about Grace's recovery would stir any heart. The love expressed by young Harry was heart melting. She replied.

Great news, Jack. I'm so happy for you and the family. No promises but I'd love to be there. Jo. xxx

She couldn't sleep. The "little things" idea kept buzzing inside her head. She made a cuppa, flopped on the settee and turned on the telly. The news grabbed her attention. There was Barry Chubb crying about his tragic loss—again—still. He made no mention of his document going public. *DI Rose's statement, my statement, has killed Barry's threat.* Jo looked at him. He wasn't acting. He was genuinely grieving.

The interviewer changed tack and asked him about another issue. It involved a man from an Eastern European country who had become a successful businessman in Australia. Some claimed he was a criminal in his homeland, that he murdered people who stood in his way, that while today he was Peter Yarberlich, years ago he was Andelko Kovac.

He fled his country, lived abroad for years then reinvented himself and settled Down Under.

Yarberlich had befriended Barry and both benefitted. Barry got donations for his favourite causes and Yarberlich got prestige and respectability from his association with Barry.

The TV interviewer raised the issue of Yarberlich not being the person he claimed to be. Barry became angry. 'I've known him for years. I've been a guest in his home. His family are a credit to him. The people who make these ridiculous claims are failed politicians in some tin pot state trying to gain power. I've rung the PM and the Minister for Home Affairs to assure them Peter Yarberlich is an upstanding citizen and the type of business leader this country needs.'

The interview ended and Jo switched off her telly. She sat in the darkness. *Barry Chubb is seriously upset about his niece's death. Karen Galbraith's sister is seriously upset about her sibling's death. Is that the link?*

She fetched her files, turned on the lamp and took notes. *Serious suffering from family*, she wrote. *Karen's sister, YES. Judge's friend Simon Beaumont, YES. Eddie's mother, YES. Barry Chubb, YES.*

She slapped the coffee table and knocked her unfinished cup of tea flying. She didn't swear because she reckoned she'd found one of those Sherlock "little things". She wrote. *Each victim seriously mourned by friend or relative.*

'That's it,' she said mopping up the tea. 'Every person murdered is mourned. But hang on. What did Pierre and I come up with before?' She looked for notes. 'Every victim is an innocent.'

Are these two facts linked? Innocent victims greatly mourned. She scratched her head literally and figuratively. Archimedes hopped into Jo's bath and she heard him cry, 'Bingo', Australian for Eureka.

She spoke aloud. 'The people murdered were killed to hurt their nearest and dearest. The motive is revenge. It's a double bluff, a code where you have the answer then add 1 or subtract 2.' Then she changed from joy to concern.

'But does it work in each case?' She applied her theory to all four murders. They all worked. 'Yes!' she cried. 'Yes, yes, yes!'

She was guessing, well making an educated guess but wrote what she reckoned were the backgrounds for each homicide.

Karen's sister, Denise, was a jury member and the killer wanted revenge for the jury's decision. Kill Karen to punish Denise.

She stopped. Simon Beaumont failed the test. His insider trading sting didn't fit the revenge theory. Jo went online. Bingo. A recent extortion case collapsed. A hardened criminal was exonerated thanks to a brilliant performance from defence barrister, Simon Beaumont.

Simon Beaumont defended a hardened criminal and got him off. Judge Slight was brutally murdered to punish his close and lifelong friend, barrister Beaumont.

Eddie Balance's mother gave an alibi which had rapist John Clington set free only for him to rape again. Eddie's Mum's punishment came when her beloved son was callously killed.

And Barry Chubb publicly supported an alleged war criminal and Barry was punished when his darling niece was murdered.

She buzzed. *But is it true? Can I prove my guesses? Can I check jury service records? Can I contact Denise in Warburton?*

Jo read and re-read her notes. She tried to find faults, anticipating the comments from her colleagues.

"What about the threatening emails to the judge? Who sent them? That person could well be the killer?"

Jo rehearsed her reply. 'True but my theory is to (a) see if the homicides are linked and (b) see if each fits the reverse revenge idea. My theory claims each victim was killed to hurt someone close to them. To find the killer, possibly a serial killer, is to discover if every victim is in the same category and I think they are.'

She flopped on the settee, so exhausted she couldn't sleep. The cure, used many times before, was to take to her toes. On with the leotard, shorts, and top-shelf runners and away she went. Her excitement at having done what she did supercharged her running. Then it was home, shower, bed and yes, sleep.

21

THE LEADER HAD FOLLOWED the fraud trial since it began. The prosecution had a solid case. The defence barrister seemed ill-prepared even disinterested. Witnesses had spoken of the ruin they endured since being fleeced by the accused. People took to drugs and alcohol, marriages ended and two victims suicided.

To the unbiased observer it seemed only a matter of the length of the sentence. The fraudster's guilt was a given. Then the unexpected happened. The defence barrister got to his feet, called a learned law professor who defined a director and stated that the accused could not be described as such.

It was a bombshell. The prosecution objected. The judge overruled. The prosecution asked for an adjournment. Her Honour agreed and asked to see both counsel in her chambers. Journalists scrambled. Victims in the public gallery despaired with many in tears.

The court resumed. The prosecutor stood and announced that no evidence would be offered. "The law is an ass" was proved again. Common sense disappeared and a guilty person walked free.

All hell broke loose. The reaction outside the court was the lead story on all TV news channels except the one with rights to football. Their lead story was about a hamstring injury to a star player.

The man following the trial, the Leader, made mental notes and that night posted on his blog. He always began with a quote from scripture. His latest being, "Vengeance is mine". The instructions which followed were clear. Or were they?

Jo woke keen to share her theory. She worried. *Am I right? If so, is there a single killer? Will my theory help find the murderer?*

She knew it was best to work through the ranks. DS Hughes had always supported Jo who was now big on reciprocity. She found Billy.

'Morning Sarge, got a minute?'

'Why am I worried?'

Jo placed her document detailing her revenge motive theory on Billy's desk. Jo pointed as she explained things. She held her breath as she waited for Billy to list the weaknesses. *What will Billy say?*

'Get it ready for the screen. I'll tell the DI.' Billy left leaving Jo speechless. Billy popped back. 'Bloody good work, Senior.'

Jo checked the document on her laptop. She entered the Incident Room where her colleagues worked on the four unsolved homicides. Rose and Hughes entered followed by Richelieu. He looked at Jo and his smile seemed to be a mix of *congratulations* and *Dinner, Mademoiselle?* Rose called the meeting to order.

'Some news, everyone. Detective Senior Constable Best has been a busy girl. She's researched the background of people known to each of the victims in our four homicides and come up with an interesting theory.' She looked at the young detective. 'The floor is yours, Senior.'

Sometimes speaking in front of a dozen people is harder than an audience of a thousand. Jo could see the faces of her colleagues. Most liked her, a few didn't. Some fancied her, others felt threatened by her ideas. And of her ideas, this shaped as being Best's best.

Her document was screened for all to read. She explained her thinking. Her points were clear. Her only fear was that someone would find a flaw she hadn't thought of which would turn her model into a house of cards. She finished. Nobody spoke.

'Well?' asked Rose.

'I think it's brilliant,' said Billy.

'It makes sense,' said Baldwin.

Justin Fleming had a query. 'How does this fit with Eddie Balance? He gave an alibi for the rapist and so Eddie is a case of a perpetrator being killed.'

'Yes and no,' replied Billy. 'Eddie only backed up his Mum. She was the real alibi giver.'

Baldwin had a question. 'If Jo's theory is correct, does this mean one person is responsible for all homicides?'

Jo responded. 'I'd argue for one group of killers—I reckon you'd need at least two people to carry out all four murders.'

'Not Eddie Balance,' said Payne. 'Whack him from behind then strangle and degrade him could have been done by one person.'

Others disagreed. Fleming quietly liked Jo and her theory. 'How do we find out if the sister in Warburton was on jury service?'

'Ask her,' said a voice from the back.

'I'm not sure we can,' said Rose. 'Anyone else?' Silence. Rose took control. 'Let's approach the court and ask if this woman served on a jury in say the last six months. Who's up for that? Jo, it's your baby. Any trouble let me know and I'll refer it upstairs.'

'Ma-am,' said Jo tingling with the way her idea had taken off.

'So ideas, people. Who is our serial killer? Who would know court proceedings and the alleged perpetrators of injustice?'

'A judge,' said Payne. That drew a sharp breath. 'Just saying.'

Fleming spoke. 'Could be a cop, a court official, a barrister or solicitor, even one of their clerks, even a court reporter.'

Baldwin contributed. 'What about someone working for the police—admin, forensics, Protective Services?'

Billy kept thinking. 'There has to be a team—a planner and the executioners.'

'But what's their motive?' asked Baldwin.

'It's revenge, pure and simple,' said Fleming.

'No,' explained Baldwin. 'What's their motive *for* revenge? Are they religious nuts, political fanatics, what? Lots of people are angry with court decisions but they don't go round killing people.'

'And certainly not someone who had nothing to do with the decision,' added Rose. She was feeling a million times better now that a breakthrough had seemingly been made.

Everyone paused. They reckoned there was serious logic behind Jo's theory. On paper it certainly made sense. But would it help find the killers? Then Payne made another, for him, astonishing remark.

'If it's a serial killer, statistics tell us many don't stop until they're stopped. And miscarriages of justice or court decisions are not gunna end any time soon. Number five could be just around the corner.'

That got people thinking. 'We 'ave to follow through with the people who are 'urting, Madame,' suggested Richelieu, sounding like the acting head of Homicide he once was.

'Okay,' said Rose. Let's re-interview the victims of the victims. That's Denise of Warburton, the barrister Beaumont, Mrs Balance and … oh shit.' Everyone laughed. 'Barry Bloody Chubb.' More laughter.

'Pardon, ma-am,' interrupted Jo. 'But we know these people have suffered. Why interview them again?'

'Your first flaw, Senior,' said her boss in as polite a way as possible. 'We need to be sure the victims are suffering and not shaming. Then we need to know all the details of the "crime" their friend or relative committed to cause the suffering. What has the shock jock done to be punished?'

'What has he *not* done?' asked Billy.

Fleming had a concern. 'How does Alvin fit into the scene where Karen's sister Denise sat on a jury?'

'He's a red herring,' said Rose.

'Sorry ma-am,' corrected Baldwin, 'but there are no herrings, red or otherwise, in the Yarra River.'

Laughter and ridicule followed. The meeting ended on a bright note. The mood was bubbling. Teams were appointed to re-interview the friends/loved ones of the victims. Jo Best started this. If her theory helped find the killer and stopped the killing spree, that would be fantastic. But hope and good feelings don't always a killer catch.

The couple huddled in front of their computer. The husband searched while his wife asked questions.

'And you're sure it's from him?'

'It's from him.'

'What's the case?'

The husband shook his head in disbelief. Once he decoded the message and thus identified the target, the husband went online to research the details. He studied them.

'This is appalling. Dozens, possibly hundreds of honest, hard-working people lose their life savings and the man responsible, the wicked, evil fraudster gets off scot free. No fine, no jail time, nothing.'

'But what about compensation for the victims?'

'Nothing.'

The wife was angry but confused. 'It's terrible but I still don't understand why we don't target the criminal.'

'If the wicked person is killed they don't suffer. This way they do. And besides, ours is not to reason why. We do the Lord's bidding.'

'Who caused the injustice in this latest case?'

'It's a solicitor. He trawled though old cases and found some legal loophole which said the accused was not a director.'

'So he got off?'

'The judge said she had no choice.'

The couple seethed. This was a massive injustice. The person who made it possible for the fraudster to walk free surely had to pay.

'Who's the target?' asked the wife. No reply. 'Who's the target?' The husband went quiet and looked at the wife. 'What?'

'It's the son of the solicitor.' The wife wanted more information. 'It's a child.'

The wife blanched. 'No.'

The people suffering from the murders were re-interviewed. At Warburton, Denise admitted she'd been on jury service but refused to give details. A visit to the Court would be required.

Barry Chubb had not been interviewed at all and Rose asked Billy Hughes to have a chat with the shock jock.

'Can I take Jo Best, ma-am? It was her theory that started all this.'

'Sure. But use her as backup. You run the interview. If it goes wrong, we know what the shock jock will do to our reputation.'

'Thanks for nothing. I'll tell Jo. She'll be chuffed.'

'She reminds me of her grandfather.'

'Interesting.'

'Why?'

'Apparently her grandfather said Jo reminds him of you.'

Rose grunted. 'What do you reckon about Jo's theory?'

'She's been right before. Made some bad blues but her instinct is good. Those who reckon a good detective is born not made would put Jo Best at the front of the queue.'

'Good luck with Barry,' said Rose and left Billy to collect Jo.

'Me, Sarge? Are you sure? 'Why not DI Richelieu or DS Fleming?'

'Stop complaining and get in the car.'

In making an appointment with Barry, there was no way he would have the police in his luxury South Yarra apartment overlooking the Royal Botanic Gardens so his radio station it was. Barry brought his team, well his manager, PA and solicitor. The police felt outnumbered.

As expected, Barry tried to run the interview. He did that for a living. He had questions and the police had bloody well give him the answers or else. Jo delighted in watching Billy handle the pompous prat. She ignored his questions.

'Before we start Mr Chubb, my colleague and I would like to say how sorry we are for your loss.'

She left it there. Bullying, bustling Barry was knocked over by sympathy and respect. He thrived on confrontation and was offered the milk of human kindness. How tricky was that?

Billy began. 'Would you be kind enough to tell us, sir, if you knew of any enemies your niece may have had?'

'None. She was a beautiful young woman cut down in her prime.'

'No boyfriends she may have upset?'

'No. Look, I gave you a list of suspects. Did you bother to even read my document?'

'We study all the advice we receive from members of the public.'

Barry fumed. *I'm not a member of the public. I'm Barry Chubb.* 'Have you interviewed the suspects I suggested?'

'I'm afraid we can't discuss the workings of the investigation. Can you suggest any friends or colleagues of your niece who might be able to help us find her attacker?'

'I don't know her friends. Ask her mother, my sister.'

'That's already in hand, sir.' He sighed. 'And was the relationship with your niece such that she would tell you if anything or anyone was bothering her?'

Barry's frustration kept building. 'What has my relationship with Pippa got to do with her death? What's it got to do with anything?'

Billy ignored his belligerence. 'Did your niece agree with the things you discuss on air?'

Barry flipped. 'Ye gods and little fishes.' His "team" worried Barry would lose it and say or do something he would later regret even though Barry's default reaction was to regret nothing. 'What has my stance on public affairs got to do with my niece's murder? I hope for everyone's sake you're not the top cop on this case.'

Billy placed her card on the desk—a power statement if ever there was one. *You call me if you've got a tip.* Barry ignored the card. Billy stood followed by Jo.

'Thank you for your time, Mr Chubb, and please get in touch if you think of anything which might help solve the death of your niece.' Billy nodded at the hangers-on.

Barry looked at Jo. 'Sorry, I missed your name.'

'Best, sir, Detective Senior Constable Joanna Best.'

Barry dismissed them. 'A sergeant and a constable—is that the best you've got? Why isn't a Detective Chief Inspector running such an important case?'

'We haven't got a DCI, sir,' replied Billy.

'What? What is the matter with you people?'

'The rank no longer exists. Homicide is run by DI Eleanor Rose.'

'A woman?'

Billy's sarcasm kicked in. 'I believe that's a truthful deduction, Mr Chubb.'

The officers moved but stopped at the door when Barry spoke. 'I know you.' He moved towards them staring at Jo. 'Where do I know you from?'

'I've no idea, sir.'

Billy knew and gave it to the ignorant bully. 'You may have seen Detective Senior Constable Best on the news recently. She expertly traced a lost child to Central Victoria, and returned her safely to her family.' That stopped Barry's cynicism, well, momentarily. 'Senior Constable Best is one of the outstanding officers working hard to bring justice to your niece.' She flashed a cheap smile. 'Good day.'

Billy and Jo walked out without a backward glance leaving Barry with nothing to say. Now there's a first.

22

ON SUNDAY, Jo's tummy turned nasty. Forget dangerous crims, jealous colleagues and smart-arse witnesses, her family loomed large. Her niece, Millie, and her father, Malcolm, shared a birthday. Her mother, Shirley, would never attend anything to do with her ex-husband with the possible exception of his funeral. In fact she already had the shoes to wear for dancing on his grave. But because her granddaughter shared a birthday with Grandpa—how unlucky was that for Shirley?—she was obliged to attend.

'Stay beside me the whole time, Joanna,' said Shirley who'd been saying that for the last however many years it was since the granddaughter was born. Jo grimaced at the thought of her social lowlight of the year. No wonder her gippy tummy was doing its thing.

Nothing significant had been discovered since Jo revealed her serial killer theory. The detectives knew Karen Galbraith's sister Denise had served on a Supreme Court trial jury but the details of the case were unknown with Jo set to investigate tomorrow.

She did feel a little better when she remembered her second social event that day, a welcome home party for young Grace Carr following her harrowing stint in hospital. Jo thought about a present. *Would that be appropriate? What if the guests bring something and I don't?*

The birthday gig was a luncheon at big sister Caitlyn and hubby Jeremy's humble mansion. For her niece, Jo settled on a book voucher. Millie always loved Auntie Jo's presents but her parents damned them with faint praise. *This time she can choose something herself.*

Jo arrived at her mother's home. 'Wait,' called Shirley, retreating.

'Hello Mum,' said Jo to her mother's back as Shirley headed inside.

'I can't find that silver necklace Auntie Bea gave me.'

Jo followed her mother into the bedroom, opened the second drawer of her dressing table and produced the missing item.

'Oh,' said Jo feigning surprise, 'here it is.'

Both women knew where it was. Procrastination was in Shirley's DNA and more so when having to be in the same room as Malcolm X. They set off for the party—finally.

The husband went through their supply of items. They rehearsed each murder known to them as a sacrifice. They needed a dry run to learn more about the victim so as to make the real thing go like clockwork. But for this fifth homicide, both killers were less keen.

Belief in their mission never wavered. Hatred of the evil criminal who needed to be punished remained red hot. And willingness to follow orders stood rock solid. But this time the person to die was a child. Even their fanaticism, their blind belief in the righteousness of their cause couldn't hide the niggles, the doubt that punishing an evil person by killing their offspring somehow didn't seem tickety-boo.

Jo parked in the street outside her sister's and heard her mother say what she always said. 'Stay beside me the whole time, Joanna.'

'Yes, Mum. Let me carry your present.'

'Haven't you got anything?'

'It's in my bag.'

The door was opened by son-in-law/brother-in-law, Jeremy.

'Ladies,' he announced without a trace of warmth in his voice. He kissed Shirley who offered a cheek. 'Mother-in-law. You look well.'

Liar, thought Shirley entering then stopping.

'Officer,' he said giving Jo a peck. His after-shave lotion yelled.

This was the moment of dread for Shirley. The spotlight stood ready to pick her out as she entered the cavernous, plush-carpeted sitting-room. Inside were her grandchildren, under restraints, her older daughter, her ex-husband, his trophy bride and their two children and Malcolm's in-laws who were younger than him and went by the unfortunate given names of Peter and Peta.

Shirley loathed being here at all but making conversation with two people she referred to as Mr and Mrs Homonym was the pits. Peter wore hearing aids with his opening line being, "Sorry, I missed that," whenever someone said Peta. Shirley considered being forced to attend the event a form of torture and wondered if she had a case with the War Crimes Tribunal in The Hague.

Presents were presented—naturally Shirley had nothing for Malcolm X although his younger daughter gave him the same gift as she gave Millie. A buffet luncheon commenced with most guests nibbling. Caitlyn boasted of the nineteen countries whose food was represented in the repast. Jo reckoned one dish was still alive. She and her mother sat in a corner and picked and pecked in silence.

After the unnatural conversation had petered out, Caitlyn asked her sister about the police activity the whole world knew about.

'So sister, when will you be on the television news again?'

Everyone jumped in. Not only because they were bored witless by the phoney dialogue but because they genuinely wanted to know the inside story of Jo and the missing toddler.

'I could tell you everything,' said Jo, 'but I'd have to arrest you.'

That produced the first snippet of laughter. Would there be a second?

Peter had a question. 'I say, Detective Best, when are we going to see you on the television news again?' Several groans were heard and his grin disappeared when told to turn on his hearing aids.

Malcolm persisted. 'So are you looking for lost kids at the moment?'

Jo sighed. 'No, Dad, that was a secondment. I'm back in Homicide.'

'And that's where we'll leave this discussion,' interrupted Caitlyn, not wanting murder discussed at a children's birthday party. Too late.

'What's Homicide?' asked the curious birthday girl, now all of 9.

Caitlyn was up and herding children. 'And now it's time to play in the garden. Millie, you can be in charge, it's your birthday.'

Jo wondered why children had to have someone in charge. *Why can't they just play?* Jeremy called. 'Play quietly and do not go near the flowers, statues or garage.' Jo thought. *Why not have them stand around like statues?*

Shirley was keen to leave five minutes after she arrived and once the cake with its candles disappeared and the singing ceased, she gave Jo the nudge. 'Tell them you've got a homicide to solve. Go on.'

Eventually they left with both feeling relief. In the car, Shirley let rip. 'I think your father's looking old.' Jo took her eyes off the road for an instant and gave her mother the evil eye. 'It's just an observation. Now what are you up to this afternoon?'

'I'm going to another party, Mum.'

'Oh?' asked Shirley with a huge dose of curiosity.

'No gossip I'm afraid. It's a welcome home party for a little girl who's been in hospital and who nearly died.'

Shirley lost interest. Jo walked her to her door, kissed her and set off for another social event. It had gone 3 when she arrived at the Carr residence. Peg opened the door but pushing in front of Grandma was Harry with a smile to kick start a flat battery. He saluted. Jo saluted in return and accepted his hug.

'Welcome,' said Peg. 'Come on, Harry, let your guest come inside.'

'It's lovely to see you both and on such a great occasion,' said Jo.

Dr Carr appeared. 'Hello Detective. Thank you so much for coming. Come in, come in.'

Jo entered the large sitting-room to be greeted by a sea of faces. Grace's friends and their parents were there, a few neighbours, Jack's in-laws and his parents of course and then the guest of honour, Miss Grace Carr herself.

Jack introduced Jo then she saw Grace and felt she should move towards her. She froze. Yes, it was little Grace. Yes, she had that beautiful smile but oh no, something was seriously wrong.

Jo fought the shock and moved to Grace who sat in a wheelchair.

'Hello Grace,' beamed Jo while her heart thumped and her mind raced. 'Welcome home. It's lovely to see you.'

Jo bent and kissed Grace who seemed to want to speak but didn't. Or couldn't. Jo struggled. *Please God, don't let me cry.*

Jack stepped forward to help the visitor. 'Grace has been waiting for you, Jo. She wants to ask you about taking Rags for a walk.' He made eye contact with his daughter. 'Is that right, darling?'

Everyone looked at Grace. Nobody spoke. Grace paused then gave a gentle nod. A wave of emotion swept over the gathering and Jo backed away afraid she would cry.

'Something to drink, officer,' said Hugh. He guided her by the arm towards the kitchen. No sooner was she out of the sitting-room then her tears appeared. She fell against Hugh and he held her without saying a word. He handed her a handkerchief which saved her.

'I didn't think,' said Jo.

'We should have told you. I guess Jack was afraid too thinking he might break down.'

Jo struggled. 'What's happened?'

'It's called an acquired brain injury. Her movements and speech are pretty bad as you saw.'

'Will she recover?'

Hugh looked and felt sad. 'We live in hope,' he said.

Harry arrived and jumped straight in not understanding the emotional distress. 'Detective Jo?'

She wiped her eyes and blew her nose then saw the handkerchief and looked horrified.

'It's yours,' said Hugh who winked and quietly slipped away.

'Yes Master Harry Carr, what's been happening?'

'Well, I've been going to school and taking Rags for his walk and practising my salute and helping Gran and ...'

Jo laughed. 'Okay, I get the picture. You're a busy little beaver.'

He was about to ask another question when his father arrived. He and Jo looked at one another. The little boy looked up at the adults. They didn't speak and Harry was confused. Silence was a foreign concept to the small chap.

'Dad?'

'Yes Harry.'

'If Grace can't take Rags for a walk with Detective Jo, can I take him instead?'

The adults did more talking with their eyes. Jo wanted to cry. Jack got in first.

'I'm sure Detective Jo would like to do that.'

'I certainly would, Harry.'

'Go and get the lead for Rags, mate.' Harry was gone in a flash. 'I should have told you, Jo. I'm so sorry.'

'I don't know what to say.'

'You being here means so much to Grace, to Harry, and to Mum and Dad.'

'And you?'

'You mean you can't tell? I thought you were a detective.'

They tried to smile and the conversation ended as Harry arrived with Rags already in harness.'

'We're ready,' said the little tacker.

The adults managed a smile. Jo looked at the over-the-moon boy. 'Lead on, young man. Let's go.'

Out through the kitchen they went, into the yard, along the drive and Rags had never been so excited. They returned tired, exhausted and full of beans.

It was an unusual party. The guests were united in their love and good wishes for Grace but as she was hardly the life of the party, the life of the party turned quiet. Again Jo got asked about her headline-grabbing exploits in rescuing the missing toddler, and again she downplayed the event. People drifted away with only Jo and close family remaining.

Jack's in-laws made their move. Jack led them from the lounge. He was out in the hallway heading for the door when the couple walked past Jo. Jack's mother-in-law, Celia, showed her true colours when she stopped and asked Jo a question.

'How is your friend we met at the school?'

Jo was thrown for a moment before she twigged. 'Oh, do you mean DI Richelieu, the charming Frenchman who wants to show me the sights of Paris?'

Celia froze. Her barb became a damp squib. Jack came back wondering where his in-laws had gone. He saw blank faces and stood aside as the fortress stormed out followed by the damp squib.

Peg pushed Grace to the kitchen and Hugh grabbed Harry. When Jack returned, Jo was alone. He sat beside her.

'Thanks again for coming. It means a lot to all of us.'

'I got a shock, Jack. I'm still upset. Your Dad said something about an acquired brain injury.'

'Yeah, it's bad, obviously, but it is what it is.'

'Will she get better?'

'Better, sure, but how much and when is unknown. Her speech and mobility are poor and that's where physio and speech therapy kick in.'

'Well she couldn't have a better family.'

Jack wanted to speak but paused, afraid he might break down. Jo leant across and placed her hand on his. He recovered and explained.

'Sadly there are thousands of people, of all ages who have an acquired brain injury. They're caused by different things—an accident like Grace, or a stroke or, with the case of babies, being shaken because the little mites won't stop crying. And because the brain pretty much runs our body—how we think, feel, speak, move—an injured brain impacts the person with the injury and usually everyone around them.'

They paused. This was a whole new world of pain and change.

'Let me help, Jack.' His eyes brimmed with tears. 'I'd love to.'

Jack put his hand to his face and held it there. He was fighting tears and stupidly felt embarrassed. Jo said nothing but squeezed his arm. She reckoned the best way out of this was to say something crazy.

'I'm afraid I upset your mother-in-law—again.' Jack recovered and blew his nose. 'She stirred me about a colleague who kissed me after I spoke at a school where another of their granddaughters is a student.'

Jack's emotions climbed onto a roller coaster. 'Ah, that's my wife's sister's daughter.'

'I told her the colleague, who grew up in France and whose mother owns a swanky apartment in the equally swanky Rue Crémieux, wants to take me to Paris for Christmas.'

Poor Jo. She was trying to take Jack out his trough of despair but instead was compounding his turmoil of unrequited love.

'Lucky you,' said Jack feeling crushed inside.

Jo realised his angst. 'Oh, I don't think I'll go. What's Christmas without a barbie and flies?'

Hugh stood in the doorway and interrupted. 'Sorry to break up the party but my grandson is threatening to riot unless he can speak with a certain police officer.'

That did bring a smile to Jack's face and they stood. 'Send him in to be arrested,' said Jo and Harry arrived in half a trice.

He couldn't stop talking and that in itself was entertainment plus. Jo felt sad but wanted to leave. She felt overcome by what she'd seen and heard and had a big day tomorrow. She felt her theory about a serial killer was about to be tested, and she had a visit to the Supreme Court and wanted to get her facts and questions right first. She made her apologies and then they went to the kitchen where Peg was feeding Grace. It was heartbreaking and summed up the impact of Grace's acquired brain injury. Here was an eight year-old being fed like an eight month-old.

Peg looked at Jo and meant what she said. Being a woman, she knew what her son and his children thought of the police officer. 'Thanks for coming, Detective Senior Constable. You've made us all feel so much happier.'

Jo refused to speak again knowing she would cry. Instead she moved to Grace and kissed her head. She managed to whisper. 'I'll see you soon, young lady, very soon.' Jo looked at the family, gave a wiggly finger wave and headed for the front door. She dared not speak. Jack and Harry followed her. The boy saluted and Jo returned the salute. She looked at Jack who mouthed, "Thank you". She turned and walked down the drive, tears streaming down her cheeks.

As she reached the street, a couple walking their dog saw this young woman balling her eyes out. They knew a doctor lived in the house. They looked at one another. 'Poor thing,' said the woman. 'She must have been given some bad news.'

23

THE LEADER SENT DETAILS. The husband studied them and explained the situation. The wife remained solemn. She willingly killed before knowing each death would hurt the perpetrators of evil. This was the only way to make a stand. God was being mocked. People flouted man's and the Lord's law. A voice needed to be heard. Vengeance was needed. Making the wrongdoers suffer was essential.

But the wife worried. The fifth victim was a child. The wife opposed the choice but relented when the husband gave the "no pain, no gain" explanation. Her heart disagreed but this was the Lord's work.

'Here's a school magazine photo.' The husband had circled the victim's face. 'They live in Melbourne with a holiday house on Phillip Island. We'll check out the home on Sunday with the family away.'

'All of them?'

'The children are boarding at school or uni with the parents at the beach. We'll wait for the judgement day timetable. Questions?'

The wife shook her head. Inwardly she despaired.

Their preparation was meticulous. They knew the ways in and out of the house, where the residents and pets were and all about the neighbours. They'd been to Warburton and knew the ideal drowning spots where the Yarra was deep enough and the current strong. They knew the layout of Judge Slight's South Yarra abode and when he was in court. They knew Mrs Balance's Carnegie home and her son's town house in Flemington. They knew the horse-riding trails in and around Monbulk. So reconnoitring the house of the parents of one master Robert Power was straightforward.

But had they studied the poem *To a Mouse* by Rabbie Burns?

But Mousie, thou art no thy lane,
In proving foresight may be vain;
The best-laid schemes o' mice an' men
Gang aft agley,
An' lea'e us nought but grief an' pain,
For promis'd joy!

Walking their dog had worked before. The pooch was quiet and easy to distract with treats. They set off a block from the target's house. It was almost dawn. A newsagent's car loaded with newspapers crawled past. The wife wore a wig and glasses and the husband a less ostentatious Groucho Marx nose, mo and specs. The dog wore a coat.

Checking the street was empty, they swung into the drive. They knew the way around behind the garage and reached the back door. The safety door was easily opened but the main door needed expert picking. Impatient, the dog barked. The hissing from its owners ignited fear in the hound and silence took hold.

The humans knew the inside layout from real estate online listings. Their goal was to study the victim's bedroom and his possessions. The couple wanted details, anything that would help in their "disposing" of the victim. "Killing" didn't sound right. What they were doing had supernatural authorisation. There were babies in the village not far from Noah's ark. Did the Lord spare them? No, this had to be done.

Upstairs, turn left and either the first or second on the left. The stairs creaked enough to add spice to their invasion.

They reached the top of the stairs. Hearts beat faster. It was dark but a touch of dawn squeezed through. They headed along the corridor unsure which room to search when the choice became irrelevant.

One of the doors opened and a person emerged. The dog barked.

Normal burglars would have sworn, exclaimed "shit" or "fuck" and reacted with surprise and a touch of fear. Not these intruders. Mind you the person who opened the door swore. He was alone and now two disguised adults and a dog stood two steps away.

'Jesus,' he said, which was not a good choice of reaction. He wanted to ask, "Who the hell are you?" but couldn't because the couple launched into action.

They'd rehearsed their emergency response for an occasion like this. The husband sprayed the victim's eyes who struggled. 'Help!' escaped his lips before a cloth soaked in chloroform was pushed hard against his face.

Not being a movie, the victim did not become unconscious in seconds but the shock of the situation, the attack and the sweet-smelling liquid being forced into his nose and mouth hampered his fightback skills. His hands were quickly bound. He slumped to his knees. His head throbbed and fear gripped his body. Fear of choking, dizziness and a headache joined forces. The invaders won.

But they had a problem. The date for the "sacrifice" as the Leader called the homicide had not been set. Now the husband and wife needed to make an executive decision.

Gavin and Dell Power were nice people. They'd been married for 20 years with an 18 year old daughter boarding at university in Canberra and a 15 year old son boarding at school in Geelong. Having the kids away during term time made life easier. With their dogs, the couple enjoyed their Cowes beach house on Phillip Island.

Gavin's career as an IT consultant was going swimmingly and Dell had gone back to teaching. Their parents were getting older but still had their marbles and muscles in good shape. You could rightly say that all was well in the Power family world.

It was a Sunday, early evening when Gavin and Dell (and the canines) turned into their street. The weekend at Cowes passed too quickly with the weather and wine in fine form.

Gavin turned the 4WD into their driveway and slowed as they approached the garage. Both the dogs sensed their destination and got excited. Their collars were set free from the restraints. Gavin hit the remote, the roller door moved and Gavin asked the dogs to behave for another thirty seconds. Dell screamed.

It was so loud and fearful she frightened herself and her husband. The dogs froze. Gavin spun around and saw what his wife saw. He tried to scream but couldn't.

In the middle of the garage, their son, Robert, 15, was hanging, suspended from a metal strut with a rope around his neck.

The parents rushed out of the vehicle and into the garage. Dell screamed at her son. 'We're here, darling. Mum and Dad are here.' Gavin picked up the chair which lay on the concrete floor, stood on it and tried to hold his son higher. It made no difference.

The shock kicked in and the parents lost control. With both front doors of their vehicle wide open, the dogs, having been released from their leash, jumped into the front, out of the car and into the garage. What's this new game? They barked and jumped adding a bizarre sideshow to the agonising spectacle.

Gavin managed to unhook his son who fell against his father. The weight was too much for the shattered Gavin who stumbled and fell. The boy helped knock his father to the concrete and the lifeless body half covered Gavin.

Dell knelt trying to revive her boy. Her tears splashed on Robert and Gavin in equal measure. The dogs joined in licking and pawing. It was beyond the parents' worst nightmare.

An ambulance arrived as did a police patrol car. A GP from four houses away came running. Neighbours helped the parents indoors. It was a time to curse God and to beg for his help. Gavin's brother arrived. His parents were too distressed to go anywhere. Dell's best friend arrived and became the switchboard operator and, depending on who was calling, would tip-toe to the lounge to ask if the parents wanted to speak to so-and-so. 'I'll call them later,' was the standard response from Gavin. Dell was in no condition to speak to anyone.

The family GP heard of the tragedy and arrived. He gave Dell something to ease her mental anguish which had quickly become a sharp chest pain. Gavin thanked the doctor and cried without hesitation as he gripped the medico's hand.

As time passed, the reality of a suspicious death had to be examined. The family GP, along with the police and ambulance, pronounced life extinct. The uniformed patrol contacted their station and reported the matter. A senior sergeant attended along with local detectives. Questions were asked.

The parents were in no position to answer any questions but the police ascertained a number of facts. The boy had no history of drugs, bullying, relationship breakdowns or other possible causes of suicide. His school grades were excellent, he liked school and his goal of studying veterinary science was set. He had everything to live for and would never have been listed as a potential suicide risk. Apart from being mind-numbingly horrendous, it was senseless.

The parents' agony intensified when their son's body was about to be removed. When asked if they wished to come outside, both parents answered by moving without hesitation. Dell wanted to brush her son's hair and noticed one of his fingernails had a skerrick of dirt. She instinctively wanted the blemish removed. Gavin kissed his son then put an arm around his wife to prevent her from smothering their boy.

''You'll have a chance to say goodbye,' said the undertaker in a soft voice. He looked at his colleagues and nodded. They paused then stepped forward and lifted the youth placing him in the van. It was unadorned and gave no indication it was a hearse.

The death was an event which would impact the parents (and others) for the rest of their lives. Right now they had to sleep tonight— an impossible task. Then they had work tomorrow—don't be silly, Gavin. Stay home Dell.

Then there was the funeral and how heartbreaking would that be? Then the reminders—his favourite TV show, his football team winning, his birthday, every Christmas, memories of a life cut short.

It was a cross to bear, seemingly forever. It was pain, unique, raw and everlasting. You could see it, smell it and touch it.

Jo was up early. She found it hard to sleep thinking of Grace Carr and the impact a single and instant event can have on a life—on lives. She contacted someone in Traffic and learnt that a driver, high on drugs, had driven through a stop sign at speed and, without breaking, smashed amidships into Hugh Carr's Volvo pinpointing Grace in the back seat. The air bag and safety belt saved her life but didn't prevent her brain from bouncing around inside her head playing havoc with the electrical circuitry. Grace acquired a brain injury.

Before Jo went to Homicide, she headed to the Supreme Court. She rang before and found she needed to go to the Juries Commissioner's Office in William Street. She reckoned the eager beavers would be there bright and early; none of this clock on at 9 routine.

She was right because a middle-aged male court official was already in harness. He looked friendly and was the man Jo needed to see as his work involved everything to do with juries.

'Good morning,' smiled Jo, flashing her ID. 'I'm Detective Senior Constable Jo Best from Homicide and wanted to ask a question about jury service. Can you help?'

'Yes and no,' replied the gent whose hair was cut with a theodolite cum razor and whose shoes doubled as a mirror. 'I can because I know pretty much everything that goes on here, but I can't because the law swears me to silence. But fire away; what's your question?'

'I want to know if somebody served on a jury.'

'Ooooh, big problem there, officer. The anonymity of jurors is sacred I'm afraid. Even jurors can't dob in their colleagues. But what's your case about?'

'Ooooh, big problem there.' Jo mimicked him. 'The anonymity of cases is sacred I'm afraid.' He grinned and Jo copied him.

'I'm Len,' he said holding out his hand.

'Jo,' she said shaking hands.

'I'm part of the furniture round here. The most common remark you'll hear is, "See Len", so if I can't help you, ...'

They spoke together. 'Nobody can.'

They laughed. Len continued. 'If you can tell me the case in broad terms, I might, repeat might be able to help.'

Jo chose her words carefully. 'We have a homicide where the victim may have been killed because of something someone else did.'

'And that something is connected to a Supreme Court jury.'

'Spot on, Len.'

'I'm good at guessing.'

Jo tried to make progress. 'So I can't discuss particulars of a homicide and you can't reveal details of jurors in a case related to that homicide.'

'Now be fair, Detective. I reckon you knew that before you got here.' He was right. 'So, are all homicide detectives as smart as you?'

Jo smiled but her brain got busy. 'How about if I get my boss to ring your boss and see if some rule bending can take place?'

Len joined the smiling club. 'Good luck with that. Plenty have tried and failed but I guess there's always a first time.'

Jo accepted defeat. 'Well thanks anyway.'

She turned to leave and he walked her to the door. 'We haven't had a murder trial for a while.'

'Are you having a dig at the Homicide Squad, Len?'

He laughed. 'No, no, I wouldn't have your job for all the tea in Christendom.' They reached the door. He opened it. 'Nice meeting you, Detective. I hope you catch your man.'

She thanked him and walked back to Homicide. She arrived to find her fellow officers being addressed by DI Richelieu. As she entered, he stopped and turned to Jo thus highlighting her late arrival.

'Bonjour, Mademoiselle. Bienvenue.' Jo took a seat. He continued. 'As I was saying, Detective Best's theory about the victims being killed to punish a friend or family member is now 'ighly likely when you consider the murder of 'is 'onour Judge Ranald Slight. Monsieur Beaumont yesterday was more distressed than when I first interviewed 'im and that is saying something. It all goes back to their friendship as schoolboys, then at university and finally with the judge 'elping to save Monsieur Beaumont's career over an insider trading scandal.'

'Questions?' asked DI Rose. Nobody spoke. 'Well the only case which we're not sure about is the Warburton drowning. Was the dead woman's sister on a jury? Jo?'

'No go, ma-am. Getting juror details is nigh-on impossible. I suggested a request from on high but even that was politely declined.'

'The theory's correct, though,' said Fleming. 'The murdered woman's sister told us she'd been on jury service but refused to give details. So while we don't know which case, if Denise Wallington was on a jury that made a decision which upset the killer, then he got back at Denise by drowning her dear sister.'

The room went quiet. Rose took control. 'And I can tell you that Barry Chubb, for all his bluster and bullying, is seriously cut up by the death of his niece. According to the pathologist, it was no accident. And we know Mrs Balance, who gave an alleged rapist an alibi, was devastated by her son's slaying.' She paused and looked at the detectives. 'So, are we agreed that someone is killing innocent people because they are much loved by someone who has done ... what?'

'Prevented justice being served,' said Fleming.

'Supported criminals,' added Richelieu.

'In Barry Chubb's case, it could be anything,' said Billy. 'But he's been going strong in defending this Peter Yarberlich guy who some claim is a war criminal.'

'Right, let's focus. What is the mindset of the killer?'

'Deranged,' said Payne.

'Fanatical,' said Baldwin.

'Per'aps we should engage a profiler, Madame,' offered Richelieu.

'Per'aps indeed. Look into it, Pierre.'

A phone rang and Jo was closest to it.

'I want us to work on the assumption that all four homicides are linked and that a serial killer or killers is responsible,' added Rose.

'Excuse me, Ma-am,' said Jo with a hand over the receiver. 'You'd better make that *five* homicides.'

24

THE HUSBAND SEARCHED FOR INFORMATION. Whenever he and the wife carried out a successful sacrifice, the Leader sent a message of congratulations in cryptic form. No two messages were ever the same and only someone with expertise in cryptography and a solid serving of luck would ever understand or link the different messages. But this time no message appeared.

'What does the Leader say?' asked the wife.

'Nothing,' said the husband still searching.

'You gave him the news?'

'Of course,' he snapped.

'You told him how we had to take action?'

'I told him, all right?'

The tension simmered. 'Maybe he's busy or forgot or …'

'Forgot? He never forgets. His planning, his case selection, his messaging and his follow-up work are faultless.' The husband looked at his wife. They didn't do much eye contact. They didn't do much of anything together except kill people. They were in love with their Lord first and second. 'He is fanatical about detail and that's why I'm worried.'

'Do you think we made a mistake?' asked the wife.

'I know we didn't. We never have. Why do you think the police have no arrests? Why do they keep making public appeals? They have no idea who we are. The Leader is a genius and the Lord is on our side.'

The wife was less of a fanatic and more of a human. She worried the Leader may be wearing big boots thereby hiding his feet of clay. She worried the loved ones of those they killed were suffering for something they didn't do. She wished the Leader chose the evildoers and not their friends and family. She wanted to pray.

'What?' exclaimed her husband staring at the monitor.

The wife hurried to her husband's side. 'What's happened?'

'The Leader is angry.'

'Why?' She pleaded as her body tensed with fear.

'Look,' he said and pointed at the screen.

The wife thought she would die.

A mini posse of detectives went to see the pathologist. DI Rose, DI Richelieu, DS Fleming and Jo Best entered the sickly-sweet smelling chambers.

'What's this,' asked Strange, 'school excursion?'

Rose cut to the chase. 'Good morning, Doctor Strange. We understand you're not happy with a suicide.'

She had examined the body of 15 year old Robert Power. His tragic death sent shockwaves through his family, friends and school, even the pathologist. 'I know nothing of the young man's life,' said Strange, 'but whatever his state of mind, I'll swear he didn't kill himself. This is a homicide.'

The detectives gathered around. 'Because?' asked Rose.

Strange could be accused of failings—she drank too much for starters—but no-one could fault her determination to find the truth.

'Slight bruise marks on his arms, slight bruise marks on his wrists, indicate he was bound and restricted. My guess is soft material, strong but unlikely to make deep impressions and which was removed once he was dead.' She indicated his throat. 'Note the lack of blood pressure marks indicating he was either dead or unconscious when his neck took the weight. You've probably seen war footage of hangings where the body convulses, legs kick, etc. We weren't there when this boy died but his external signs are that this was a gentle hanging.'

'What's a gentle hanging?' asked Fleming.

'It's the same as a suicide where the victim shoots himself four times in the head.' Fleming shut up. 'See here,' said Strange pointing. 'There's discolouration in the eyes. A foreign liquid causes a reaction.'

'What sort of foreign liquid?' asked Rose.

'Pepper spray, chloroform, mace.' Strange picked up a bowl with a body part. 'But the kicker, if you'll pardon the expression, is this.' Jo wondered if the organs were put back for the undertaker. 'His liver shows signs of injury. See here and here.' The detectives looked enthralled yet repulsed by the pathologist's display of a young man's once thriving organs. 'Again, something like chloroform can cause such an injury.' She returned the liver to its place. 'So, those who have listed the young man as a suicide may not like what I put in my report. This death is another for your collection.'

She looked at them. The police fell silent. They thought they were closing in on the killer when up pops another body. That's assuming this lad was victim number five.

'When might we expect your report, Doctor?' asked Rose.

'In the fullness of time, Inspector.'

Jo remembered the pathologist making that reply before.

'Thank you,' said Rose. 'We appreciate your outstanding work.'

'Bloody hell,' gasped Strange. Everyone stopped and looked at the pathologist. 'Your predecessor never thanked me, and as for paying a compliment, well that'd be when *Frozen* gets filmed in Hades.'

Billy Hughes and Jo interviewed Robert Power's parents. Gavin and Dell Power had dealt with uniformed officers and local detectives. They were still in shock and now confusion made it worse.

'I don't understand,' said Gavin after Billy and Jo introduced themselves. 'We've told your colleagues everything we know.'

Billy paused. Jo admired the way she set the pace for a conversation whether to a witness, a suspect or now, to suffering family members.

'Mr and Mrs Power, we need you to understand. We are homicide detectives.' She let that sink in.

Dell twigged first. 'Homicide? But they investigate murders.'

'Yes, we do.'

'But Robert took his own life,' countered Gavin. 'He wasn't murdered.'

Billy paused again. 'We have a report from the pathologist who examined Robert and there are doubts about his death being a suicide.'

Wow. If Billy had slapped the parents hard, she could not have shocked them any more than she did with that last statement. They gasped and stared, dumbfounded. Jo was glad to remain anonymous.

'No,' groaned Dell. 'No!' She wailed and her husband hugged her as she sobbed. Jo thought. *How much suffering can they endure?*

She kept quiet, but looked at Billy who didn't invite her junior to speak. With the parents in serious distress, chances of a productive interview were low. Driving to interview the parents, Jo and Billy talked about how they could find out what, if anything, someone had done to bring about Robert's murder.

Was this murder linked to the others? Had the parents served on a jury and acquitted a dangerous suspect? Had they given an alibi to a criminal? Had they supported an evil person or covered up a crime? Or something else? And if so, would they admit that? Hardly.

When the initial shock and anger began to settle, Billy tried gentle questioning. She was walking on eggshells.

'Forgive me asking sensitive questions, Mr and Mrs Power.' She wanted to call them Gavin and Dell but it didn't seem right. 'Can I ask if you or your children have been in any dispute lately?'

'Dispute?' asked Gavin. 'What sort of dispute?'

'Have you or your family upset anyone? Have you made an enemy or been involved in any court action?'

'No,' protested Dell. 'Nothing like that.'

Gavin was trying to make sense of the questions. 'Are you saying we did something to upset someone who killed our son?' The parents were desperate for answers, and the interview headed towards a disaster.

'Not at all,' replied Billy in an even softer voice. 'But if Robert didn't die by his own hand, then we have to consider the possibility he was killed and if so, our job is to find out what happened.'

More pauses, moans and sobs. Billy gave Jo the cue.

'Was Robert good at opening up to you?' she asked. 'Would he tell you if he had a problem at school or with a friend?'

'Always,' said his father.

'Always,' repeated his mother. Jo hit a dead end so swung onto another tack. 'And your daughter is away studying, I believe?'

'In Canberra,' said Gavin.

'And if she had any major issue, would she talk to you about it?'

This was too much for the parents. Their son's suicide brought unbelievable pain. Now the possibility he was murdered because of something they did made the horrific situation worse. Billy took over.

'And was Robert due to be picked up by a school friend and driven to Geelong?'

Gavin snapped. 'Yes. Look we told all this to the other detectives. Why are we going over it again?'

'Because we want justice for your son, Mr Power.' Billy's soft voice and sympathetic understanding kept the parents from losing it.

Gavin shook his head. 'Robert was to call his friend if he needed a lift and when he didn't call, they left without him.'

'But how could he ask for a lift if he was dead?' shouted Dell.

'Mr and Mrs Power, we apologise for asking such difficult questions. We'll take our leave and contact you later.' Billy looked at Jo and they stood. 'Thank you for your understanding and again, please accept our sincere condolences.' The parents looked at the police with faces of despair. 'We'll be in touch as soon as we have any news. Here's my card.' She placed it on the dining room table. 'Please call if you have any questions or just want to chat. We'll see ourselves out.'

They left quietly. Neither spoke until they were in the car.

Billy spoke without looking at Jo. 'Telling parents their child is dead is tough. Telling them he was murdered is worse.'

'If it's murder, there's no obvious link to the revenge killing theory.'

'Give it time,' said Billy who started the car.

'Assuming it's the parents the killer wants to punish, they sure didn't give the impression they're covert criminals or evil people.'

'Don't get carried away with your theory. This death might not be a murder by the serial killer, if he exists.'

That thought attacked Jo's thinking. 'Bugger,' she murmured.

It took only a few seconds for the husband to figure out what went wrong. He was shocked and couldn't speak. He looked at his wife.

'What's wrong?' she dared to ask.

He told the wife and the shock hit her hard, the guilt even harder.

'What have we done?' she gasped.

'Nothing that can't be fixed.'

'Fixed?' she screamed. 'Fixed? We've killed the wrong person.'

The husband growled. 'Don't raise your voice to me. It was a genuine mistake. We wait till the Leader gives new instructions.'

'But we've murdered the child of innocent parents!'

He looked at her. He suspected she was weak. 'We took an oath to do the work of the Lord. Our hearts have always been pure. We want vengeance for the sins of the world. Do not even think about wavering.'

She couldn't bring herself to look at him. She felt torment, wanted to rage and curse her husband, their Leader and yes, even the Lord. She left the room and the house slamming doors en route.

The husband waited for the Leader to comment.

Rose called the squad together. They were eager for details about the suicide now listed as a murder. Was this #5 on the serial killer's list?

'Right, we have four homicides all possibly victims of a serial killer with the motive of killing people to punish those who have done what someone reckons is the wrong thing. If true, how do we find the killer?'

'Ma-am, are you saying this latest homicide is not part of the revenge theory?' asked Baldwin.

'We don't know. There's no obvious reason to punish the parents.'

'Are they seriously upset?' asked Fleming.

'What sort of dumbass question is that?' snapped Billy Hughes. 'They thought their beautiful boy killed himself and now they discover he's been murdered. Of course they're seriously upset.'

Fleming explained. 'So because their pain is traumatic, it adds weight to the theory they've done something to inspire the killing.'

Billy conceded. 'Sorry, Justin, point taken.'

'So 'ow do we discover if the parents 'ave done something to inspire murder?' asked Richelieu.

The room fell silent. Payne had a thought. 'Is there any DNA evidence from the supposed suicide? Sooner or later the serial killer has to make a mistake.'

'Billy?' asked Rose.

Billy shook her head. 'Forensics found nothing. And I think there has to be more than one killer. There had to be two for the drowning, two for the judge, certainly two for the equestrian on the horse, and now two for rigging the hanging.'

'Eddie Balance needed two,' said Fleming. 'He's young and fit. He would have fought and one killer would have been too risky.'

Rose sucked in breath. She was treading water. She was new to the job, had bodies piling up but no persons of interest or evidence, and was left with one interesting but as yet unproven theory.

'Help me, somebody. The head of Homicide is sinking and fast.'

The others knew how she felt. Prayer was looking like the best option and to a bunch of atheists and Callithumpians, that meant they had diddly squat.

25

JO WAS FLAT OUT trying to prove her vengeance theory and identify the killers. But she kept having thoughts about little Grace Carr who was all of 8 and confined to a wheelchair needing countless hours (years?) of therapy to learn to speak and walk again. Whoever reckoned that *Shit happens* knew what they were talking about.

At home that night she wanted to call the Carr family to see how things were and to offer any encouragement she could. Her specific offer was to take Harry out and thus away from the unhappiness in the home. She took the plunge and made the call.

Peg answered. 'Hello, Carr residence, Peg speaking.'

'Peg, it's Jo Best. How are you?'

There was an ominous pause. *Not more bad news, surely.*

It was and even the stoic grandmother had a tremble in her voice. 'Jo, it's awful I'm afraid.'

A panic attack gripped Jo. She struggled to breathe, her finger tips tingled and her heart started pounding. She didn't want to hear the news but seemed drawn to the scene. 'What's happened, Peg?' Jo dreaded hearing the worst. Then she heard crying. It was Harry. That bright soldier, Mr Effervescence, was crying loud and with pain.

'It's Rags,' said Peg. 'He's run away.'

Jo was in two minds. She was expecting terrible news but instead got … no, that *is* terrible news. More crying came from the background and then the boy's plaintive cry.

'But he might be scared, Daddy, we can't leave him alone.'

'Poor Harry,' said Peg. 'He and Hugh had the dog in the park and they threw a ball. Rags raced after it, dived into the bushes and didn't come back. They called and searched but he disappeared.'

'Oh God,' said Jo, 'how awful.'

'Harry thinks it's all his fault and won't go to bed without his mate.' Jo announced. 'I'll come over, Peg. I've got a really strong torch.'

'No, don't Jo. I'm sure he'll turn up in the morning.'

'But Harry'll go to bed if he knows I'm looking for Rags. Will you tell him?'

'Of course, he'll be thrilled. And thank you, Jo. You're a darling.'

'I'll see you soon. Bye.'

Jo found her runners, tracksuit and torch. In her car she rang Michael Chan, the IT genius who refused to use caller ID on his phone.

'Michael Chan speaking.'

'It's your favourite cop, Michael. How are you?'

'Worried. No, doubly worried that you're ringing at this time.'

'How do you fancy finding a lost dog? I can pick you up in ten.'

'A lost dog?'

'Afterwards the pizza's on me. Come on, get a bit of fresh air.'

'I need a course in assertive training on how to say "no".'

She laughed. 'I'll be there in five. I'll toot. And bring a decent torch.'

Michael was excited. He made all sorts of complaints about Jo's tasks but secretly he loved them. He thought he loved her and his pulse picked up at the thought of their meeting albeit looking for a lost dog.

She did toot and he stepped from the shadows being ready well in advance. He hopped in the car and she floored it.

'Whoa, what's with the speeding, officer?'

'How are you, Michael?' she said. 'And how are your folks?'

It was a while since Michael's parents had been brutally assaulted and kidnapped by the criminal Sim brothers only to be rescued, in part at least, by one Joanna Best.

'They're fine, thanks. But what's with the lost dog?'

'It belongs to some friends and the little boy who's pushing six, won't go to bed until his best mate is found. So I'm going to find Rags and need another pair of eyes.' She indicated her passenger, 'Du-dah!"

'So no fraud, no criminals and no IT expertise required?'

She laughed and headed to Mont Albert.

The Leader explained, in code, that the husband and wife had killed a Robert Powers instead of a Rupert Powers. Having the two boys at the same Geelong school didn't help but the mistake had been made. The husband had mild dyslexia.

"Do not accept previous order," wrote the Leader. "Await next message". The husband took the news in his stride; not so the wife.

Jo and Michael stood at the Carr front door. Michael was impressed with the real estate. Jack opened the door with Harry wiping tears but overjoyed to see his favourite police officer.

'I've brought reinforcements,' said Jo. 'Jack and Harry, meet Michael, IT guru and dog finder extraordinaire.'

The big boys shook hands and all went inside. 'This is really kind of you, both of you,' said Jack feeling slightly concerned that Jo had arrived with another male person in tow.

Harry hugged Jo. 'Thank you for looking for Rags, Detective Jo.'

'You're welcome, Harry. And Michael's going to help too.'

'Thank you, Michael,' said the boy and held out his hand.

Michael shook it. 'I only hope we can find him.'

'So do I,' replied Harry. 'He doesn't like being out on his own.'

Jo bent down to eyeball Harry. 'Now, young man, where did Rags go missing?'

'In the park.'

Jack took over. 'I'll give them directions, old man.'

Before he could describe the situation, Michael produced a phone and asked for the name of the park. Jack told him and seconds later they looked at a map. Jack pointed to a place. Michael zoomed in and Jack explained where the dog had disappeared.

'And we're ... here,' said Michael hitting the screen and pulling up the street and house in which they now stood.

Jack looked at Michael and then Jo. She smiled. 'We won't get lost.'

'Fantastic,' said Jack. 'Come on, Harry, let's wave them goodbye.'

They headed to the door. 'How's Grace?' asked Jo in as nonchalant way as possible.

'She's okay. I told her you were coming and she smiled.'

Harry took off and the adults thought the strain was too much for the boy but he returned in no time holding a lead. 'This is his lead.'

Jo took it. 'Thanks Harry. Keep your fingers crossed.'

They waved goodbye and headed down the drive.

'I hope you find him,' called the voice of a desperately sad child.

They reached the park. Jo felt happy to have company and such an ordered brain beside her. Her torch was powerful but Michael had what she thought was a theatrical spotlight.

'This is where he disappeared,' said Michael. 'How about I head this way, you go that way and we circle the park and meet back here?' He looked at her. 'Am I taking over?'

'Yes, and I like it,' smiled Jo. Their eyes met and Michael felt happy.

'Rags,' he called and started to search.

Jo did the same, their bright lights picking up the bushes, trees, seating and playground equipment. So far no sign of any dog and no sign of blood or fur from a fight or dognapping.

The park was large and searching took time. Jo worried that the roads were nearby and while she dreaded not finding Rags, she dreaded more finding his body having been hit by a car and dumped.

After 20 minutes, both had covered as much of the park as they could and were heading back towards one another. There was traffic nearby but the sound of cars was not noticeable until a roar began.

A car was travelling way too fast. It came from a fair distance away but the sound got louder and quickly. Jo worried. Any person or dog in the vicinity of such a speeding vehicle would have no chance.

Then a police siren joined the airwaves. Jo was instantly alert. She left her dog search and headed towards the sound of the speeding vehicles. Michael saw her in the dark and followed.

The spectacular finale happened in a flash. A squeal of brakes, a car lost control, hit the curb, took the airborne route and flew into the park, missed trees and smashed through the side fence of a house. The cop car with lights and siren followed but in a much safer way.

Jo and Michael sprinted. Two occupants of the crashed car got out. In the darkened park, the escapees saw two bodies hurtling towards them and heard the cop car doors slam. They were in strife. One dashed into the park and the other dived inside the backyard of the house with the damaged fence.

'Stop! Police!' cried Jo as she changed direction to tackle the nut case heading for freedom.

The escapee felt better hearing a woman's voice and kept on his course, confident he could swat any female fly that dared to cross his path. She came out of the night and tripped him. His momentum saw him take a dive. He tasted grass. His hands were grabbed. He screamed in pain and then frustration as cable ties locked his arms behind his back.

A uniformed officer from the chasing patrol car arrived to arrest the escapee. His torch illuminated a young woman in a tracksuit kneeling beside a well and truly restrained suspect.

'Bloody hell,' said the uniformed officer, panting.

'Senior Constable Jo Best,' said the woman, not panting.

Together the cops assisted the seriously annoyed runner to his feet and all three headed back to the now heavily populated crash scene. Stickybeaks have always been a dime a dozen and that night they joined forces with the rubbernecks.

'My friend chased the other guy but I didn't see what happened to him,' said Jo.

The constable used his radio to call his colleague. 'Under control,' came the reply. 'Some bloke's made a citizen's arrest. I think he's a kung fu expert. What's happened with you?'

'Ditto,' said the constable and Jo grinned. 'Only my helper's a cop.'

The journalist was alone in the news room, the office of a current affairs TV show on commercial television. It was late and hot tips were conspicuous by their absence. A phone rang. The journo answered it. *'Tonight at Seven.'* He listened then grabbed a pen and scribbled. 'Hang on, say that again.'

'Someone I know was murdered. The police haven't arrested anyone but I know why the victim was killed.'

'Okay, madam. Could I have your name please?'

Denise didn't want to give her name. 'I'd rather not say. But the police have a number of unsolved murders at present and if they're anything like my situation, then someone is killing the wrong people or killing people for the wrong reason.'

153

The journalist was fascinated but frustrated. 'So how do you know this information?' Denise went silent. 'Hello? Are you there?'

Denise decided to go against her conscience or at least the instructions she received. 'I was on a jury which voted Not Guilty. That upset a lot of people because the crime was cruel ... really cruel.'

The journalist had questions but his training taught him to let the witness talk. He took notes and recorded the conversation. She spoke.

'Somebody close to me was murdered. I don't know who killed them but I can see no other motive for the murder apart from hurting me.'

'Because you were on that jury?'

Denise spoke slowly. 'Because I was on that jury.' She'd been stewing over her sister's drowning ever since it happened.

Why would anyone kill Karen? She had no enemies—a cheating husband but he couldn't run a bath let alone arrange a murder. This was no accident. The killer hated me because I was the person who asked questions which helped turn other jury members. Somebody on that jury leaked information that I was the person who argued for a Not Guilty verdict. That meant someone wanted to get back at me and make me to suffer. They found out my sister meant the world to me so killed her to punish me. And drowning is a terrible way to die. They knew I wouldn't be able to get that image out of my mind. I was punished for what I did on that jury.

The journo struggled. He wanted more details, at least her name and number, but feared pushing too hard.

'Look, I'd like to help,' he said. 'I understand your wish to remain anonymous but if what you say it true, you must want to see your friend who was killed—it was a friend you said?'

Denise nearly blurted, "No, it was my sister", but stopped and spoke quietly. 'Yes, a friend.'

'You must want justice for her.' The journo used the feminine pronoun hoping for confirmation or correction. Denise didn't bite.

'I do,' she replied.

'My name's Greg and how about I call you Jane?' The journo paused. He didn't want to lose the connection. More silence from Denise.

'Okay,' said Denise feeling happy with a pseudonym.

'I would like to talk to my producer, Jane, and try to help you get justice for your friend. Would you like that, Jane?' He was good this journalist. He could sell bibles to believers.

'Yes, I'd like that.' She grew in confidence. 'I want that.'

'Well I'll give you my number and you can call me tomorrow morning whenever it's convenient. Can you get away from work, Jane?'

She was hooked now. 'I'm retired.' Greg scribbled.

'I'll be here from 10 am, Jane. Here's my mobile.' He had her repeat it. He knew he was taking a chance by not getting her number but he wanted her to trust him. He turned on the charm.

'I hope you won't mind me saying this, Jane, but I think you are a very courageous lady and I think your friend would be tremendously proud if she knew what you are doing for her. She would be grateful and love you even more.'

Denise was crying. 'Thank you,' she whispered.

'I'll wait for your call in the morning, Jane. Goodnight.'

There was goodwill and kindness in spades, all contrived, and Jane felt warm inside and uttered, 'Goodnight,' as the call ended.

The media had a sniff.

Jo, her police colleague and prisoner reached Michael and his two pals. Two ashen-faced car thieves were not happy. Onlookers gawked. The crooks were captured by a girl and a geek and faced a string of charges. The uniformed officers thanked the have-a-go-heroes and departed with their captives.

'Well done, you,' said Jo slapping Michael on the arm. 'So you're not just a pretty face.'

'All those judo lessons I endured as a kid finally paid off.'

'Well we might have bombed in the dog finding but we sure nailed it with catching crooks.'

'Not true,' said Michael in his usual deadpan manner.

Jo froze. She didn't know what to say. 'Michael?'

He gestured with a finger. 'Walk this way.' He led her into the back garden of the house with the smashed side fence. The runaway vehicle made itself at home beside the pool with patio furniture now floating therein. Jo followed Michael towards an open shed full of firewood. Michael shone his torch and crouched. 'Look.'

Jo bobbed down and looked where Michael's torch shone. They saw the terrified face of a frightened dog. Jo was about to speak.

'Shhhh,' said Michael. 'Don't spook him.' He shone his torch at the corner of the property. 'See that broken paling. I reckon Rags came in there probably being chased by a bigger dog.'

'Or dogs,' said Jo.

'The owners have two dogs and this little fella's too scared to move.'

'You're a star, Michael Chan.' She kissed his cheek with some serious intensity then moved closer to the dog and whispered. 'Rags, come on Rags, here boy.'

He whimpered and tried to get his tail wagging. Jo put her hand closer and he leant forward, hesitated then licked it. She made a kissing sound and he came out from underneath a pile of red gum, crouching and sweeping the ground with his busy tail. She scooped him up and copped a lashing of licks.

The owner of the property arrived with his two dogs keen for action. Jo explained their real purpose but the owner was far more interested in his rearranged back yard.

Jo and Michael, with Rags on his lead, went back into the park. Jo handed the lead to Michael and made the call. Peg answered and relayed the news. Jo could hear family members shouting their joy with Harry in ecstasy. Rags headed home.

Harry's joy exploded. He found it hard to hug and thank the dog rescuers as he wouldn't let go of Rags.

'Time for bed, Harry,' said his grandfather and the dog, the boy and the Pop said their farewells and headed upstairs. There was a large dose of happiness in the Carr household right now, a nice counter to the sadness of Grace and her condition.

Jack was overwhelmed with relief and gratitude. He offered coffee and Peg turned barista. Jack had been reminded by his parents that Michael was Jo's partner in finding the lost toddler. Jack was curious to know what Michael did and about his relationship with the senior constable. When Jo gave Michael a huge rap for his IT skills, Jack reluctantly took a punt.

'It's an awful cheek, Michael, but my hard drive is as slow as a wet weekend. I don't suppose you could have a quick look.'

Michael stood. 'Lead the way, Doctor.'

'Are you sure? And I'm happy to pay.'

'Go, Jack,' said Jo. 'He's the best there is.'

'Excuse us,' said the excited GP and led Michael to the study.

Peg sat closer to Jo. 'You've been the best thing this family's had in a long while, Jo Best.' She raised her coffee cup. 'Cheers.'

Jo responded in kind. 'Thanks but it was Michael who found Rags.'

The women enjoyed their coffee and basked in the good news. Both had plenty to say but saying nothing seemed right.

'Listen, young lady, I'm speaking out of turn here but hopefully I'll get away with it because of my age.'

'That sounds interesting. Are you confessing to a crime, madam?' teased Jo. 'You know you have the right to remain silent.'

Peg smiled. 'I know you copped a serve from the other grandmother so at the risk of even more bashing from a grannie, here's my two bob's worth.' Jo sensed Peg was serious.

'Do I need my lawyer?' she tried to be flippant.

Peg declared albeit softly. 'I wouldn't dream of telling you how to live your life, young lady but I reckon you should think about things before you make any big decisions.'

Jo paused. The women looked at one another. Jo thought she knew where this was going but didn't want to make a fool of herself.

'Whatever you're trying to say, Peg, I'm sure you mean well.'

'Don't get me wrong. I'm probably Jo Best's biggest fan, although Harry might dispute that.' They kinda smiled. This *was* serious. 'We all love you, Jo, but sometimes, being a tiny bit selfish and looking after number one is not such a bad idea.'

This got Jo thinking. *Is she warning me off? And if so, off what?* She looked at the older woman. 'You should be a philosopher, Peg or maybe a poet.'

They both smiled and said no more as Hugh arrived followed by Jack and Michael.

'Children and canine in bed and asleep,' said Pop.

'Michael has my hard drive skipping through fields and singing,' beamed Michael.

It was a good mood all round. 'That's great,' said Jo standing. 'But I have a big day tomorrow and must a good night's sleep have.'

Hugh took Jo's hand and kissed it. 'Good night, good night! Parting is such sweet sorrow, That I shall say good night till it be morrow.' Everyone laughed. Michael and Jack would have enjoyed doing that routine and they all headed to the front door.

Jo kissed Hugh and Peg then Jack. 'You are a star, Jo Best,' said Jack. He grasped Michael's hand. 'And you Doctor Chan are a gentleman and a scholar.'

The family waved and Jo and Michael headed for her car.

'*Doctor* Chan? What was that all about?' asked Jo.

'Minor appendage from years ago.'

'Michael, sometimes the humble routine is unnecessary. Blow your own trumpet.'

He yielded. 'Okay, I did a doctorate in an obscure field of computer science—now completely useless—and thus is never mentioned.'

'Jack Carr got it out of you?' They got in the car.

'He tricked me.'

'He tricked you?'

'I saw some of his academic paraphernalia on the study wall and commented on it. He said I must have been at Melbourne and he prised out my academic adventures.' They drove.

'You're good at secrets, Michael Chan. You keep your expertise and thinking close to your chest.'

'You mean my cards.'

'No, I mean your feelings. You're hard to pick, Doctor Chan.'

She took a quick look at him. He was already looking at her. 'So you're a psychologist too,' he said.

'More like an agony aunt.'

They laughed and she drove him home.

Will I accept his offer of coffee? Too much caffeine, I'll never sleep.

26

THE HUSBAND WORRIED. He misidentified the teenage boy. "Robert not Rupert is an easy mistake to make" he told himself. But now there were consequences. His flaky wife was flakier. His boss, the Leader, sounded angry in his latest message.

The husband scanned the blog. Nothing. *Has the Leader dropped me and my wife? Are we no longer worthy to do the Lord's work?*

The wife stood beside her husband. 'What?' he snapped.

'I don't want to do this anymore.'

'Don't be ridiculous,' he derided her comment.

'I mean it.'

'You must. We took an oath. We must obey.'

'Killing a child is terrible but killing the wrong one is unforgivable.'

He stood and grabbed her arms. His grip hurt her but physical pain was nothing to her mental anguish. It pounded her brain.

'If the Leader heard you, he would be extremely angry. Imagine how our Lord is reacting to your wilful disobedience. Obey,' he shouted and shook her. 'Obey!'

She defied him and yelled in his face. 'I don't believe our Lord wants us to kill children. And why does our Leader only communicate online? Why does he not give orders in person?'

The husband instinctively went to strike her. "Wives obey your husbands" flashed across his brain. She stared at him, daring him to do his worst. He froze. Striking her now would wreck their mission. How could he explain that to the Leader? The husband knew why the Leader remained at arm's length. It was a tactic if ever the police got lucky. The disciples worked apart.

Speaking of the Leader, the zealot studied his next attack. Forget the death of the wrong victim. Move on. *Now, who next deserved the vengeance, the wrath of the Almighty?*

Gabrielle Strange worked late. Being a single woman without a family, going home had no appeal. Her friends were few. Drinking too much as she did appealed to fellow soaks but the pathologist never suffered fools. She was finishing her examination of the teenage boy.

Having checked so much of the young man's body, she felt glad that while her liver was in dangerous territory, her heart continued to respond whenever a tragic death crossed her examination table. She referred to Robert as a beautiful boy. She understood the pain his parents now suffered and would forever. Then she saw it.

'It can't be,' she exclaimed. 'How could I have missed that?'

Using a powerful lens and a bright light she parted the healthy hair on the boy's head. 'Yes, it is,' she said with growing excitement. She was alone and had no-one to share her excitement. With difficulty, she collected her discovery and stored it.

'Better late than never, my dear,' she murmured. 'And have we found the key to identifying our killer?'

Jo prepared for bed. There were three text messages on her phone. Peg Carr was blunt. *Please ignore any advice from an old woman. Love Peg xx.* From Peg's son came, *A million thanks to you and Michael. Love Jack.* And the third message, a Strange one. *I may have found the missing link. Ring me. TPP. xoxo.*

All three made her smile but the one from TPP (The pathetic pathologist) got her excited. Did it ever? She looked at her clock radio. 2227 hours. *Well, she did say, "Ring me".*

The doctor did her spooky voice thing. 'Hello, I'm Strange.'

'It's the Deranged Detective here.'

'Tell me, Mizz Best, how many teenage boys do you know? Sorry, I'll re-phrase that. How many teenage boys have you encountered in your work as a police officer?'

'You could cut to the chase, Doctor.'

'I could but I'm excited.' Jo sensed that in her voice. 'When you talk about the skin of teenage boys, what's the first thing you think of?'

'Acne.'

'Not dandruff?'

'Dandruff?'

'Our supposed suicide has dandruff, not much mind but enough to remove and hold in store awaiting analysis.'

Jo got the excitement bug. 'You mean it's the killer's dandruff?'

'No idea but I'll be gobsmacked if it's the victim's.'

'But if it's someone else's, how does dandruff change heads?'

'Why do you keep asking me to do your job? When was the last time I asked you to carry out a spleen biopsy? Or dissect a brain, or ...'

'Yes all right, I get the picture.'

Strange then did exactly what she had objected to doing and became a detective. 'There was a struggle. Even when drugged, the kid fought. The killer, being an adult with un-shampooed hair, had some of his or her dandruff dislodged. It took off and settled in the victim's luxuriant locks.'

'And medically that's possible? Dandruff can travel?'

'We shed skin cells all the time, under the shower, when asleep, when trying to commit murder.'

Jo bubbled. 'That's brilliant news. Who have you told?'

'What a ridiculous question. Surely you know I only deal with the top detective. Now I suggest you get to my emporium first thing in the morning and have Forensics examine this gold dust. Copy?'

'I copy. And many thanks, Doctor, you're the best.

'No, you're the Best, I'm the Strange. Sleep well.' Click.

Jo remembered her mistakes of the past. As much as she loved being given the scoop, she now put her superiors in the loop. Her text to DI Rose, CC'ed to DS Hughes read—*Speaking with Dr Strange, we may have a DNA breakthrough on the 5th murder—Robert Powers.*

Jo found it hard to sleep. Mixed in with the excitement of some evidence which might solve the case or cases, she kept returning to one place and person—Forensics and Alastair Dean. *Can he help me?*

Greg from *Tonight at Seven* emailed a report to Laurel, his producer about his chat with Denise known as Jane. The next morning he was waiting in her office.

'I reckon this could be big,' said Greg. Laurel was not convinced.

'How?' she asked.

'If Jane is telling the truth, and her friend was murdered to punish her for voting *Not Guilty*, that's a bombshell right there. If these other unsolved murders are in the same boat, then this is dynamite.'

Laurel was a hard bitten operator. If she had a dollar for every journo who reckoned their scoop was the story of a lifetime, she'd be filthy rich.

'If Jane rings, get her to agree to an interview. Offer money and anonymity. Then come and see me.' Laurel got on with something else but Greg hadn't moved. She looked at him. 'What?'

'One of the unsolved murders is the niece of Barry Chubb.'

Talk about a game changer. The producer came alive. 'Right, this is our lead story. If somebody killed Bazza's niece to get back at him, this will rate through the roof. Go.'

Greg departed hoping like hell his phone would ring.

Jo and Billy went to see an unhappy Rose. 'How come the pathologist rings a junior officer? She should be ringing me or at least DS Hughes.'

Jo was thinking on her feet. 'Ah, she knows ringing me at all hours won't cause an issue, ma-am and besides, she knows I'll immediately pass any news to my senior officers.'

Rose looked unimpressed. 'That sounds like bullshit.'

'And Dr Strange and I go back a long way, ma-am.'

Billy laughed and Rose scoffed. 'A long way? You were still in nappies when I started working with Doctor Strange.'

Meekly, Jo replied. 'I'm sorry but that's not true, ma-am.'

Rose headed towards being angry. 'Yes it bloody well is.'

'I'd moved from nappies to knickers by then.' The joke died.

'Right, get that dandruff sample to Forensics and use your feminine wiles to speed things along.' Jo hesitated. 'Problem, Senior?' Billy smiled. Rose remembered. 'Oh that's right. You've got the love puppy scientist. Well, catching violent killers is your day job, Missy. Handling amorous co-workers you do in your lunchbreak.'

Jo wasn't happy and drove to see her favourite pathologist. Both buzzed. Strange fetched the container with the sample of dandruff.

'Don't know why I missed it before. I'm getting old, Joanna.'

'Never.' *Something's up. She called me Joanna.*

'When you get affected by a corpse, it's time to give it away.'

Jo didn't have an answer. She changed the subject. 'This could the breakthrough we need.'

Strange spoke with her back to Jo. 'I'm thinking of retiring.' She turned and faced her young friend. 'Well say something. At least try and talk me out of it.'

Jo moved to the medico and hugged her. They held the embrace for some time. When they separated, Jo looked at Strange. 'I want you to do what you want to do.'

'Coward,' said Strange and returned to sorting her equipment.

'How about I come round with your favourite Chinese one night this week?'

'Whatever,' was the response which Jo found scary. This wasn't the sarcastic woman she knew. But now wasn't the time to probe.

'I'll give you a call,' said Jo and left. Her worried state increased. If being upset by a clearly upset friend wasn't bad enough, now the Senior Constable had to contend with her lovesick Mummy's boy at Forensics. His cards and bunches of flowers were sweet when from someone you fancied. But Alastair, with his mother came too, failed to get Jo's carnal thermometer out of the dead zone.

Greg's mobile rang with caller ID blocked. 'Hello? Greg Norfolk.'

'Hello Greg, it's Jane. I rang you yesterday.'

He felt fantastic. 'Oh hi, Jane. Thanks for calling. How are you?'

'I'm nervous. I didn't think I would make this call.'

'Well I'm glad you have and I've got some great news. My producer thinks you are a very brave and deeply caring person and wants to help you get justice for your friend.' There was no end to his malarkey.

Denise felt better, relieved, her heart beat changing from anxious to elated. 'Thank you, that's wonderful.'

'Let me tell you what we'd like to do.' Greg explained an anonymous interview with a made-up name, disguised voice, hidden face, etc. Denise was treated gently and sold the benefits. 'You've come this far, Jane,' oozed Greg, 'don't give up on your friend now.'

Denise fell across the line. It took all of journalist Greg's baloney to get her to agree. But she had conditions. No way would anyone collect her or drive her home. And she wanted a written guarantee that her identity would never be revealed.

She agreed to be in the Melbourne studio at 2 pm for a recording. Already the promo for her segment—it would open the show—was being written. A commercial current affairs TV show was about to give the Victoria Police Homicide Squad a serious whack, and a certain shock jock would be seriously pissed to boot.

Jo arrived at Forensics clutching her dandruff sample. To add to her distress, she remembered that the lovely Alastair used to sport some of the flaky powder within whatever hair he had left. "Hello Mr Dandruff, here's some more". She entered the lab where Mr Bland usually worked. *With any luck he'll be on leave or sick or out buying more flowers.* No such luck as he saw her.

'Detective Best,' he called and hopped down (he wasn't a giant) from his stool to greet the visitor.

'Hello, sir,' said Jo trying to be polite but formal at the same time.

'It's lovely to see you. I was beginning to think you'd forgotten me.'

'Never,' said Jo with mock enthusiasm. 'And I've evidence for which we desperately need an analysis, please.'

She remembered the smile and fluttering eyes she used before but locked them away. *Steady girl. No sex please, we're police officers.*

'And is that the evidence?'

Jo handed him the container. 'Doctor Strange believes the young boy we initially thought to be a suicide but now appears to be a homicide, had someone's dandruff in his scalp.'

'Someone's dandruff?'

'That's what we'd like your brilliant scientific skills to discover.' Jo cringed at her flattery. 'I understand you have the young boy's DNA. We're hoping this dandruff came from his killer.'

Alastair seemed distracted. 'I'm so glad you're here. Mother was asking about you only yesterday.'

What! Mother doesn't know me from Adam.

'Oh?' was the best the Best could offer.

'She was saying how nice it would be if that lovely young policewoman could come to tea next Sunday.'

He's making this up. 'How kind,' said Jo regretting her reply.

164

'Would you like me to collect you?' asked the emboldened and slightly aroused scientist. Without realising it, he was a natural salesperson. Never ask, "Would you like to come?" Instead ask, "What time will I collect you?"

I haven't accepted yet. 'Oh please don't bother.'

'It's no bother. Would 3 o'clock be suitable?'

Hell's bells. 'That's very kind. I'll give you my address.'

'Oh I know that,' he smiled. 'I told Mother and she was most interested.'

Now he's a stalker. In her past romantic encounters, Jo had fought the odd amorous prawn with the arms of an octopus but this example of submarine life appeared dangerous and fishy with a touch of creepy. *Help me, somebody!*

27

'YOU MIGHT WANNA SEE THIS,' said Billy poking her head around Rose's door. The two women went to the Incident Room where other officers were watching a monitor. 'From the top please, for the DI.'

Rose and the others looked at a promo for tonight's episode of *Tonight at Seven*. A woman, heavily disguised, gave her testimony with a digitally re-mastered voice.

Denise Wallington, sister of Karen Galbraith, who drowned in the Yarra River at Warburton, told a part of her story. "I served on a jury in the Supreme Court. I voted Not Guilty and then someone very close to me was murdered."

Then a Voiceover message was heard over file footage of Homicide detectives at a crime scene, including some now watching the promo.

"Does Melbourne have a serial killer? Is someone killing the friends and family members of people who made decisions affecting criminal trials in our city? Witness the shocking truth on *Tonight at Seven*."

The monitor was switched off. Everyone looked at Rose. Not only did she have five unsolved homicides with a decided lack of leads, she now had the media running her cases.

'Pardon Madame,' said Richelieu, 'but this calls for an injunction, n'est-ce pas?'

'It does, Pierre. See to it, s'il vous plait,' said Rose breathing fire. Richelieu left. The pressure was getting to Rose and it increased when her secretary interrupted. The AC Crime was on the line. Rose left.

'That's Denise Wallington,' said Fleming. 'I interviewed her in Warburton. She's the sister of the woman who drowned.'

'She's in trouble for breaching jury confidentiality,' added Baldwin.

'Their legal people will have covered all the bases,' said Billy.

The police were not the only people discussing the promo. Simon Beaumont checked it out online. He rang his solicitor who too had been a good friend of the late Judge Slight. Then Barry Chubb got wind of the promo and turned livid. 'They've stolen my story,' he thundered, which was rich coming from the copyright thief of the millennium. Len from the Jury Commission was in discussion with his superiors each of whom demanded to know who the person in disguise was and what if any of her claims were true. But the piece de resistance involved Gwenda Balance who saw the clip and was on the phone to *Tonight at Seven*. 'I've got a story to tell,' she spat into the phone. 'And I don't want any stupid disguise. I'm not afraid of anyone.'

Jo returned to Homicide still hoping to get out of tea and cucumber sandwiches with Mother and her balding, cardigan-wearing offspring.

'How did you get on?' asked Billy.

Jo explained her visits to the pathologist and Forensics. 'If the dandruff provides a DNA result, we might have our killer.'

'We might have him or her or them anyway,' replied Billy. 'Somebody else agrees with your theory about vengeance.' Jo was gobsmacked and Billy explained the TV promotion.

'And it was the sister of the woman who drowned?' asked Jo.

'Didn't you and DS Fleming interview her in Warburton?'

'We did. And you reckon she's saying what I reckon is the motive for the killings?'

'Spot on. But she's only one.'

'For now,' replied Jo. 'If any of the other friends or family members see the programme and come forward, we'll be investigating a serial killer on live television.'

'True but it might not go to air.' That stopped Jo. 'The boss asked Maurice Chevalier to follow up an injunction.'

With her law degree, Jo knew about these things. 'Wow, that's rare. Victoria Police doesn't often ask the court to stop publication of a story.' She used a mocking tone. 'The public has the right to know.'

'The boss is talking to the AC. She's earning her money that girl.'

Jo had an idea. 'Sarge?'

'Yes?' mimicked Hughes with an upward inflection.

'Is it worth a second visit now a jury member has outed herself?' Hughes wasn't sure. 'What's the point in the Jury Commissioner's Office denying access to a case where the jury member has told the world who she is and what she did?'

Hughes argued. 'She hasn't told the world who she is.'

'Yet.'

'Okay. And it's pointless me ordering you to not cause a scene.'

'Sarge?'

They both remembered when Hughes once gave Jo a specific order to not arrest anyone which she promptly did.

'Go on,' she said.

'Thanks, Sarge,' grinned Jo who headed for the Jury Commission.

Barry Chubb discussed tomorrow's radio show with Tippy Wagstaff, his producer, and the new TV promo featuring Denise. Barry went ballistic. 'I ran that story. I raised the fact that Pippa was murdered. I told the world about our incompetent police.' His producer let him go. Trying to stop Barry never worked.

But Tippy worried. She twigged that Barry had not put two and two together such was his anger about being gazumped.

'I want Pippa's murder as the lead story,' he thundered.

'Barry, listen to me. I know Pippa's death has hit you hard, but attacking the cops is not smart.'

'I don't care about smart. This is personal and I will not be fucked over by those TV leeches. They'll run their story tonight and I'll go even harder tomorrow. I have inside information on Pippa's murder.'

'You're missing something, Barry.'

He ranted, oblivious to the bleeding obvious. 'I set the agenda on this and every other story of importance. I'm in control.'

Tippy went for it. 'Take a deep breath, darling. It's truth time.'

Barry stopped. His producer's blunt speaking snuck under his guard. 'What?' he demanded. 'What did you say?'

Tippy struggled. How could she tell her star performer he caused his beloved niece's death? She tried but proceeded with caution.

'The disguised woman on TV reckons someone she loved was killed out of revenge.'

'I know that. That's my scoop, my story.'

'*Tonight on Seven* reckon there's a serial killer murdering people who are close to people who have done something wrong or bad.'

'Stop telling me what I already know. Stop treating me like an idiot.'

You are an idiot, Bazz, thought Tippy. Barry blundered on.

'I know the woman in disguise voted Not Guilty on a jury and because of that somebody killed her friend,' he said losing steam.

Tippy paused. Barry still hadn't got it. It was time to say it. 'Maybe Pippa was murdered to get back at you.'

There, she said it. What followed was a first. Barry Chubb fell silent. He was programmed to fire off a reply whenever anyone spoke. The saying, *Engage brain before opening mouth* was never explained to Barry. His approach was reply first and with attitude. Now he couldn't.

Quick, somebody call *The Guinness Book of Records*. Barry Chubb is lost for words.

Did Bazza have a heart? He loved his niece as would a caring, adoring parent. Her death belted his soul, the one he always denied having. But this latest revelation was beyond belief.

I killed Pippa? Something I said or did caused someone to murder my girl? No. No. Noooooooooooo!

The Leader's phone pinged. On Twitter he followed various people and institutions. There was a tweet with the promo for the segment on *Tonight at Seven*. The Leader had little reaction and studied the clip.

Then he got busy. He knew the disguised woman. Of course he did. She'd been handpicked to suffer. Her sister had been drowned as a punishment for setting free an evil and guilty criminal.

But now, for the first time, the Leader worried. His revenge plan had been discovered. If the media knew, did the police? Tonight's television viewing had a must-see show.

Jo walked through town. As she approached the Jury Commissioner's Office her phone rang. She saw the caller ID.

'Good afternoon, Doctor Carr.'

'Good afternoon, Detective. Am I interrupting a major crime bust?'

Jo laughed. 'No, not quite. How are the kids and how is Rags?'

'We're all fine, thanks, and speaking of Rags, the whole family is taking him for a walk on Sunday to his least favourite park but this time with Grace in her new wheelchair. About 4 is the ETA and we'd love you to be there if you're free.'

Shit. Double, triple, quadruple shit.

Jo remembered her mother telling her how to behave when she accepted a birthday invitation from a girl in her class, someone she didn't particularly like, and then got an invitation from her second first-best friend. Naturally 8 year old Joanna wanted to dump the first birthday event and attend the second.

'You can't, Joanna,' said Shirley. 'You've accepted the first invitation so you have to go.'

Now she faced the same situation. She accepted Alastair's soiree invitation meaning she must decline the Carr family outing.

'Oh Jack, I have an afternoon tea on Sunday. I'm so sorry.'

'Not a problem. I can understand why everyone wants the beautiful detective at their social event.' The phone call had both of them disappointed. Jack didn't fancy telling his family the special person would not be there.

Jo stopped outside the Jury Commissioner's Office. 'I've got to go, Jack. Please give my love to your family and tell Grace I'll see her soon. Bye.' She hit *End* feeling miserable and walked into the building.

Only a short walk away in the Supreme Court, Victoria Police applied for an injunction to stop a television segment from going to air. It would feature an unknown juror and screen on *Tonight at Seven*. The TV Network's lawyers protested with limited facts as they scaled the moral high ground. They trumpeted the line that the public has the right to know.

In the end, His Honour ruled in favour of the cops. Having the media investigating a case or cases in which the police were yet to make an arrest did not appeal to His Honour, particularly when one of the unsolved murders involved a Supreme Court judge. The TV scoop died, at least for now.

DI Rose was over the moon, the team at *Tonight at Seven* was ropeable, and Barry the Grub was still in shock thinking he caused his niece to be murdered.

Unaware of the legal injunction ruling, Jo entered the Jury Commissioner's building and couldn't remember the surname of the man she met there two days ago.

'Can I help?' asked a woman in Reception.

'Is Len available?' asked Jo flashing her ID.

One name was enough as Len was, as he claimed, part of the furniture. 'Who's calling?'

'Detective Senior Constable Best,' said Jo. 'We met the other day.'

A message was delivered and soon the famous Len arrived. 'We meet again,' he said offering his hand to Jo. They went into the corridor. 'I bet you're here because of a certain television programme.'

She smiled. 'You should have been a detective.'

'So before you ask, the answer I'm afraid is still no. Now, do you fancy a cuppa?'

'Please,' smiled Jo.

They settled in his cubbyhole which was as immaculate as his hair and shoes. He had a range of teas and biscuits you would never find at Homicide. They sat and chatted.

Jo chided him. 'Why do I get the impression you're second guessing the police on this matter?'

'When you've been involved with juries and trials for as long as I have, you get a sixth sense about these things.'

'My boss was hoping if a jury member outed herself, you might treat a police request more kindly.'

'Nice try,' smiled Len. 'Have a biscuit.' She did.

'Are you able to stop a former jury member from breaking cover?'

'With prior knowledge, perhaps, but with the instant nature of social media, a jury member could go public without warning, and stopping them would be pointless.'

She was thinking. 'Do you know who the jury member is?'

He smiled. 'Of course but it matters not as your colleagues won their injunction.'

'Oh?' Jo wondered how a jury official knew before she did.

He sensed her surprise. 'Nothing much happens in the Supreme Court without us knowing.'

'I think you're being overly modest, Len.' She paused. 'So are you worried a jury member has gone public?'

He thought about his answer. 'Yes and no. It's more what they want to say or gain from going public that concerns us.'

'Well from the TV promo it seemed that her voting *Not Guilty* caused the death of someone she loved.'

'I think you're playing games, Detective.'

Mock shock from Jo. 'Me, sir?'

'I think you already know the identity of the talkative jury member and who was killed and why.' He paused. 'Am I right?'

Jo milked the moment, sipping her tea. 'If I tell you, Len, I'll have to arrest you.' He laughed. 'And then who would run the jury service?'

They both smiled. He turned serious. 'I don't envy the police. Criminals plead not guilty, witnesses lie, barristers harass, judges capitulate, victims suffer and the Law is mocked. From the crime being committed to sentencing, the police face opposition at every turn. And now you've got the media running the show. I tell you Detective, something is rotten in the state of Denmark.'

Wow! I didn't think Mr Shiny-shoes had such a passion for politics.

'Well thankfully, Len, I've only got one job and that's to catch killers.'

He sort of smiled. He wasn't sure of her thinking. He chose to open up. 'We watched the TV promo and wondered if it's true.'

'What's true?'

'That the media is leading the police, that this revenge motive is driving the killer to murder people close to those who break the Law.'

Jo paused. 'I'm not sure I follow, Len.'

He looked at her. 'Liar,' he said with a hint of levity.

'But I can assure you of one thing, the media is not leading the police. We've been investigating several murders on the assumption you mentioned long before the media ever took an interest.'

'I'm pleased to hear it.' They paused. 'So is it four or five cases you have now? The media reckon it's five.'

'Now Len, are you trying to get me into trouble? To quote F.U., "You might very well think that; I couldn't possibly comment".'

Len knew the television series *House of Cards* and the fictional British PM Francis Urquhart known as F.U. He laughed with vigour. Jo's mother had the series on DVD.

Len walked Jo out of the building. 'I've enjoyed our little chat. Tell me one secret, please. How close are you to making an arrest?'

They stopped at the front door and Jo looked at him. She liked him and decided to be truthful. 'Of motive, Len, we are confident. Of suspects,' she shook her head.

He grimaced. 'Then I wish you well.' They shook hands and he vanished inside the building.

28

IT WAS CRUNCH TIME for Jo. Later that afternoon she was to be collected by the boyfriend from hell, the balding, boring boffin from Forensics. He would collect her, drive her to his home and there enjoy—surely *enjoy* is the wrong word—tea and cucumber sandwiches with the domineering dragon called Mother. Jo had a brainwave. Thanks to her mother's insistence, Jo couldn't get out of the invitation she'd already accepted. But she could make things a little better.

She rang Alastair and began explaining about a sick girl and immediately he sensed she was trying to back out.

'Oh, detective,' he said, 'Mother is so looking forward to meeting you. Please, please don't tell me you are unable to attend.'

'No, Alastair,' she quickly moved to allay his fears, 'but I have a small request to make.

He paused. 'Oh?'

'The little girl I know has been involved in a terrible car accident and I have the chance to visit her after I come to your house. So I was thinking if I drive to your place, then after my visit to you and your mother, I will be able to drive to see the little girl. It would save you the trouble of driving me and ...'

'It's no trouble. I want to drive you.'

Bloody hell, thought Jo.

'That's most kind, Alastair, but if the little girl who's now in a wheelchair'—Jo was hoping some plaintive violin music would magically appear beneath her voice—'would like me to stay and read her a story, having my car would make things so much easier.'

Alastair was stuck for a reply. He wanted to control the situation and have the detective dependent on his chauffeuring services. 'Well,' he said, 'as it involves a sick child, I suppose it might be better for you to drive yourself.'

Jo breathed a huge but silent sigh of relief. 'Thank you Alastair for being so understanding.' Then she lied. 'And I'm looking forward to meeting your mother at three o'clock this afternoon.'

'Please don't be late. Mother is such a stickler for being punctual.'

I bet she is. 'I'll be on time, Alastair, and thanks again for your kind invitation.'

She ended the call feeling relieved but slightly guilty. *Did I lie? Possibly. How do you tell someone who wants to be friendly, the feeling isn't reciprocated? Is it better to be blunt?*

She wondered about ringing Jack to tell him the good news. Then she thought it might be easier escaping from Colditz than from Alastair and his mother so she held fire on calling the Carrs.

The Leader stewed. He was following a Supreme Court trial. A woman was charged with running a brothel involving Asian women brought to Australia on a visitor's visa then forced into prostitution. The women were sex slaves and treated appallingly. With passports confiscated by the evil Madame, knowing nobody and having little or no English, these wretched souls suffered and slaved.

The woman, Lee Wong, threatened her slaves. 'If you speak, your families in Asia will be punished.' (Read killed). The witnesses refused to speak and the evil woman was found not guilty of the serious charges and merely fined for not complying with brothel regulations.

The Leader fumed. His research discovered that Lee Wong had an elderly mother who was the light of the wicked woman's life. The 87 year old was earmarked as victim #6. Lee doted on her elderly mother. The brothel owner escaped punishment for her wicked slavery but a much harsher penalty was just around the corner.

Jo stared into her wardrobe. What does one wear to meet the tyrant of a mother, the scary shrew of Surrey Hills, the woman who turned her son into an automaton? Jo thought about upsetting Alastair's mater by dressing tarty. Jo once went to a fancy dress party as an escapee from St Trinian's. *What about a St Trinian's look*, she thought? *It would inflame Alastair but horrify his dragon of a mother who would in turn order her son to dump the Jezebel forthwith.*

Then Jo remembered her visit to the Carr family afterwards. She settled for jeans, her favourite shirt, not tucked in, and sneakers. As always her hair was up and this time topped with a cheeky cap.

En route she tried to devise a strategy for dealing with Mother and the unwanted suitor. Multiple thoughts crossed her mind including abusing the woman for being an unbearable bitch to congratulating her for successfully training the Wimp of the Year. Sarcasm and abuse seemed her best options although anything which would turn this visit into her only visit rated highly.

She parked a couple of doors away from the house in question and imagined Mother to be a curtain-twitcher and pretentious snob.

In terms of style, the house and garden were neither one thing nor the other. As she rang the doorbell, her hands seemed to shake. High speed car chases, confrontations with gun-wielding, violent criminals, and a brutal attempted rape were some of her work experiences. Meeting an ardent suitor and his tyrannical mother was hardly in that class. But yet, her hands revealed her nerves.

The door opened and there stood a smiling Alastair. He dressed exactly as he did at work minus his white coat. He opened the door until it could open no more.

'On time, Senior Constable Best; congratulations and welcome.' He gestured and Jo entered.

Jo lied. 'What a lovely house.' The décor and furniture were so unremarkable they were remarkable. Of taste had they none.

'Mother is looking forward to meeting you,' he said in a loud voice.

Is he warning her?

Jo's only thought at the time was *60 minutes*. She determined to be back in her car before the expiration of 60 minutes.

'Come through,' said Alastair who was like a child at Christmas. His nose was red, his sleeveless cardigan featured a television test pattern, and his aftershave reeked of pine needles.

Jo stepped into the lounge expecting to see Mother Christmas on a giant wing-backed chair looking down her nose at yet another harlot who dared to entrap her son.

Hang on. Where's mother? Alastair knew. 'Mother, this is Detective Joanna Best, the policewoman I told you about.'

Only then did Jo spot her quarry. Mother was the exact opposite of who and what Jo expected. She was tiny, sat in a small chair in the corner and looked less offensive than a polite church mouse.

Jo smiled. 'Hello Missus Dean. I'm pleased to meet you.'

Mother nodded. She might have spoken but if so, Jo heard nothing.

'Do take a seat, Detective,' said Alastair. 'There, next to Mother,' indicated the Fat Controller.

Jo sat and in so doing entered a scene from a novel by Charles Dickens. All that was missing was mother's name which should have Annabella Fiddlesticks or Dorothea Clacking-Downminster.

Mother wasn't the tyrant in black from the ghostly mansion by the marsh. She was the shrinking violet widow from the rose-covered cottage at Dimble Downe Dell. Alastair wasn't controlled by his mother—he controlled her.

After some meaningless small talk, Alastair announced the serving of afternoon tea. Mother shuffled through the opened frosted-glass double-doors into the dining-room. Alastair smiled and Jo took her cue and followed Mother. He held a chair for Jo and left his mother to make her own arrangements.

The "spread" was so large, Jo assumed she was in the first sitting. Buttered scones which could have doubled as yonnies in a skim-the-water game eyed her and growled. *Touch me, sister, and you'll be sorry.* Pikelets supporting what looked like a jam topping with tears begged to be put out of their misery. Sandwiches with use-by-date fillings, and crusts removed as if being punished, were curling at the edges. But the piece of greatest resistance was the sponge cake propped precariously centre stage on the strongest table in the land. The cake began life as a multi-layered creation with cream filling between floors. Alas an earthquake or equivalent culinary disaster had caused an implosion with the filling fleeing for its life. Four layers became one. Jo wished her firearm was by her side.

Mother passed a plate of this and that by moving it two inches allowing Alastair to reach across and complete the journey. He was in his element with his guest in shock. The penny had dropped.

Mother didn't drive away any possible brides for the boffin—he did. He was his own worst enemy. Jo realised that Mother would never have scared away any women but instead welcomed them. She desperately wanted any female—fat, old, hostile or hermaphrodite— just to escape the life of living with the Barry Crocker of the burbs.

Time didn't drag, it went backwards. Jo took up prayer. She tried to think of an exit strategy. *Why didn't I have someone call me and pretend there was a murder in Mildura?*

At last, at long, long last she got the chance to leave. Alastair suggested that Mother might show Jo the garden but the senior constable turned that idea on its head.

'We could do that when I come again,' she said with a straight face. She planned to stick pins in her eyes rather than make a second visit. Alastair savoured the idea of a second visit from the sexy policewoman and reluctantly agreed to her exit.

Jo thanked Mother and their eyes spoke volumes. The older woman apologised for her son and the younger woman sympathised.

Alastair accompanied Jo to the front gate and watched as she walked to her white VW Golf. He waved as she got in her vehicle then stepped back out of sight. She didn't look and did a steady three-point turn before driving away. She threatened her car a la Basil Fawlty. 'Break down and I'll thrash you.'

She didn't see the scientist race back along his drive to the rear of the garage where he grabbed a helmet, hopped on his motorbike and took off. Mother potted with the detritus of the afternoon tea while her son became a part-time stalker.

Jo decided not to ring the Carrs but simply drive past the park on the off chance she might see them. The surprise would be all the more satisfying for both family and visitor. She got closer. It was a gorgeous afternoon with perfect weather to push a wheelchair. Jo's luck was in. She saw the family in the park—grandparents, father, son with dog on lead, and daughter travelling by wheelchair courtesy of Hugh, Pop.

Jo parked, crossed the road then called. 'Hello!' She waved.

The family saw her. Harry got excited with Rags even more excited. The little boy set off with his father worried the dog might escape again. Jack chased Harry and called for him to slow down. Jo increased her walking speed. Harry had trouble with Rags. Jack caught up with his son and Jo got closer.

Jack checked that Harry and Rags were okay then stepped forward as the senior constable arrived.

Across the road, a motorcyclist pulled in behind Jo's car and looked at the park. Alastair couldn't see the grandparents with the girl in the wheelchair or the boy with the dog. He could see his favourite police officer and a man meet in a park and embrace. They even seemed to run towards one another.

'The bitch,' said the motorcyclist, 'the fucking bitch.' He revved his machine, spun around and roared away causing a driver he cut off to sit on his horn. The couple in the park took no notice. They embraced happiness.

29

NEXT MORNING BARRY CHUBB WAS off-air during a commercial break. Carrying an envelope, his producer entered the studio, something she rarely did during the programme.

'You might want to read this.'

'What is it?'

'But put on a music track first.'

That caused him to hesitate. Tippy nodded to the panel operator who'd been primed, then handed Barry the envelope. He read the contents. When the last commercial finished, music began.

'Is this true?' Tippy shrugged. 'Well true or not this puts me back on top. Barry Chubb is the go-to man when it comes to solving crime.'

'I've rung the legal department and the cops.'

What?' Barry spat. 'This is addressed to me. It's a private letter.'

'Keep your shirt on. Legal said there's nothing defamatory and the cops said they'll send someone to collect it.'

'They'll need a warrant.'

'And they asked us not to handle it.'

'It's not a bomb, it's a bomb*shell*. I've solved a major crime—me.'

The panel operator held up a hand indicating the music was coming to an end. Tippy worried. She knew Barry knew he might be the reason his niece was murdered and now, having the murderer write to him, well that could make the unpredictable shock jock even more unpredictable. Tippy left the studio and the music finished.

At Homicide, most of the squad gathered to listen.

DI Rose was an emotional mess. Five unsolved murders created significant pressure. Being new to the job didn't help. And now, out of the blue, the case was solved. Or was it?

'Play it again,' she said once Barry Chubb had finished reading the letter confessing to all the homicides. They listened to a replay.

'It's a hoax,' said DS Fleming.

'Not until proven otherwise,' argued Billy Hughes.

'If it's true,' said Baldwin, 'why confess anonymously?'

'Killers often feel obliged to tell someone,' said Jo. 'Or else he's taunting us as in "you can't catch me".'

Richelieu put down a phone. 'Parcel at Reception, Madame. Allow me, s'il vous plaît.'

'Thanks Pierre,' said Rose who felt the pressure mounting. That buffoon Chubb was running her case and worse, solving it. 'Right, until we have Forensics, a profiler, handwriting expert and the world and its Mother check this letter, we assume it's a hoax and continue as per normal. Yes?' Agreement sounded around the Incident Room. 'So crack on. And Jo, we'll need an analysis of the letter and envelope. Can you make sure your friend at Forensics gives it top priority?'

Jo was a pretty good actor but even she couldn't disguise the feeling of dread that flooded her body. Less than 24 hours after her nightmare in afternoon-tea land, she was ordered to renew her acquaintance with the monster from the beige lagoon. And little did she know the monster had changed from admirer to jilted lover.

Lee Wong got out of human trafficking and prostitution—for now. The heat was too much. The Sexual Offences Team didn't take kindly to her *Not Guilty* verdict. They were like the Leader, bent on revenge, and while the cops were keen on legal means of redress, the Leader had murder on his mind.

The details were sent by code to the husband who told the wife. She showed little interest. Sacrificing a child and the wrong child at that had shattered her belief in the Lord's way. Why would the Leader give them instructions to kill a child and why would the Lord allow them to make the mistake which lead to the wrong sacrifice? The husband never admitted his error to the wife.

'You'll have no qualms this time,' said the husband as he explained the wicked ways of the brothel-owner daughter and the fact that her beloved mother was almost a nonagenarian. The wife didn't agree to participate but she didn't disagree either. Lee's ma was for the chop.

With the letter and its envelope secured, Jo began the journey of a thousand cuts. She parked at Forensics and entered the building. Her sanity remained in place only because she had no idea that Alastair's love or lust or whatever he held for her had turned to hatred and jealous rage. He was surprised to see her and the shock of her unexpected presence knocked his anger sideways. He stuttered.

'Detective Best.'

'Good morning, Alastair.' Her smile and body language hid her fear and disquiet.

'Is something wrong?'

It was Jo's turn to be surprised. 'Wrong? Not at all. And thank you again for a lovely afternoon.' The other forensic officers were all ears.

Alastair recovered. He decided to test the two-timing bitch. 'Did you manage to catch up with your little girl in the wheelchair?' He was sure Jo only caught up with her boyfriend—the rat.

'I did. But right now I have a special favour to ask. A man has confessed to all the unsolved homicides and ...'

'What, all of them?'

'Yes, all five.' She indicated the protective envelope. 'And this is his confession. It was sent to Barry Chubb the radio broadcaster.'

'I know who he is,' said Alastair taking the package.

'We haven't identified the sender so anything you find that helps us catch him before he kills again will be a fantastic result.'

'Assuming his confession is not a hoax.'

'Of course,' said Jo feeling pressure as she grovelled. 'If you could give this your immediate attention, Alastair, we'll be ever so grateful.'

Alastair was thinking. *She said "we'll" be grateful. Once she would've said "I'll" be grateful and fluttered her eyelids at me. Bitch.*

'Leave it with me,' he said producing a fake smile.

Jo wondered why he didn't spend even a little money on his teeth. 'Thanks a million, Alastair. If I may, I'll give you a call later to see how you're going. But please feel free to call me if you get a breakthrough.'

There was no hand on his arm. There was no imaginary kiss. She fought hard not to give even the merest hint she fancied him. This was tricky. 'And any luck with the dandruff?'

'DNA takes time,' he said in as flat a voice as possible. Jo sensed a problem. With a chaste smile and another platitude of gratitude, she left. He tossed the package on his bench. *I'll fix you, minx.*

Barry Chubb went OTT. He was a braggart and self-opinioned at any time but now he exploded. 'I've solved the serial killer case. I've done the work of the police. Even mass murderers come to me because they know I care. I'm the man of the people.'

Listeners called to congratulate him. Those who called to tell him the letter was from a crank were never put to air. When one slipped through and told Barry he'd been fooled, Chubb gave the caller an almighty spray.

On and on he went. DI Rose kept Stephen Payne listening and recording the diatribe and making notes. 'Let me know if he says anything remotely plausible,' she said.

AC Crowley rang Rose demanding to know the facts. 'The letter's been sent to Forensics, sir. We've booked a handwriting expert and profiler.'

'We have to take this seriously, Inspector.'

'I'm well aware of that, sir.'

'But don't neglect any and all other avenues.'

'Already in place, sir.'

He worried she was too inexperienced to oversee what had become a crime that dominated the media. People were asking if the police were up to the task. The Chief Commissioner contacted the AC Crime asking blunt questions who in turn pestered DI Rose.

'Regular updates, please Inspector,' ordered the AC, 'and don't hesitate to contact me if you need any help.'

'Thank you, sir, will do.'

He ended the call and Rose stifled a scream. She was ambitious and jumped for joy when appointed. Right now her self-confidence was being prodded by fear and doubt. The prods became jabs.

Lee Wong parked her Mercedes at the end of the deserted car park off Beach Road. Her mother could stare at Port Phillip Bay. 'Look at the water, Mamma. I will get you an ice-cream.'

Lee kissed her mother. The shop was across Beach Road. Lee had stopped in this place many times before and knew the ice-cream her mother enjoyed. The shopping would take three minutes.

That was all the husband and wife needed. They'd followed Lee, parked in a side street, slipped across the road and approached the Mercedes from the thick "forest" of tea-tree. It was a weekday and cold and beachgoers were missing. If only Lee had locked her car.

The passenger door opened and the elderly woman turned not so much in fright as in surprise. She was elderly and while not demented, slow and unaware of most things around her. Having a doting daughter made it easy to live a life dependent on others.

She didn't scream as the cloth was pushed into her face. She barely struggled as the needle plunged into her flaccid arm. This was taking candy from a baby. This was murder made easy. The drug took effect. The victim's pathetic attempts to maintain her breathing barely raised a ripple. Her raspberry ripple was now en route and the husband and wife closed the car door and disappeared into the tea tree.

The old woman died quickly but being held in place by the safety belt, remained as she was when her daughter left.

Lee took some time to discover the corpse. Getting into the car, closing her door, and passing an ice-cream to her mother all took time. The daughter chatted. 'I have your favourite, Mamma. This is the ice-cream you love. Here you are, Mamma.'

Mamma didn't respond with much movement at the best of times but even less so when dead. Again it took Lee time to twig. Her mother was her usual unresponsive self. Lee turned in her seat offering the ice-cream to her mother whose eyes were wide open. Lee took hold of her mother's right hand to lift it and place the ice-cream therein. The hand wasn't cold just unresponsive. Lee stared at her mother who had never looked like this. She was as unresponsive as one could be—she was dead.

The brothel and slave-owner screamed in a way that would have scared the daylights out of anyone within earshot. There was no-one within earshot and the top-of-the-range Mercedes meant Lee's anguish remained private. The ice-creams were of no further use.

Eventually an ambulance came. Eventually because Lee couldn't accept her elderly mother was dead. Lee pleaded. 'Oh Mamma, wake up, please Mamma.' All this begging was between copious amounts of tears, and from a woman who tricked young women to come to Australia where she placed them in sexual slavery. These women pleaded with Lee and she ignored them. Their tears meant nothing.

If only the husband, the wife and Leader could see this. Here was the Lord's work in action. *Vengeance is fine,* the motto of the killers, now came true in living colour. The wicked sinner was being punished. Boy did she suffer.

The ambos examined the old woman and pronounced life extinct. Lee begged them to try resuscitation. The local police arrived. She grabbed them by their uniform, ordering them to order the ambos to revive her mother. It was full-blown emotion. The cops wouldn't allow Lee to drive. She was a mess.

'Do you have a family member who can come and collect you?' they asked. She didn't. Her ex-husband lived in Hong Kong and Lee's son had disowned his mother. Her loneliness compounded her grief.

This was tricky for the cops. Lee's car was locked and she went with her deceased mother. As for the raspberry ripple ice-creams, they melted in the Merc.

30

THE WOMAN WENT TO HER LOCAL POLICE STATION. The young constable on duty smiled. 'Good morning, madam, how can I help?'

'My brother's the crank who sent that letter.'

Never has an opening statement needed more detail. The woman explained that the letter sent to Barry Chubb claiming the writer was the serial killer bumping off everyone including a supermarket worker and a Supreme Court judge, was a hoax. It was written by her brother. He was a fantasist, a dreamer, Walter Mitty's love child.

'And how do you know this?' asked the constable.

'He told me.' The cop wondered if she too was a fantasist. 'Look, I know him. When Barry Chubb talked about the letter on his show, my brother confessed. He always confesses to me.'

'Confessed to what?'

'Oh please, arrest him and tell the police looking for the serial killer to forget my brother.' She stared at the constable. 'He's a fraud.'

The constable paused. 'Wait here, madam.' He fetched his sergeant who took the woman seriously. A statement was taken, calls were made and DI Rose's phone rang.

'You're kidding,' she said. Homicide's one and only lead was a hoax, a dead-end. She took some details then ordered Fleming and Baldwin to arrest the loopy loser.

Rose addressed the remaining squad members. 'At least we know. A useless lead is worse than no lead. Jo, can you please chase up the DNA of that dandruff found in the teenage boy's scalp.'

'Ma-am,' said Jo via clenched teeth. *Not another visit to Ally Pally.*

Rose rang the AC and told him the letter from the serial killer was a fake. They discussed the dandruff. Crowley was not pleased.

Jo toyed between ringing Alastair or visiting. She didn't know he was a changed man. Where once he thought her to be the girl of his dreams, he now believed she was a liar and a two-timing bitch.

Alastair had the DNA of the dandruff shedder and worked extra hard on the envelope and letter from the hoaxer. Multiple people had handled the goods including Barry Chubb. Sorting the good guys from the criminals would take time. He cheated. He broke the law. He didn't care. He wanted to embarrass the woman who flirted with him, led him on while all the time simply used him.

He took a tiny amount of the dandruff and placed it on the sticky seal of the envelope. The two samples matched. They had to, they were the same material. The person who murdered the teenage boy was the person who sent the letter.

He asked a colleague to check his findings. She agreed. 'Brilliant work, Alastair,' congratulated his colleague. 'Your favourite senior constable will be super grateful.' Alastair felt good. He wrote a report.

The Homicide detectives arrested the hoaxer without incident. He was surprised they found him so quickly, not smart enough to know his sister had grassed him up. The police knew he would be charged with wasting police time and possibly other offences but saw him more as a simpleton who was lucky to have a sister who cared. The drive back to Homicide was a treat for the hopeless hoaxer.

Back at HQ, Billy Hughes took a phone call. It was her mate Toby Weatherhill from SOCIT. 'This is getting to be a habit,' laughed Billy. 'Are you trying to get a move to Homicide?'

Toby expressed mock horror. 'And work with you again?—never.' More laughter. 'Listen, Billy, a mate of mine at Brighton gave me a call. They attended a sudden death where the daughter is the notorious brothel-keeper, Lee Wong.'

'Right,' said Billy wanting more.

'She got off our charges for trafficking and worse, but apparently she was pretty upset at her mother's death and I wondered ...'

'... if the old girl was killed to punish the wicked daughter.'

'Just a thought.'

'Just a brilliant thought, Toby. I owe you.'

Toby gave Billy the details and she knocked on Rose's open door. Her predecessor, DI Steele, disliked contact with his detectives and never had an open door.

'Make it good news or go away,' said Rose sinking deeper into depression by the hour.

'We may have victim number six.'

Billy explained and Rose insisted on Strange being involved. 'Get the strange pathologist. We must know if it's a homicide.'

Things happened. The body count rose. Barry Chubb cranked up his rhetoric. Alastair Dean took a call to advise his mother had suffered one of her turns. He asked his colleague to ring Detective Best and give her the news of the DNA match. The detectives arrived with the hoaxer in custody. Gabrielle Strange was asked to conduct an autopsy on Lee's ma. Rose rang AC Crowley to inform him of a likely murder victim number six. His stress added to Rose's stress. It was depression all round.

Jo got the call from Forensics and burst into her boss's office. Hello bedlam. Forensics had a match.

Rose and Hughes didn't believe her. She explained how two officers from Forensics double-checked the data. Rose snatched her phone and called AC Crowley. He too had doubts but the DNA doesn't lie. The hoaxer in custody had no idea he was now a star.

In the Incident Room, Justin Fleming was rabbiting on about Simple Simon, the hopeless hoaxer when in came DI Rose followed by Hughes and Jo with a following wind. The brown stuff hit the fan.

'We've got him,' said Rose who was a mix of elation and fear.

'What? Who?' responded her detectives.

'Forensics confirmed the DNA at the boy's hanging murder and the DNA on the hoax letter is a match.'

Fleming scoffed. 'No way is that dickhead a mass murderer.'

'Are they sure?' asked Richelieu.

'And we may have victim number six,' said Billy explaining the sudden death on the foreshore. From nothing to something went the investigation. The feeling of relief was tempered by disbelief.

Jo and DI Richelieu were sent to see the pathologist. Dr Strange was hard at it. She looked up, saw the detectives then resumed her work. 'I'm demanding double time and a half. What is it with you people?' The detectives looked at one another.

Richelieu spoke. 'Do we 'ave another 'omicide, Madame Doctuer?'

'Tricky,' replied Strange. Not sure of her age but one document says 92. She's had open heart surgery and God knows what else. Apparently her daughter insisted on every op going, money no object. I call it elder abuse.'

'So it could be natural causes?' asked Jo.

'It could be any number of things including homicide but it's not definitive. An elderly frail person given a fright could die. Is it possible she was murdered? Yes. Is it possible she died of natural causes? Also yes.' She looked at them. 'Sorry. And the only out-of-place material on her body was some ice-cream. Raspberry ripple if I'm not mistaken.'

The detectives thanked the pathologist and left. They headed back to Homicide with the DI behind the wheel. His offer of a Christmas in Paris had not been mentioned by either party. Richelieu decided to stick his head above the parapet.

'Tell me, Mademoiselle, s'il vous plait, 'ave you given any more thought to 'aving a Merry Christmas in Gay Paree?'

Jo genuinely felt torn about succumbing to his Gallic charms. Before she could speak, her phone rang. Relieved, she answered it and heard a familiar voice.

'Detective Best, it's Alastair Dean.'

'Oh hello, Alastair. Thank you for your prompt DNA work.'

'That's why I'm ringing.'

Jo worried. 'Oh?'

'There's been a terrible mix-up. My colleague got the data wrong. There is no DNA match.'

'What?' Jo yelled. Richelieu pulled over such was his concern.

'I apologise, it was a genuine mistake and we wanted to correct it before any arrests were made.'

'But your colleague said that both you and she had double-checked the data. How could such a dreadful mistake occur?'

Richelieu felt the heat. 'Mademoiselle?' he enquired.

Jo didn't look at him but held up her spare hand. 'Alastair, I told my boss and she told the Assistant Commissioner and we've arrested the man who wrote the letter.'

'But how did you know who he was? Is his DNA on file?'

He was right. The sister had dobbed in her brother. It was nothing to do with the DNA.

She backed off a little. 'No, we got some intel.'

'I've rung you the moment we discovered the error. Now you can get on and find the real killer. Bye.'

He ended the call. 'No wait,' said Jo, but he was gone. His plan worked a treat. He believed she played him for a fool. He struck back.

'I'm not saying it's your fault, Senior Constable,' said Rose, 'but not going to Forensics, not seeing the evidence in person, not being there to ask questions, left you open to getting wrong information.'

Jo wanted to argue her case but didn't. She didn't know Alastair tailed her after their soiree but got the feeling he was angry. Her conscience got chatty. She'd flirted with him to get preferential treatment. She led him on. He didn't like being used. There was no way she would admit that to her boss—to anyone.

'I'm taking you off front-line duties,' said Rose. Jo died. 'Learn from your mistake. Be better for the experience.' Jo didn't speak. She didn't want to cry or swear or both. She stood assuming the "discussion" was over. Rose continued. 'Some penance will do you good.'

'Ma-am?'

'You can look over some cold cases.'

What? A desk job? Count paperclips? I'm a detective!

Jo joined the real world and responded. 'Thank you, ma-am. And I apologise for the mistake.'

'Go, before I throw something.'

This was a first. Jo was out but still in.

31

'MICHAEL CHAN SPEAKING.'

'Hello stranger,' said Jo.

'I'm sorry. Who's speaking?'

'Ha, ha.'

'I thought you'd run away and joined Interpol.'

'I have.'

He was serious and groaned. 'Oh you haven't been sacked again?'

'Sort of.'

'What's happened *this* time?'

'I think I'd rather tell you in person.'

'Will I need a box of tissues?'

'Are you at home?'

'I'm always at home except when looking for kidnapped children and lost canines.'

'But are you home alone?'

'How dare you ... and yes.'

'I'm on my way.'

Jo's suburb of Clifton Hill was next to Michael's suburb of Northcote. She could walk to his place in thirty minutes and drive there in ten—five if the lights co-operated. She stood beneath his old-fashioned door lamp, straight from Hitchcock's version of *The 39 Steps*.

They chatted. Jo avoided Michael's relationship with Connie Bryant and he avoided her current employment situation.

'So what shall we talk about?' he asked knowing she had something important to discuss. He liked her as a person and loved the challenges she threw his way.

'I've been working on these homicides where everyone reckons a serial killer is responsible.'

'But you don't?'

'I do although I've been removed from the front line and sent to study cold cases.'

He wanted to know why but didn't push the issue—yet. 'Are they related to the current murders?'

'I doubt it.'

'So will you tell me why you've been dumped or would you rather crack on and solve the current homicides?' She grinned. 'Gotcha.'

Jo laughed. She liked Michael and loved his expertise and willingness to get stuck into a puzzle. She told him all she knew about the homicides plus her theory about revenge killings—punish an evil person by killing someone the baddie loves.

'And you've got no suspects?'

'No but I reckon it has to be someone who is political or religious.'

'Or both.'

'Or both.'

'Because?'

'There's no theft involved. The victims are law-abiding, decent, normal people.'

'Whatever that means.'

'True, and the teenage boy doesn't fit the theory and the only link between the other victims is their closeness to someone who has broken the law or offended someone and got away with it. That's why I'm thinking politics and religion. It has to be a fanatic, someone who reckons we're disobeying God or the Law or both and needs to be punished.'

Michael grimaced. 'Sounds possible but finding the weirdo could be tricky.'

'And as you know, said Jo, 'that's precisely why I'm here.'

Of course he knew that and already his mind was racing. 'It can't be a lone wolf. So how many killers are there?'

The game was afoot as they thought aloud. 'At least two with a boss as the planner.'

'It won't be members of the Greens or Quakers.'

She loved the way they bounced ideas off one another, the way his mind worked. If Jo ever got sacked from Homicide, she'd convince Michael to join her in a private investigation business. *Best and Chan* or *Chan and Best*.

She challenged him. 'Is it possible the killers will boast about or comment on their work? I mean some serial killers keep trophies, talk about their deeds because they have news they want to share.'

'So it's fringe political parties with ultra-right-wing views or small religious groups where obedience to Old Testament law is de rigeur.'

Jo blew air. She loved the discussion but felt an answer or clue was a million miles away. *Help me, Michael. Please, release your genius.*

Michael's cat, Alan, joined the conversation. The humans drank coffee and discussed tactics. Jo felt they were looking for half a needle in a paddock of haystacks.

The Leader was pleased. The latest killing worked like clockwork. And the photos and news footage of the distraught daughter, the evil, sinful harlot, were pleasing indeed. But the Leader had a problem. The husband dropped hints the wife was losing faith in the work of the Lord. If she confessed, that would be a disaster. The Leader considered his response. It included having the husband offer up the wife as a sacrifice. Needs must in the work of the Lord.

Michael pondered the task. He would contact Jo if he found anything. He would use his IT genius to hunt the fanatics who wanted to right the wrongs of Society. But that could take forever and any zealots found may not be the killers. Better to have the fanatics find him.

He thought about creating a web page extoling right-wing religious hard-line beliefs and loopy law-and-order policies but then reckoned that'd be too obvious. And would the killers be looking for such a site anyway? No, subtle was the way to go.

As the murders were in or close to Melbourne, then the murderers would likely be local. Michael found Melbourne-based blogs and websites which promoted extreme right-wing, law-and-order issues or religious fanaticism with doom and gloom rantings pointing out we're all on the road to Sodom and B'gorrah me lads.

He studied these local sites then posted in their Comments' section. His nom de plume would appeal to politicians and the religious—*The Right Way Rules.*

Jo rang her grandfather which made his day. After the usual chat about his health and Jo's dementia-ridden grandmother, she asked if she could visit. Silly question.

She always brought chocolates having remembered how he used to spoil Jo and her sister whenever they came to visit their grandparents as kids. Pop was the king of the chocolate frogs.

They enjoyed a cuppa and Jo told the retired DCI exactly what had happened to her with the mistaken report from Forensics. She didn't talk about her flirting to make a shy middle-aged male give her forensic results priority, and Robbo didn't ask. She loved him the more for that.

'So what have they got you doing, lass?' he asked.

'I'm working on cold cases, Pop. I've been told to make notes on anything I think should be looked at again.'

Robbo turned sad. 'And you're going to ask me who murdered Maggie Stephens in Collingwood in 1996.'

Jo looked at her grandfather. It was more than 20 years since that case, and yet he knew every detail. His feelings of regret lingered. She trod carefully wondering how he felt. Now she knew. 'We don't have to discuss it, Pop.'

'Yes we do.' He paused. 'I hated retiring leaving that poor girl's murder unsolved.'

'The case notes suggest it *was* solved. The boyfriend killed her, couldn't handle what he'd done so committed suicide.'

'Sometimes the facts, the notes in the file say one thing and your gut instinct screams "wrong". Even after all these years, that inner voice keeps haunting me. It's a bit like the coroner recording an open finding. But in my opinion, we still don't know for sure who murdered Maggie. To me the finding was too neat, too tidy. The victim was a part-time prostitute and single mother. Her family were in jail or scroungers. Maggie was a loser. Her death wasn't important. Why are you complaining? We got a result. Her loser boyfriend did it. Close the file, folks. Move on.'

Jo sat and listened. Robbo's passion burned bright. She loved that and hoped she could capture it. She would go back to the file.

Robbo switched gears. 'So what's news? How's your mother and her new boyfriend and, as your mother would say, what's happening with *your* boyfriends?' His eyes sparkled. 'Or shouldn't I ask.'

Jo laughed. 'I'll make you a promise, Pop. As soon as there's any serious evidence, you'll be the first to know.'

The Leader sent another cryptic message via the church's web site. The husband read it and froze. *That can't be right. I've made a mistake in translation. No, the Leader's made a mistake in naming the target.*

The husband checked and checked again. There was no doubt. He was to remove the possibility of his wife forsaking the work of the Lord. How? Sacrifice her. What?

The husband thought about querying the latest instruction. Then reckoned that would be disobedience. *I must do what the Leader commands. His instructions are from the Lord.*

The Leader too was online. He wanted to post a message about the group's next meeting. Both men checked the comments. There were the usual non-believers with their caustic remarks. These were deleted. But one comment stood out. It had all the signs of being written by a believer. Hallelujah.

The Leader re-read the post. He had no idea the writer was an ABC (Australian Born Chinese) in Northcote, Australia with a cat called Alan named after a mathematical genius called Turing. In fact the ABC and Mr Turing could well have swapped theories and ideas challenging one another. The post inspired the Leader. He replied trying to attract the writer to his flock.

Jo concentrated on her new role, investigating cold cases. Her colleagues were left to find the killers. She ignored her former friend turned foe in the FSD (Forensic Services Department). Hiding away amidst the boxes of files of cold cases, she heard a familiar voice.

'Anyone home?'

'In here, Sarge.'

'Where's here?'

Billy Hughes found Jo and asked about her work. They avoided the elephant in the room but someone had to crack and Billy was it.

'Look, we all know you were set up by that bloke in Forensics.'

'Sorry Sarge but I set myself up. Leading him on sent all the wrong signals and he hit back.'

'What changed? Did he catch you in the arms of a certain DI?'

Ouch. Billy wished she could take that back. Jo felt even worse. They looked at one another. Both tried to change the subject.

'So how goes the serial killer hunt?' asked Jo.

'It's not. DI Rose tells everyone she's under pressure, hoping that'll make us feel sorry for her. It ain't working. Only a breakthrough and a genuine arrest will fix the problem.'

'Just between you and me, I've got my friend Michael investigating a couple of possibilities.'

Billy looked at her younger colleague. 'Trust you. But if you find something, you'd better tell the boss. In fact, finding something could get you out of jail.'

Jo knew she had a friend. 'Thanks Sarge. I appreciate the visit.'

Michael's machine pinged. His programme told him when his blog posts got a reply. He clicked on *Disciples of the Lord* and read.

> *Welcome Michael. We value your thoughts and prayers. If ever in Melbourne, please join us for worship. Sundays at 3. PM me for details. Ezekiel.*

Michael contacted Ezekiel and was given the address of the meeting place for *Disciples of the Lord*. This was the fourth invitation to join a group. He heard from two political and now two religious groups, each desperate for members and relevance. They seized on anyone who showed the slightest interest in their whacky activities.

He chose a far-right political Party for Saturday and the *Disciples of the Lord* for Sunday. He decided against telling Homicide detective Best. She would insist on coming and that spelt trouble.

The political group might well have housed a serial killer or three but Michael—*how stupid am I?*—never got past the door. Being of Asian appearance, only because his parents are Chinese, meant the ultra-ultra-right wing racists were never going to have a member the likes of Michael Chan in their midst. *Still*, he thought, *worth a try*.

The next day he rocked up to meet the zealots in the *Disciples of the Lord* church. They rented a room in a scout hall. It wasn't big which didn't matter because the worshippers could have met in one of those ancient red phone boxes and still been able to swing a cat.

Michael entered and stood out like a giraffe at an ants' wedding. 'You must be Michael,' said a man. 'I'm Ezekiel.'

'Hello,' said Michael shaking hands.

Before the meeting, Michael watched YouTube clips of off-the-wall religious groups and practised saying aloud some of the jargon. *Praise the Lord, Hallelujah* and *Amen brother* were his stock-in-trade replies.

The service began, Ezekiel preached and Michael reckoned he gave a pretty good impression of a believer according to that olde time religion. Later, Michael shook hands with the other 11 congregants, and departed promising to keep in touch.

For Michael, this was a successful first step. No serial killer said, "Hi, I'm Abraham, the mass murderer," but he felt he had an in. If anyone killed people out of vengeance, there was a chance they attended a group like *Disciples of the Lord*. Michael wanted more of this group. Ezekiel was keen too but for a different reason.

At home, he opened his computer. Something about Michael Chan rang a bell. Ezekiel searched. Bingo. 'I know you,' he said staring at a report about a missing child being rescued near Castlemaine. The caption beneath the photo read *Detective Senior Constable Joanna Best and Mr Michael Chan*. 'Hello Michael,' said the Leader. 'So you're a friend of the police.'

32

BARRY CHUBB HAD PROBLEMS. He boasted about finding the serial killer but knew he probably drove the madman to murder his niece.

The Leader had problems. One half of his execution squad wanted to quit and outsiders were trying to infiltrate his band of believers.

Michael checked the *Disciples of the Lord* blog. He had a message thanking him for attending a service, inviting him to come again, and to contact Ezekiel for exciting news. Michael reckoned "exciting news" was code for scam, danger or rip-off. He would be told the news in two days. A time and date were set. For Michael it was time to holler for a marshal and he contacted you know you.

'I can't believe you've got a lead already,' said Jo.

'How dare you,' replied Michael with his tongue in his cheek.

'Is it any good?'

'Be here at 8 and keep tomorrow night free,' said Michael.

Jo tingled. This man had a brilliant track record of finding people and unravelling things. She stood at his front door at 1959 hours.

'You're early,' he said opening the door.

They sat for a chat with the cat on a mat. 'And this is tomorrow night?' asked Jo.

'I've decided to take you with me in case they really *are* serial killers and as I can only handle six at once, I may need backup.'

'Surely a religious group doesn't engage in cold-blooded murder?'

'I've met their leader, Ezekiel.'

'Ezekiel? That's his name?'

'Good Old Testament stock.'

'Good Old Testament mass murder. Don't you know your bible?' He didn't, at least not that well. '"Slay utterly old and young," and include the women and kids.'

'And that's in the Book of Ezekiel?'

'You may have done it again, Michael.'

He took a deep breath. 'We may need the SOGGIES.'

'Tell me about the *Disciples of the Lord*.'

He did and she asked questions developing an itch in her hunch department. Only by attending a special meeting in the Scout Hall would that itch go away. *Should I tell DI Rose or Billy Hughes? But I'm off the case. And what if it's a wild-goose chase?*

The next night, she collected Michael at 7. The drive across town to Dandenong would take 40 minutes or more depending on traffic and route. 'Any more blog posts,' she asked.

'Not for me. And I've posted nothing.'

'So they're only expecting you, there's no mention of ... who am I by the way—wife, girlfriend, bodyguard or what?'

'You're the person who will save me making a citizen's arrest when we discover the serial killers. Are you armed and dangerous?'

'I thought you said they were quiet church-going folk.'

'I'm allowed to change my mind.'

They drove in silence. Both knew this could be a waste of time. Religious and political fanatics are no more likely to kill people who have done immoral or illegal things than non-believers or those who never vote. Jo was aware of criminal statistics about serial killers and not a lot were regular God-fearing bible students. They parked in the dark street beside the Scout Hall.

'What's the drill, Officer?' asked Michael.

'It's your party, Michael. I'm only the decoration.'

He looked at her. He always thought she dressed down, not dowdy but understated. He wondered how she'd look with one of those makeovers—clothes, hair and makeup.

They walked across the grass to the rear of the Scout Hall. Neither spoke. Their heart rates increased. They stopped at the door. Michael looked at Jo. She was good at hiding her feelings but fear kicked in as he knocked. They heard two voices then the door opened.

'Hello Michael,' said the husband. He saw Jo. 'Oh, who's this?'

'This is Jo, my friend. I'm sorry, I can't remember your name.'

'Call me, brother.' Jo entered and Michael followed. The wife stepped forward distracting the visitors as the husband closed the door and, unseen by the visitors, softly turned and removed the key.

'Hello Michael,' she said. 'Call me sister.'

'Hello sister. And this is my friend, Jo.' The women shook hands.

The husband moved to the end of the room in front of the pulpit. 'Come and sit. Brother Ezekiel apologises but will be here soon.'

Michael and Jo sat on the two chairs with their back to the mini stage. The husband and wife drew another two chairs closer and sat facing their guests.

'We're so pleased you want to join our group, Michael,' said the husband. He turned to the wife. 'Aren't we?'

'Yes,' she said as if on command but with little enthusiasm.

'Ezekiel said there was something special he wanted to show me,' said Michael, wanting to cut to the chase.

'He'll be here soon,' said the husband who seemed on edge. Jo sensed the tension but couldn't see how the middle-aged couple posed a risk. Jo was fit and trained and Michael was the Kung Fu king from Northcote. The couple were lightweights and hardly intimidating.

The conversation centred on what Michael thought of Ezekiel's sermon when the husband asked the wife to make some tea. She moved behind Michael and Jo, pottered then began pushing a trolley towards them. The husband pointed to the trolley and asked what they would like. Michael and Jo turned to look at the trolley and the religious couple took off.

The husband produced a can of mace and squirted. Plenty landed and the stinging sensation was acute. Michael and Jo were blinded and rubbed their eyes making the pain worse.

The wife slipped behind them and pulled two bolts. The back legs of Michael and Jo's chairs collapsed as the floor, a trapdoor, dropped revealing the baptismal bath two metres below. With their weight on their chairs, the visitors fell backwards. Instinctively they threw out their arms and clutched at one another. It was in vain. Michael being taller whacked his shoulders on the edge of the frame of the bath. Jo belted her head.

There were yells from victims and attackers. Surprise, the mace and a loss of balance gave the killers the advantage. Ties were slipped around hands. Michael and Jo struggled to stand. They were dragged from their baptismal "jail", had their ankles tied then rolled onto their stomachs with streaming eyes, and hands and feet tied tight.

The hint of fear they felt when they arrived was now full-blown. Michael and Jo reckoned death was a real possibility. They were sure they'd found the serial killers.

Michael tried reason. 'Look, all I wanted to do was find out what went on here.'

'Silence,' ordered the husband. 'We know you are of the Devil.'

'I'm a police officer,' called Jo struggling to see. 'Assault is a serious charge. Let us go now and you may get a suspended sentence.'

The wife stunned everyone including her husband, not by speaking but by what she said. 'How much do you get for eight murders?'

'Silence,' snapped the husband.

She ignored him. 'Might as well be hanged for a sheep as a lamb.'

The sting in their eyes and the discomfort of their ties vanished as Michael and Jo faced death. Jo told no-one about this excursion. No-one at Homicide knew she was doing her loose cannon routine. The six victims of the serial killers would soon have a couple more bodies to add to the pile. Jo shuddered, imagining Gabrielle Strange performing the autopsy on Jo's soon-to-be lifeless body.

Then hope sprang eternal as someone knocked on the outside door.

Michael and Jo thought being in a church, or at least a building used for religious purposes, meant that prayer might have a better chance here than anywhere else. Their atheism came under attack.

The door was opened and footsteps were heard. The person who entered surveyed the scene. 'All good I see?' Michael knew the voice of Ezekiel. Jo shuddered instantly recognising the voice. The door closed and the footsteps got closer. They stopped a smidgeon from Michael and Jo's heads. The mace impact was still strong but Jo squinted. She could see—just. Right beside her head were the shiniest shoes in Christendom.

'Hello Len,' she said.

The visitor stamped his foot in anger. He wanted his real name kept secret. The husband and wife wondered why she called him Len. He took control. 'Do it now,' he commanded.

The husband dragged Michael by his ankles towards the baptismal bath. The wife stood firm.

'Help your husband,' ordered Len a.k.a. Ezekiel a.k.a. the Leader.

'No,' she said and defied him.

The husband forgot about Michael and went to his wife.

'Woman,' he growled, 'you must do as Ezekiel says.'

She was having none of it. 'I want to know what wicked things the friends and family of these two people have done for them to be killed.' The Leader and the husband were stuck. 'Tell me,' demanded the wife.

The Leader pointed at the trussed captives. 'Her mother runs an abortion clinic and his brother's a rapist.' Meet Len the liar.

The response was dramatic and the wife lost her defiance. The husband grabbed her. 'Now come on. Let the Lord have vengeance.'

He grabbed Michael's tied ankles and dragged him towards the open baptismal bath. Being dragged, hurt. 'Take her,' snapped the Leader and the wife dragged Jo. Michael was flipped on his back and went feet first into the empty bath. He tried to get out and the husband struggled. 'Help him,' yelled the Leader. The wife stepped behind the husband in order to help.

'Help me,' demanded the husband. He bent to push Michael down as the wife turned to the pulpit and grabbed the giant King James version of the bible.

'Hey!' cried the Leader. The wife swung the book with the husband's head the target. Bullseye. She dropped the scriptures.

Into the empty bath went her husband half landing on Michael who hopped up the side steps. Ezekiel roared at the backsliding woman and set out to tackle her. Jo turned her head, and as the Leader strode to exact punishment, Jo's tied feet tripped the fiery preacher from the Jury Commissioner's Office. He lost his balance pitching head first into the bath landing on the husband.

The wife was on her toes, slipped her hand into the handhold on the moveable floor and had the lid raised and locked before the boys below knew what was happening. They got busy in the vocal department.

Michael and Jo had their ties removed. The wife handed them a bottle of water each and they sought relief from their stinging eyes. The wife collapsed on the floor against the wall. Her battle was just beginning.

Jo looked at Michael. 'You all right?'

'Fine, never better. You?'

'Has what I think happened, happened?'

'Possibly. So how do you fancy getting out of reviewing cold cases?'

She grinned then looked at the wife. 'Thanks for your help, sister. You saved our lives.'

'Yeah, thanks,' said Michael. 'Oh and not that it matters but I haven't got a brother and her mother wouldn't say boo to a goose.'

The wife slumped. Jo put ties on her hands. 'I'm sorry but you're under arrest on suspicion of murder. You do not have to say or do anything but anything you say or do may be given in evidence. Do you understand that?'

The wife remained slumped but felt relief. Her ordeal was over. The killings were no more and the blind obedience to belligerent men was a thing of the past.

'Killing a child was the last straw,' she said. 'And killing the wrong child …' Her face screamed pain and she cried silently. The sounds from the locked baptismal area continued with threats, pleas, banging and cries.

Jo found her phone and rang Billy Hughes.

'What now, Senior? Have you solved a cold case?'

'No, this one's pretty warm, Sarge.'

'What's that noise? Sounds like someone's locked in a loo.'

'Close Sarge but no cigar. I've arrested the three people responsible for all those homicides we've been trying to solve.'

Disbelief sounded in Jo's ear. 'Why am I not surprised?'

'One's wearing cuffs and sitting on the floor next to me and the other two are locked in a baptismal bath in a scout hall in Dandenong.'

There was a long pause from Hughes. 'The crazy thing is I'm totally convinced it's true. Where are you?

Jo told her.

33

24 HOURS LATER THE FRENZY KEPT BUZZING. The media blew a gasket when DI Rose made the stunning announcement that two men and a woman were in custody charged with multiple homicides.

Jo and Michael were feted although they asked to be kept from the publicity. Michael insisted. DI Rose grovelled in making an apology to Jo and re-instating her Homicide role. AC Crowley had a toothpaste ad grin. Robbo Robertson shed a tear at the news of his granddaughter's success. Barry Chubb raged from anger and frustration at having missed the scoop. The staff at *Tonight at Seven* chewed glass.

Jo loved the lack of limelight. Weeks ago she was thrilled at finding the missing toddler but hated the TV lights and bombardment of questions with journalists wanting to know the name of her boyfriend, favourite football team, whether or not she wanted children and, if so, how many? Not having that pressure again was great. People in the force knew what she and Michael did. In time, the story would come out but by then the hullabaloo would have settled—a tad.

But little did Senior Constable Best know that an investigative journalist wanted the goss. Who caught the murdering missionaries and how? Loose lips sink ships and folding stuff lubricates tongues. Jo's name was leaked because some police are only human.

Two days after the trio were nabbed, Jo was relaxing at home, still buzzing from the success (and luck) of her arrests thanks to the IT wizard, one Dr. Michael David Chan.

Her phone rang. 'Is that Joanna Best?'

'Who's calling?'

'Hello Joanna. My name's Katie Maguire. I'm a journalist writing a story about the serial killers you arrested and wondered if you'd agree to an interview?'

'Can't help you. Sorry.' She went to end the call but stopped.

'We have all the details, Jo. The story's going to run tomorrow and we'd like to give you a chance to put your side.'

'What?' Jo fumed. It sounded like the journalist was accusing Jo of something and before telling the world, was giving Jo the chance to defend herself.

'I know you're not allowed to accept money but you can nominate a charity and we'll make the donation. How does $100 grand sound?'

Jo went from furious to flabbergasted. 'I'm not interested.'

'You could nominate research into acquired brain injury. Would you like that?'

Talk about the last straw. Some foot-in-the-door journo had been digging around her private life and wanted to get a scoop on the serial killers and the woman who discovered, disarmed and detained them. The journo knew intimate details of Jo's life, and flaunted it. Not much of swearer, Jo made her feelings clear by shouting 'Fuck off!' and hitting *End*. The journalist had recorded the call and purred. Jo seethed.

Her phone rang again and she drew on her ration of expletives ready to sally forth a second time. She looked at Caller ID and knew the number. She took a deep breath and tried to be as polite as possible.

'Bonsoir, Monsieur.'

'Hello Joanna.' She froze. This definitely wasn't DI Pierre Richelieu, the gallant, flirtatious and somewhat scrumptious police officer.

'Pierre, are you okay?'

There was a silence before he spoke, again with an unusual voice.

'I am ringing to apologise, ma chère. With regret I must withdraw my invitation to show you Paris at Christmas.'

Jo was genuinely disappointed. She hadn't accepted the invitation as yet but to have it withdrawn made her sad and curious.

'There's no need to apologise, Pierre. And thank you for asking me in the first place.' She paused. 'Will you still be going?'

'Non.' He had lost his boyish charm, his suave manner.

'Is something wrong, Pierre?'

'Oui. I 'ave just 'eard.' He paused. 'My mother, she 'as died.'

Jo fell on her settee. 'Oh Pierre, I am so sorry. How awful for you. Make I ask what happened?'

He was crying now. 'I never got to say au revoir, to tell 'er 'ow much I love 'er.'

'That is so sad, Pierre.'

'She 'ad the 'eart attack and died on the floor in 'er apartment.' Jo was feeling his pain. 'The doctor said she was there for maybe two days.' His voice cracked. 'Per'aps she could 'ave been saved.'

Jo decided. 'Would you like some company, Pierre?'

That seemed to throw him. 'Oh, oui, that would be wonderful. Merci Mademoiselle, Merci.'

'I'll see you soon.'

He opened the door of his magnificent apartment and looked terrible. Jo embraced him and grief and sympathy overrode romance and lust. They sat in his sumptuous sitting-room drinking black coffee. He again congratulated her on the arrests but she steered him to his mother.

Richelieu opened up. It was a time for home truths, back stories and reminiscing. Death focuses the mind.

'My father is Australian and my mother French. He was working in Paris where they met and married. Then my father's company promoted him and he returned to Australia where I was born 'ere in Melbourne. When I was three, my parents divorced and my mother took me back to France. Today, my father lives with his third wife in Florida but my mother never re-married. I grew up in Paris and after university, and to my mother's 'orror, I joined the Police Nationale.' The mention of his mother brought on more tears. He wiped his eyes.

'So what brought you back to Australia?'

He almost smiled. 'Ah, Mademoiselle, what else causes a man to move 'alfway round the world?' He stared at her. 'J'étais amoureuse.' He paused then translated. 'I was in love.' He let the words linger, pocketed his handkerchief and gave her that special stare.

The grief and sympathy mood shifted a tad. Jo wanted to ask but didn't. 'It was, 'ow you say Mademoiselle, unrequited love. I was defeated by a better man.'

206

Jo wondered what that better man looked like, where he was today and if Richelieu's former lover ever regretted her decision. 'So will you return to Paris?' She asked with more than a passing interest.

'Naturellement. I 'ave my mother's funeral to arrange, 'er apartment to sell and much more besides.'

'But you'll come back?' Her interest peaked.

'Naturellement. I 'ave my career 'ere, my friends, and especially my favourite Senior Constable.'

The occupants of the apartment were aware of the mood swing with sympathy and grief now heading stage left.

'Well I'm sure everyone at Homicide will want you back whenever you're ready—sir.'

'Sir?' He seized on her choice of word. 'We are not on duty now, Mademoiselle. Please, you must call me Inspecteur or even Commissaire.' She smiled. He moved and sat beside her. Her heart started jogging. 'I 'ave an idea. Why not come with me to Paris now. It may not be Christmas but Paris is always beautiful. Please Joanna, tell me you will think about it.'

'Oh Pierre, I'm not sure.'

'So, now you 'ave thought about it. What is your decision?'

She laughed. *It's true. If a man can make me laugh, he's halfway to winning my heart.*

'I need to think about it, Pierre.'

'Okay, I will give you 24 hours, no, less.' He kissed her hand and stood. 'Merci for coming to see me. You are a true friend.'

She stood and he kissed her cheek and then the other. They walked to her car. She remembered a night not so long ago when they did as they were doing now. He remembered running through the rain and two thugs trying to attack him. She remembered a certain kiss.

They reached her car. He seemed reluctant to repeat the former farewell routine. He again kissed her cheeks then opened her door.

'Remember, Mademoiselle, my invitation to take you to Paree remains. We leave in three days' time. Au revoir.'

She smiled and drove away. In her mirror she saw him waving. All the way home she thought of all the reasons why she couldn't, wouldn't and shouldn't accept his offer. She got home, parked and walked to her front door. She sensed movement and turned. A woman approached.

'Hello Jo, I'm Katie Maguire. We spoke earlier ...'

Jo's hackles leapt to their feet. 'Go away.'

'We know what you did, Jo. Let us tell the world your story.'

Jo thought about arresting the woman then reckoned there'd be a photographer in the wings ready to milk the moment. There was.

Say nothing, get out of here.

Jo struggled with her key. The journalist moved closer continuing to harass. The guy with the camera appeared. A light flashed. Finally the door opened and Jo escaped inside slamming the door. The woman outside called.

'Think of all the money you can donate to acquired brain injury research.'

Jo fumed. She was caught in a publicity nightmare. She was about to have her face plastered over web sites, TV screens and newspapers. She was being invaded. This was hell. Then an idea pinged.

I can avoid this nonsense. I can escape this unwanted exposure. Talk about perfect timing. Of course. What a bloody good idea.

A trip to Paris.

To be continued

Epilogue

Karen Galbraith answered a knock on her door. A distraught woman had hit a cat and could someone please help identify the owner. In the street, the husband swung into action and Karen was kidnapped.

Judge Slight raised his garage door. His killers were hiding in the garden. As he opened the door of his Bentley, they raced inside waving fake but real-looking handguns. His Honour was bound and gagged then murdered in a cruel and gruesome way.

Gwenda Balance got the dinner date wrong due to her being absent-minded and being prompted by her former neighbour and mother of the rapist. Weeks later, as Eddie Balance alighted at his local station at night and headed for home, a woman walking towards him dropped her shopping. Kind-hearted Eddie stopped to help allowing the woman's husband to step out of the shadows and knock the poor bloke unconscious. The rest was easy.

Pippa was enjoying her ride when hailed by a woman who claimed to be lost. Pippa pointed the way not noticing the knife-wielding husband approach from behind. With her beloved horse under threat, Pippa dismounted, was drugged then murdered and her horse made lame.

Eric a.k.a. Ezekiel was perfectly placed to know what went on with criminal trials and the discussions within the jury room.

The emails sent to Judge Slight were from a rival to the Attorney-General. Politicians from the same Party are the most duplicitous.

The glass in the two watermelons was put there by an employee angry at being refused extra hours. Alvin only pinched them.

The husband had mild dyslexia. Robert not Rupert was a simple reading error. People with normal intelligence can have mild dyslexia.

Eric, the husband and the wife all received life sentences. *Disciples of the Lord* disappeared.

The Detective Joanna Best Mysteries

www.cenfoxbooks.com

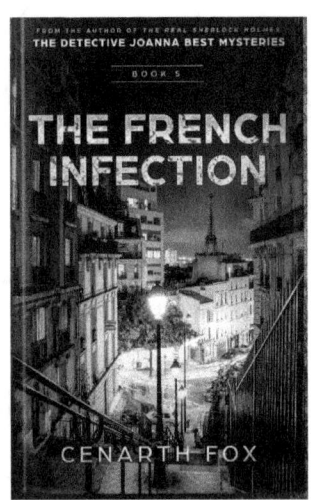

WW2 Thriller set in Paris

The father of the Brontes

www.cenfoxbooks.com

Shakespeare Down Under

Political thriller

www.ingramcontent.com/pod-product-compliance
Lightning Source LLC
Chambersburg PA
CBHW071108100726
47908CB00008B/2310